# REBEL VAMPIRE

# REBEL VAMPIRE

## 2

### BROGAN THOMAS

This is a work of fiction. Names, characters, places, and incidents either are the product of the author's imagination or are used fictitiously.

No part of this book may be reproduced or used in any manner without written permission of the copyright owner except for the use of quotations in a book review.

Published by Brogan Thomas
WWW.BROGANTHOMAS.COM

Copyright © 2023 by Brogan Thomas

All rights reserved.

Ebook ASIN: B0BWK956XY
Paperback ISBN: 9781915946027
Hardcover ISBN: 9781915946034

Edited by Victory Editing and proofread by Sam Everard
Cover design by Luminescence Covers

*For my hubby*

# CHAPTER ONE

I REGRET my life choices as a mottled orange-and-red tentacle swings at my head. I duck and neatly dance out of the way just as another tentacle sneaks out, grabs hold of my calf, winds its way around my leg, and gives me an ever-so-friendly squeeze. I wince as my bones grind together.

Yeah, it has a heck of a grip. It tugs. *Uh-oh. Oof.* I hit the tarmac with a thud.

My jumper bunches and the rough surface sloughs off the skin on my back as the monster drags me along the road and towards the portal. With gritted teeth, I tense my abs, dig the heel of my left boot into the road, and my rapid trajectory grinds to a sudden halt as my foot finds a convenient pothole.

*Thank fate for the poor state of British roads.*

I pull out a knife and, as carefully as I can, slide the flat of the blade between my leg and the sticky limb.

*Uh, it's really sticky.*

The muscles in my forearms strain as I use both hands to yank the knife sideways and wrench myself free. I roll to the side and scramble to my feet. Hands on my hips, I take a second to catch my breath. I click my tongue against the roof of my mouth. *Ew.* I can taste the alien creature; its briny scent is that pungent. Gross.

Cringing with a mouth full of bile, I put the knife away. I peer over my shoulder and fake smile at the Land Rover to reassure the young occupants I have everything under control.

*There is no problem here.*

The pixie children are out of their seats, bundled up in their coats, and all three kids have their noses pressed to the Defender's back window.

Page, the youngest, gives me an encouraging wave.

I wave back.

A wide-eyed Jeff grins at me, and then he scowls when Novel, the oldest, grabs a piece of popcorn from his hand and stuffs the kernel in her mouth. He yells, there's a scuffle, and it looks like... Yeah, he gives the rest of the popcorn in his hand a big lick.

Technically, the snacks were strictly only to be eaten at the cinema.

My eyes drift away from the kids' antics as I scan the quiet street and side-eye the portal with its wiggling tentacles. My stomach flips, and again I feel sick. The portal is big enough to swallow the entire Defender.

I look back at the kids. It was a close call. *They could have died.*

We were driving to the cinema to watch the latest must-see

kids' movie. Just as we passed the coach station and the row of new houses on the left, the beam of the headlights showed the tarmac ahead was frosty and the road underneath the bridge glittered like diamonds. *Black ice?* I took my foot off the accelerator. After the Land Rover slowed, the road ahead cracked and disappeared.

I slammed on the brakes, and we missed the ragged rogue portal by a scant inch.

After I moved the Land Rover a safe distance away, called for a gateway witch to close the portal, and blocked off the road with a temporary ward, the tentacles busted out.

*Ha.*

*Tentacles.*

I wash my hand down my face as I rack my brain for a solution that doesn't involve me up close and personal again with an alien. I come up blank. The spells I have are useless. I can't use them to contain him as it will destabilise the already-dodgy portal.

My nostrils flare as I take in another stinky breath. I fill my lungs with much-needed oxygen, swing my arms, roll my shoulders, and turn back to my task with grim determination.

"Right, let's do this. I can so do this." I rub my hands on my jeans and squint. *Bloody hell, are there more tentacles?* In my head—so I don't freak out—I've convinced myself this creature is a bigger, otherworldly cousin of our octopuses.

I have my sword in the car, so I could, if inclined, chop him into tiny pieces, but... I don't want to hurt him. I like octopuses.

I grunt, and my tentacle-squeezed calf throbs as I take a running jump and throw myself at the creature. *I'm having so much fun.* A manic grin tugs at my lips. I use my entire body to ram, push, prod, and poke him back into the hole in the tarmac.

"He's just a giant, cuddly octopus." Uh-huh. A tentacle wiggles out of my grip and slaps me in the face. A suction cup takes the skin off my cheek with a pop. *Ouch.* "I think I'll call him Fred." I give *Fred* another full-body shove. "Get back in the bloody portal, Fred."

Hands full and face stinging, I give the creature a final well-aimed push, and it slithers back into the gloom. *Yes! Woo-hoo.* I scramble out of the way.

"Now!" I yell to the waiting gateway witch.

She sniffs and shuffles her feet.

*Gah. Anytime now, Ethel.*

Her magic swells into the air, the streetlights dim, and with a flick of her wrist, Ethel's power slams into me.

*Oof.* The magic sears. *Ow! Ow! Ow!* I feel like I've been vigorously rubbed with grade-40 sandpaper. Like I've been microwaved. I taste blood in my mouth.

*Great. Bloody great.*

With teeth-clenching agony, I swallow down the pain, and the pain flips into anger. She didn't have to zap me like that. My hand twitches towards the knife, the urge to bury the blade in the witch is almost a living thing inside me. I have the "You hurt me; I'll hurt you back and harder" mentality down pat. It's my mantra.

My breath shudders with the pain again, and my hand trembles as I slide the knife back into the thigh holder. *No. I don't need to do anything daft.* Taking out the witch is not worth the paperwork. I bite my tongue so I don't swear at her and rapidly blink my blurry eyes to focus on the portal.

Ah, I see some of her magic has made it. I watch as the illegal portal snaps closed. "Bye-bye, Fred."

I sag. With my hands on my knees, I hunch over.

Out the corner of my eye, I spot a determined sapphire-blue creature zipping out with a stick of chalk over her shoulder. Story. Her paper-thin rose-gold wings flutter as she flits about, drawing a complicated circle around the now-damaged ley line to ensure it cannot reopen.

I sag a little more. The icy road looks mighty comfortable. I want nothing more than to drop to the ground in a sweaty, exhausted heap and sleep, but I don't. I can't. 'Cause the kids are watching.

*Yay. I'm having so much fun.*

Yep. This is just what I wanted to do on a Friday night: wrestle with an alien octopus and have my skin burned off by a vindictive witch's spell. I shake my head. My back clicks as I stand straight and plaster my professional mask back into place.

*All I wanted was a single night off. Was that too much to ask?*

I prod at the round injury on my face with a wince. I need to shift. My body feels like one enormous bruise. I have sucker marks and road rash, and my poor skin is still burning from the spell. The pain is making me angry. I want to pound Ethel in her smug face.

The demon kiss—the royal mating mark on the back of my hand—has been throbbing for the past hour. Kleric is worried. I try to ignore it. The demon kiss insistently throbs harder. It's itchy. I groan, clench my fist, and rub the back of my hand against my jeans. *Eff off*, I think—then moments later utter a silent apology in my head.

Last month I found a way of blocking Kleric. I learnt to build a wall, a shell around my mind. The nosy demon was perfectly okay with it. He said whatever makes me comfortable. It's a relief not to transmit every dumb thought that enters my head. He still gets the occasional flash, especially when I'm asleep or in pain. I sigh and poke at my face.

Scowling, I allow a trickle of my memories to escape my hold—of the portal, of Fred the otherworldly octopus—with a clear *I'm fine* thrown in at the end. That should shut him up.

*I have a demon mate.*

And just like that, my temper recedes. I chuckle and shake my head again, this time in disbelief. *Mate. What a load of crud.* I mentally scoff. We haven't even been on an actual date. I don't even know the guy. I fidget.

*At least this one likes me.* Yeah, not like the angel. My cheeks glow with embarrassed heat.

Having a mate doesn't mean shit. I soul-bonded to an angel, and look how that turned out... Prison. White torture. Yeah, all the fun stuff.

A niggly pain of my thumb reaches me, and I stop picking at the skin around my cuticle. Now *that* is a hard habit to break. I shake out my hand and allow it to flop against my leg, pressing each finger against my thigh so I don't start picking again at my poor bleeding digit.

The bond with the angel is broken now, so it doesn't matter.

I scuff the kerb with my boot as I watch Story finish the last curve of the circle—she's getting superfast at circle work.

I wish fate and magic would butt out of my nonexistent love life. Why can't I just be normal? I've had enough magic nonsense for a lifetime.

Everything would be better if Kleric were here on Earth. Talk about a long-distance relationship. Ours is out of this world. He was called back to his realm to answer some questions. And not just him. All the demons—apart from the scarce few born here—have returned.

Months ago, I stumbled upon some lower-level demons who used a hidden portal to enter Earth illegally. Then, while they were on *holiday*, they had the bright idea of setting up a blood ring to make money.

Yeah, who does that? Exsanguinate the locals and sell the blood to the highest bidder to make a few quid? I close my eyes and blow a breath through my nose. They killed a lot of good people.

The fallout has been a political nightmare. We've been on the cusp of war. Kleric has been away for three endless months while they all try to fix the problem.

I miss him.

Not seeing him makes me twitchy.

*Of course I'm twitchy.* I laugh under my breath and tilt my head back to stare at the night sky, sighing when I can't see any stars because of the light pollution. I've no idea if what we have is real. If it's magic pushing us together or... or I'm trying to replace the angel-shaped hole in my chest.

Kleric said I'm his mate.

No one said he was mine.

And Xander. I try not to think about the angel. There is something to be said about loving somebody too hard. Too much. Especially when they don't love you back.

The entire experience with Xander broke something inside me. And the love I had for him? It crumpled like an old paper cup. Xander. Why did I think of him? It's like I can't shrug him off no matter how much I try. I must stop obsessing. It's like my mind is stuck on him.

Hate will do that, and deep down I know it's unhealthy and a waste of my time.

Mental anguish will send a person like me barmy. I swallow down the lump in my throat and push the thoughts of Xander away, along with the yucky feeling of my stupidity.

A few kisses and a demon mating mark do not make a relationship, and if I'm honest, I don't trust myself.

It takes a special kind of bravery to try again with someone else.

I'm sure things will be resolved—if we get to see each other. Meanwhile, these random portals popping up all over town aren't helping matters. It freaks everyone out. Whoever is doing this needs to get a life.

I have an inkling it's because we shut down the first illegal portal, and now they think it's fun to play games. I make the easiest target. Yeah, whoever is doing this won't be laughing when I chop off their effing head.

Tonight someone opened that portal with the sole intention of swallowing my Defender. I glare down the street. Don't they say arsonists and criminals hang around at the scene to revel in the chaos? That's something this portal idiot would be doing. I bet a bale of timothy hay they are still here. Watching.

No matter what some creatures think, magic isn't infallible, and it's only a matter of time before they make a mistake. I smile. I'm glad I have micro-cameras recording everything.

"Why didn't you do your job and kill it?" says a bitter, whiny voice behind me.

*How nice. Ethel has come to chat.* I have to stop my hand from reaching towards my knife.

# CHAPTER TWO

I ROLL my eyes and stiffly turn to meet the witch's accusing blue gaze. Why didn't I kill it? It would have been quicker, but I've got a thing about killing innocent creatures. I won't if I can help it. Fred just saw a hole and poked his tentacles into it.

Ethel's eyes narrow with spite, and her lip curls with disgust. "Executioner." She scoffs.

*Executioner.*

My heart misses a beat with the title, but I lift my chin at her scorn. I deserve a pat on the back—aka a fist to the face—for taking on the role.

Oh, it offers me a level of protection, and no one is throwing me back into prison anytime soon. But if creatures hated me for being the weird unicorn-vampire hybrid, they sure do love me now as the executioner. I snort. Not only am I an abomination, but I'm also now a sell-out.

Literally *everybody* hates me.

Fun times.

Ethel doesn't bother to hide her abhorrence. No, she makes it perfectly clear which side of the fence she's on. And it's not the pro-Tru side. *Figures.* Her blonde hair is plastered to her temple with sweat, and dark grey circles shadow her eyes. In trying to hurt me, she used a heck of a lot of magic and hurt herself.

Ethel then dares to stare at the pixies and Story as if they are dirt. I sidestep to stand between her and the Land Rover, blocking her view.

I narrow my eyes. "Don't," I say in a creepy, soft tone.

Ethel puffs up from my warning and pushes her sweaty hair from her face. "Ever since you took over this region as its executioner, I've never been busier. You really need to start doing your job."

Story zips up from the road like a bullet. Under the glow of the streetlights, the dust from her wings sheds like sparks of glitter as she zooms past my nose and aggressively flies towards the witch's face.

*Uh-oh.*

"Do *your* job, Ethel, and shut up," Story snarls. "I don't know what you are moaning about. You're getting paid well." With sapphire-blue hands and arms covered in chalk, Story points her finger, wagging it millimetres away from the witch's button nose.

"You're on call, and it took you fifty minutes to get here. Fifty minutes! My kids are in that car." Story points behind her. "If we are going to chat about who's not doing their job properly, you might as well look in the mirror."

Ethel's mouth drops open.

I stand awkwardly while I watch the pixie and witch stare-off.

Story wins—of course she does. Ethel clears her throat, adjusts her fancy cream coat sleeves, and drops her gaze to the road and the finished circle. With a wiggle of her fingers and a pulse of magic—I'm proud I don't flinch—chalk puffs into the air, and the lines crackle and glow a pale blue as the spell locks on.

The magic fades, and I do my best to ignore the pain I feel as I go back to scanning the street.

"Let's talk about you hitting the executioner with your portal magic." Story continues her tirade. "Did you do that deliberately, or are you that shit?"

*Oh heck.*

"You are lucky the executioner is strong enough to shrug your magic off and has the grace to ignore your petty arse. Anyone else would have been hurt or killed with that stunt. What were you thinking? How stupid can one witch be? Pick a fight with the executioner? Next time you come out to close a portal, let's hope you don't trip and fall in." Story smiles.

It's not a friendly smile.

Ethel squeaks, spins on her heel, and hurries to her car.

"You're useless," Story shouts at her retreating back, "and I'll be speaking to Carol Larson about your negligence. We've got you on camera."

I wince and scratch the back of my neck; the grit from the road collects in my nails. That isn't an idle threat. Carol Larson is one scary lady. She's on the Grand Creature Council, and over the past five years, she has become the head of all the English covens.

Ethel's car door slams shut behind her, trapping the cream

coat in the door. She over-revs the engine, and the gears grind painfully as, with a flash of sparks, the red Fiat 500 careens through the ward and down the road, out of sight.

I don't think she even paused to put her seat belt on.

I hum as I root around in my heavy magic kit and grab a water bottle to wash away the chalk. My hand hovers over the first part of the circle. I could use a cleaning potion, but those spells are expensive, especially when water and a shuffle of feet will do the job. Plus I can say I used the spell and use it instead to clean my house. Win-win. I hate cleaning.

"Tripping into a portal, huh?" I say nonchalantly. The cheap plastic bottle crunches as I squeeze it. I rub the wet chalk with my boot—then frown. I'm making a right mess. This was a lot easier in my head.

"Well, she was rude. She could have seriously hurt you." Story drops onto my shoulder. "Are you okay?"

"Yeah. I've had worse." I glance down at my favourite jeans—or they were. I wasn't dressed for a battle this evening, and they're now ripped and dirty. I notice Story's chalk-covered hands and dribble some water onto one of Kleric's white monogrammed handkerchiefs I keep in my pocket like a weirdo, then pass it to her so she can clean up.

"Oh fancy. Thanks. Your face looks sore." She scrubs her arms.

"Yeah, I'm surprised I have any skin left." I scuff the last bit of chalk, now a blotchy mess, and sigh with self-disgust. I glug the remaining dregs of water. "Will the kids be okay for another few minutes? I need to shift." I'm hurting. I don't think I'll be able to concentrate enough to drive, and I can't wait to get home.

"Go for it. They are fine."

Story returns the handkerchief, and I stuff it back into my

pocket. I dig my phone out and place it on the kerb—the clothing-retention spell doesn't like technology, and to save the phone from becoming a mangled mess, it's best not to shift with it in my pocket.

"Thanks for scaring the witch and telling her off. You're my hero. I'm sorry this happened, and I'm gutted the kids missed the film."

Story glances at the car and grins back at me. "They're not. They haven't had this much fun in weeks. Such a wonderful time watching you fight an alien. I've never seen them so enthralled. The entire school will know about this adventure by the end of the weekend. If not the entire town." She nods at the ward, and I can make out the glint of a news van.

*Great.*

There's a pixie wail from the Land Rover, and an argument ensues.

Story groans. "I spoke too soon. Let me sort them out. Shift so we can go home. You're like a beacon with your poor skin glowing. It's so red." Story pats me on the cheek, and her toes dig into my shoulder as she springs into the air and flies back to the kids.

I watch until she disappears inside the car through the partially rolled-down window. "Jeff! Stop biting your sister. Did you open that popcorn?"

I grin. My face stings, so I allow the shifter magic to wash over me. Before an average person can blink, my molecules vibrate, and my vision goes black as I go from my human form to unconnected microparticles of matter floating around, then re-form into a unicorn.

My iridescent hooves clatter on the tarmac—gah! Such a slippery surface; I don't like roads. My rainbow mane blows in a salty gust of wind from the sea, and my tail whips against my hind legs.

I blast a big equine snort that echoes off the surrounding buildings and the bridge. Then it's a full-body shake. I'm overdue for a gallop and some field rest.

When my friend Forrest shifts, she can snap back into her human form without becoming her wolf. Each time I shift, I try, as my unicorn form is cumbersome, but it's something I've yet to crack. With a yawn and a last swish of my tail, I shift back into my human form.

Ah, good as new. The pain in my face and body is long gone. I adjust my tattered jumper and bend to collect my phone.

My scalp prickles.

"Watch out!" screams a woman's voice.

# CHAPTER THREE

My heart pounds as I spring to the side and spin. There's a *bong* sound of curved metal hitting flesh, the creature sneaking up behind me scrapes me on their way down to the ground, and their head hits the pavement with a splat.

*Oh no.*

I take in the trembling form of my rescuer: a girl with a *frying pan*. The sales tag, still attached to the handle, flutters in the wind as she holds the pan above her head, readying for another swing.

There's no need. The creature she brained—a man—lies deathly still. There's nothing I can do for him. His brains are leaking all over the pavement.

He's dead. Very dead.

The girl has a sweet, pretty round face with cheeks rosy from the cold. Her panting, panicky breaths fill the cold air with puffs of white, and her wide, innocent, frightened eyes stare at me in utter shock as she clutches the pan in one hand and the plastic bag it came from in the other.

My lips twitch as I note that she took the frying pan out of the bag before hitting him. Cute.

Her breathing makes me worry she will have a full-on panic attack, and I hold my hands up and keep my voice soft and soothing, so as not to freak her out further. "You're okay. It's okay. You saved me. You stopped him, you can put the pan down."

The hand above her head shakes, and she blinks up at the frying pan. I wince when a drop of red blood splatters against her cheek.

"Oh." Like a marionette with her strings suddenly cut, both her hands flop to her sides, and the girl slowly blinks at the downed creature. "Oh." Her knees wobble, and she lists to the side.

Crikey, is she going to faint?

"Here, sit down." I take hold of her elbow and guide her from the body to the edge of the pavement. After a few steps, her knees buckle, and she plops onto the kerb.

"I..." Her head rolls back, and big brown eyes stare at me with disbelief. Her mouth opens and closes like a fish gasping for breath, and her eyes fill with tears.

I shuffle between her and the dead guy, blocking off her view.

Heck, I've really messed up this time and turned a sweet, innocent kid into a killer. How horrific. This is bad. Really, really bad. Awkwardly I twist my hands and clear my throat.

"You didn't kill him. He's still... erm... breathing." I side-eye the dead guy.

Eh, what's one little white lie? Right? *Right?*

I am such a bad person.

She nods, drops her head between her knees, and gulps the frosty air. Her long, silky dark hair sweeps across her face. Still in her grip, the deadly frying pan clangs and scrapes on the road, leaving a macabre trail of residual blood and chunks of scalp—with hair. *Gag.*

Ah, poor girl. Her entire body is really shaking now.

"Everything is going to be okay." I awkwardly pat her back. "I appreciate your help." I back away from the girl, grab my bag, and pop on some blue medical-grade gloves. "There you go; that's it." I gently tug the pan out of her hand and ever so casually slip the blood-splattered kitchen utensil into a plastic evidence bag.

There. *I'll buy her another one*, I promise myself.

I don't know why I put things into evidence bags. It's something I do. Professional. I've not got a clue what I'm doing. I'm purely emulating what I see on television.

"I'm Tru. What's your name?"

"Caitlyn. Caitlyn Croft," she mumbles into her knees.

"Can you tell me what happened, Caitlyn?"

It takes her a few seconds to answer me. "I'm s-sorry I hit him so hard. I panicked. He had a potion ball and a knife! He was going to hurt you." She lifts her head, and I meet her earnest brown eyes. "He was creeping about outside my window for the past ten minutes. I'd just come home from shopping at Asda." The plastic bag with its green supermarket logo crackles as she hugs it to her chest like a teddy bear.

Gosh, I feel terrible.

"I heard the tyres squeal and saw that a portal had opened

under the bridge, almost underneath a car. I realised immediately that you were a professional when you put up the ward, so I stayed in my house, out of the way, and watched you out my window. I'm glad you didn't hurt the octopus."

*See, see? Not everyone thinks I should have hurt Fred.* I hide my smile behind my forearm.

"I noticed the man lurking. He disappeared using a Don't See Me Now spell. But I could still feel him on the other side of the glass." She frowns. "His magic felt rotten. He stepped away from the spell when you picked up your phone and crept towards you. He was holding a knife and an orange potion ball. I know enough to know an orange potion is bad. When he moved to throw the spell... I... I grabbed the nearest thing, ran out the door, shouted a warning, and whacked him on the head." Her eyes drop to stare at her hands.

Within the row of brightly painted terraced houses, I clock the open door behind us. What she's saying makes sense.

"Will I get in trouble?" She cringes and ducks behind her hair.

I turn back to her. "No. You did great. You saved my life."

Guilt swims in my chest. She shouldn't have had to save me. He shouldn't have got so close. I'm so used to Dexter, my beithíoch—fae monster cat—watching my back. Aside from tonight's cinema trip, he hasn't left my side since Kleric left.

I've become lackadaisical.

My vision swims. I'm so damn tired. The shift didn't fix that. It's been a hell of a few weeks. I force myself to keep talking. "If everything checks out, which I'm sure it will, you won't get into trouble. Are you okay for a second? I'm just going to... erm..." I stare at the dead guy. *Come on, Tru, think.* I click my gloved fingers and grin. "Move him into the recovery position."

My smile must be so fake, but her eyes are glassy with shock, and she doesn't seem to notice.

Thank fate.

"Yes, yes, of course. Thank you, Executioner." She waves me away, and her head slumps again between her knees. Yuck. I get that same uncomfortable feeling in my chest hearing the title.

I grab my kit, stash the pan, and kneel beside the dead guy. I peek over my shoulder. Lucky for me, Caitlyn doesn't move and keeps her back turned.

"So you're strong?" I ask her as I pat down the corpse. I empty his pockets, placing his personal effects into another evidence bag. Huh, no wallet but a massive collection of expensive spells. He's well connected.

"Not really," she mumbles. "I'm human. I have three brothers, and they used to make me play with them to even the numbers on teams, so I developed a good swing."

"Nice." Now that's kind of strange. I ignore the warning bell that clatters in my head. Humans can't feel magic, and she said his magic felt rotten. If Caitlyn doesn't want to tell me the truth about her heritage, I won't go poking. I spent seventeen years playing human, and I'm not about to out her.

No way am I going to be a hypocrite and out someone who has helped me.

If I had to guess, I'd say she's fae. I peek at her. Maybe part elf? Creature heritage can be a touchy subject, and I know from experience that people do not like different. I'm a strange unicorn-vampire combo, a true hybrid. Hybrids are usually hunted and killed on sight. Some old inbuilt fear about our magic has everyone in a tizzy. I think it's an old wives' tale. For all my research and my grandad's research when he was alive, we couldn't find anything, but it's a fear that goes back millennia.

I'm lucky to be alive.

Story is also different. She's pure fae. Her mother was a fairy, her father a pixie. After her mother's death, her troupe excommunicated her when they discovered the secret of her beautiful wings. Getting thrown out for a pixie is a death sentence. They dared to call *her* an abomination.

*Dicks.*

If pixies shouldn't have wings, then perhaps her father shouldn't have mated with a fairy.

She showed them. Not only did she survive, she thrived and is loved, with a troupe of her own who embrace and celebrate their differences.

I nudge the guy's leg. Next to the body is a silver knife and an intact orange marble-sized potion ball. Oh! Caitlyn was right. I poke the spell. It is a nasty melt-your-face-off potion.

If Miss Pan-a-lot hadn't helped, I might have been in a pickle.

The nasty potion goes into a specialist anti-magic bag along with all the other spells—my new job does come with some perks—and the knife goes into another evidence bag.

"I'm an only child. I would have loved brothers."

"I'm lucky. They are great."

Ah, that's good to know. Perhaps I'm supercynical. Not everybody has a crap life, and maybe she's just a magic-sensitive human with a great swing.

"Do you want me to call them? Your brothers?" I ask.

Caitlyn hunches. "God, no. I'd rather you don't. They are protective and will be mad I left the house."

I roll the dead guy over so he's face up and so the microcameras filming the scene can see him. *I bet they've already scanned him and taken his DNA.* As soon as the thought enters my head, my datapad pings. Ava.

The tech witch, like Story, is now an official part-time employee of the Office of the Executioner. I need all the help I can get. Even if I constantly worry about their safety.

I groan scrolling through the information, then wince. The man was a witch. Male witches are exceedingly rare; I'm going to get a lot of blowback from his death.

A powerful dead male witch. Great.

Not that this idiot wasn't a bad guy. According to the data, Marcus was a gateway witch. If I'm right—and the witches can confirm his magical signature—he's the one who's been popping open portals all over town, causing havoc, fanning the flames of war. A right pain in the arse.

I hope the witches will see Caitlyn has done them a favour bashing in his head. Marcus was a PR nightmare. And if that's not bad enough to warrant his death, the dickhead tried to kill me.

Let's hope things will return to normal with his death. *Maybe a certain demon can come home?* The witches are going to have to suck it up.

At the end of the message, Ava adamantly states she will not help further with this case, citing a conflict of interest. Wonderful. That's just great.

At the fluttering sound of wings, I glance up—Story hovers behind my shoulder, reading the report.

"That the portal guy?"

"Yeah. I believe so. He's a gateway witch. I'll have to get ahead of the storm and debrief Carol Larson as soon as possible." I do a full-body shudder. I hate speaking to people. I especially hate talking to Carol Larson. "I bet Ava will have already informed her."

"I'll speak to Carol." Story interprets my shudder perfectly. "So glad he's dea—"

"Unconscious," I blurt with a wave and frantic nod towards the shaking girl.

Story narrows her eyes. I widen mine and do another weird nod at Caitlyn. She rolls her eyes when she finally catches on. "Yeah, so glad he's *unconscious*," she deadpans. *Did she kill him?* she mouths.

I nod.

"Sooo I rang for an *ambulance*"—now she's laying it on a bit too thick—"and a team of hunters are on their way to take over and clear the scene."

Great. They can finish up. My role as an executioner isn't to investigate, it's to kill people.

"It's okay," comes a mumble behind us. Caitlyn wobbles to her feet and points at Marcus. "I know he's dead. Stuff is leaking from his ears, and..." She straightens. "Executioner, you are a terrible liar."

"She's not wrong." Story grins at me.

*An executioner should never apologise or admit any liability.* That's a line in the training handbook. I groan. I might have read the thing and stuffed it into a drawer to never be seen again.

Eff it. I've never been one for following the rules.

"I'm not sorry I lied, Caitlyn." I lift my chin and square my shoulders. "I'm sorry you had to kill him. I'm so sorry I put you in that position. If it's any consolation, he was a bad man."

"I know."

"Have you got somewhere else to go? I can arrange a safe hou—"

"No," she snaps, thrusting out her palm to stop me.

"Oh okay." I rock from foot to foot.

Caitlyn has had a nasty shock. I'll try to convince her, even if it's a temporary relocation, tomorrow. I doubt my employer, the Grand Creature Council, will help as she claims to be human. I know from experience they won't even put a guard on her door. I'll get Story to ring our contact within the human police and see if the local patrol can at least keep an eye on the house.

"I just want to stay home," she whispers. Caitlyn backs away from us and towards the open front door. "Look, I'm freezing. Is it okay if I... Do you need anything else from me?"

I shake my head.

"Will the Hunters Guild want to speak with me?"

"Yes, as a formality. No one else should bother you if they do." I dig into my pocket and pass her an official business card. The corners are slightly curled at the edges, and the card is a little worn. It has seen better days, but at least it's clean—no blood or goo. "Call me anytime. I'll try to keep you out of everything as much as I can."

"Thanks." She taps the card against her palm.

A nagging instinct twists my insides and insists I need to do more. "Oh, and here." I stuff my hand into the kit bag. I don't trust the witches not to retaliate. *Aha.* I pull out a ward. We can't be too careful, and like most creatures in this area, she hasn't got a barrier on her home. "This ward should last a few weeks." I hand her the expensive potion.

She blinks. "Thanks."

"No, thank you. I owe you one." I gently squeeze her arm and give her a small, reassuring smile.

Caitlyn nods, and with a floppy, sad wave, she goes inside.

"Don't worry." Story tugs a strand of hair away from my cheek and tucks it behind my ear. "I'll speak to Ava about getting her a place at the Sanctuary."

I nod. "That's a good idea. Thanks."

The Sanctuary is a pocket realm. I've never been myself, but from what I've heard, it accepts and protects anyone who genuinely needs help. It could be an excellent option for Caitlyn until we sort things out. After a few minutes, the ward pops into existence.

She's safe.

For now.

And you never know; everything might *pan* out. Inwardly I smirk. Everything tonight has gone wrong, but at least my mental pan puns are on point.

# CHAPTER FOUR

"They're here," Story singsongs from above my head as two giant, beefy black Land Rover-style vehicles enter the ward. The ward spits and sparks but allows the cars through as it's set to all authorised personnel.

Ah, yes, the hunters. Backup has finally arrived, and it's about time. It's been well over an hour since Story made the initial call.

Story lands on my shoulder as they pull up to the kerb and disgorge as a unit from the vehicles, wearing black fatigues and loaded with creature-killing weapons that glint under the streetlights. I refrain from rolling my eyes. They look ridiculous.

Eight hunters. They sent two teams. How nice.

One team splits into two, peeling off to guard each end of the ward, and a single hunter hefts the portal equipment from the back of the car. It looks like a big Geiger counter, but it's made to monitor ley line activity.

Helpfully, as if it isn't apparent, I point at the splodgy chalk mess underneath the bridge. She acknowledges me with a chin lift and gets to work.

The remaining hunters stomp towards us. I've seen all three around but have yet to work with them directly, so I don't know their names. Two eye the dead body while one guy, a smarmy-looking vampire, stares at me like I ate the last piece of birthday cake.

*That one is going to be trouble.*

"Executioner." The big guy in the middle lifts his gaze from the dead witch and snarls a greeting while he looks at my torn-jeans-and-jumper combo like I should be ashamed for not having a matching outfit.

*Oh, and perhaps that one too.*

Going off the simple stripes on the shoulder, he's the team leader and a cat shifter from the look of his magic. "What do you have for us?" he barks, overaggressive and highly combative.

*Who the heck does he think he's talking to?*

My sudden rise to the lofty heights of the executioner had to have come as a surprise. It's not like anyone knows I was a super-secret black ops assassin. They don't know what I can do, and if they don't know, how can they respect what I've done?

The dramatic public display of me outing the demons could be taken in various ways, and it would not be a stretch to presume wrongly the Creature Council paid me off with a fancy title and a job that I don't deserve.

It's iffy and confusing. I get it. So I try not to take it

personally, but... I sigh. This entire hostile thing is getting old real fast.

On my shoulder, Story shuffles, and her bare toes scrunch the material of my top. The animosity in the air is choking.

The team leader narrows his eyes. Impatient.

I stare back at him.

He scowls and makes a get-on-with-it hand gesture.

Ah, so that's how it is? Would it hurt them to introduce themselves? What has the world come to when they can't even be arsed to pretend to be polite? Frustration bleeds out of my pores, but I keep my professional mask on. If I took offence over every little thing... I'd get no work done.

I sigh again and, as professionally as I can, give them the rundown.

While I'm talking, the male witch's brains are scraped off the pavement, and everything is sealed into a body bag.

"I'll let you get on with it," I finish. I'm ready to go home. My stomach is cramping with hunger, and even though it's still early, I'm willing to call today over and done. Go to bed and hide under the covers to contemplate what the heck I'm doing with my life.

"I'll send you the video evidence and reports within the hour," Story adds, still on my shoulder, tapping away on her datapad. She doesn't even bother to look their way.

The team leader grunts.

*All righty then.*

I hand over the collection of evidence bags and turn to leave.

"Bitch," someone says under their breath.

Story stiffens.

Name-calling? Seriously? My tolerance level for maiming

or insulting Tru Dennison today has reached its peak. Oh, and I think Story's head is going to pop off she's so mad.

When I turn back, the smarmy vamp goes so far as to smirk and give me a finger wave. His eyes sparkle. "Bye-bye, Executioner. You have a nice night."

*Funny guy.*

This hunter is having a wonderful time at my expense. He thinks I'm some kind of joke. He also thinks I was born yesterday. Calling me a bitch will not get a rise out of me, no way, and the jokes on him. I don't care what some random hunter thinks. He can't bait me.

I stare back blankly.

What I really want to do plays out in my head: I mentally punch him in the face. No... I pause the fantasy and rewind it. That isn't good enough, not a punch. The idiot deserves a bitch slap. *There.* I smile picturing the blooming red glow of my handprint on his face—no one wants to be slapped—followed by the embarrassed flush to his cheeks. The tang of blood on his breath means he's recently fed; the blood in his system should give his skin a nice glow.

Yeah, all I want to do is slap him around a bit. That isn't too much to ask, is it? But that'll just prove to them I lack control, and they win. I will remember his face.

I keep staring.

It has been so long since the vampire wiggled his fingers. It's as if the entire world has gone silent in anticipation. It holds its breath.

The vampire rocks from foot to foot.

Silence is an underrated psychological weapon. He's finding it hard to continue to hold my gaze. I might not have a reputation, but something instinctive happens in his brain as he looks into the eyes of a killer and begins to feel like prey.

Life was so much easier when I could open my mouth and let what I thought vomit right out. Biting my tongue and playing these professional games is tedious.

I turn to leave.

Oh, and the vampire doesn't like that. "That's right, leave us to clean up your mess. Next time you open your legs for someone, maybe leave the Hunters Guild out of it. We all know your job is a reward for you lying on your back." He belly laughs, gripping his stomach, and elbows his colleague.

*Nice one, very smart.*

His laugh gains a creepy edge when I don't react. Then I yawn, and he snaps. He pulls out a silver knife, slides into a fighting stance, and points the blade at my face.

*Cute.*

My lips twitch, and it takes all my control not to bust out a laugh. "Hunter, are you threatening me with that little silver blade?" I blink innocently. "Story, are you seeing this, or do my eyes deceive me?"

"Nope. That's a knife."

I hum.

*Come, let me kiss you with my fist or tickle the side of your head with my toes.*

My manic smile is so bright the other two hunters step back. I grin toothily at the three of them and clap my hands. They flinch. For good measure, I give my shoulders a little shimmy. "Finally. Something goes right."

*Thank fate. The handbook was very clear about dealing with threats.*

I chuckle.

The vampire's Adam's apple bobs with a nervous swallow, his hand gripping the blade for grim death ever so slightly shakes. He takes a deep breath—and lunges.

Story leaps from my shoulder and zooms into the air.

My left hand snaps out, and as if I'm grabbing a naughty toddler, I use his prominent Adam's apple as a handle to pull the vampire out of his leap. My fingers grip either side of the cartilage, and my nails dig into his throat.

I control his knife hand with a quick twist of his wrist, then hold him easily above my head—arm's length to avoid his flailing legs—and manoeuvre him over to slam his back against the wall of the house next door to Caitlyn's.

The vampire's feet dangle a foot off the pavement.

I jerk his blade arm to the side of the fresh new ward and let it zap him. With a lovely, satisfying scream, he drops the knife.

*There, that's better.*

"Don't," I growl as his pals move to help him.

They back off.

The vampire's blood trickles underneath my nails and dribbles down to my wrist. I could pop his larynx right out. *All it would take is a quick twist.*

"Anyone else?"

Grumbles of "no, Executioner" come from the surrounding hunters. All seven of them. How lovely; the gang is all here. Sometimes people need a demonstration.

I turn my head and glare at the cat shifter—this idiot's team leader. "I can't address you by name because you haven't introduced yourself. You really need to learn some manners. So, unknown cat shifter, is this how you run your team?" I give the whimpering vampire a little shake.

"No, Executioner."

"No?"

The shock on his face is priceless.

The vampire's blood is now dripping to my elbow. I turn back to the struggling hunter. "And you, you need to learn discipline. Learn to keep your mouth shut. You wanted a reaction. Huh? Was this what you wanted?" I shake his dangling body, and his shoulder brushes the ward. *Oops.* He moans when the magic bites him again.

"If I ever hear your dulcet tones again, I'll do more than squeeze your throat." I drop my voice and lower him ever so slightly so we are nose to nose. I wrinkle mine. The guy stinks of onions, garlic, blood, and a smidge of rot.

If you have a keen nose, bitten vampires smell a touch dead. Like the faint, barely perceptible reek of early decomposition. Cells dying before the vampire virus kicks in. I was born part vampire, so I'm not half-dead or whiffy.

My fingers brush the side of his cheek, and I turn his head, lean closer, and whisper creepily in his ear, "If I see you again, I'll kill you. And then I'll find and kill everyone you have ever loved just because I can. Whatever story you've made up in that little pea brain of yours"—I poke him in the forehead—"or whatever bullshit the gossips are saying behind my back, be aware: I didn't get the job by lying on my back."

My nails dig in a little more. Gosh, I wish I had claws.

"No, I got the job because I'm good at killing things. I'm good at sneaking around in the shadows during the dead of night. You're only alive now because I choose to spare you, and frankly, I can't be arsed with the paperwork. Think about that. Your death isn't worth my filling in a ten-minute form."

With disgust, I move back, open my hand, and drop him.

Now I'm all gross with his blood. Without thinking and with my anger riding me, I shift my sticky, bloody arm. It doesn't change into a hoof. Instead, it snaps back to a clean human hand.

Story lets out a little gasp and covers it with a cough.

"Later." I'm too mad to think about what I just did. I file it away to puzzle over later and raise my voice. "Hunter, you are done. Report to the Guild to sign the paperwork. You're dismissed from service for gross misconduct."

"You can't do that," chirps another hunter.

"I can't? Well, funny that I just did. Section 8.682: Attacking a superior is grounds for instant dismissal." Okay, so I memorised the bloody manual before chucking it into a drawer. "And for attacking an executioner with silver, he should be dead by rights. But today I'm feeling generous. However, please continue to argue. I might change my mind and kill him."

I wait for any comeback, but wisely, the hunters keep shtum.

"Now clean this scene up and get the road open." I step back, spin, and prowl back to the Land Rover with a bouncing, elegant stride.

I make sure Story is ahead of me.

I can feel the judgy, hate-filled gazes on my back. Meh. They can judge, gripe, and moan all they want. I'll still be the person who comes to clean up their mess when things get too tough.

# CHAPTER FIVE

I LEAN against the dirty Land Rover, arms and chin resting on the roof. My cheek is wet with Page's slobbery goodnight kiss, and I haven't the heart to wipe it off. The pixies make their way down the winding, solar-lit path to their fancy state-of-the-art home. I like to ensure they get there safely.

Their burrow is hidden within the tree roots of a small orchard grove of nine ancient apple trees to the left of the driveway.

The trees were a mess when we first purchased the house. My eyes drift across the sleeping winter branches. Carefully pruned and trimmed, they are now healthy, and with the surrounding soil organically fertilised and sown with wildflowers and wild garlic, the area will be extra beautiful come spring.

I'm so looking forward to the apple blossoms. Who doesn't love apple trees in bloom?

The café where I used to work—and where Story still decorates the wedding cakes on occasion—is owned by a dryad friend. Tilly has branches of her apple tree stretched across the café's ceiling. Due to Tilly's magic, the branches are forever in bloom.

The scent of blossom and coffee and cakes is memory-inducing for me and will always remind me of safety and... throbbing feet. I wiggle my toes. Crikey, I clocked some hours at that café. I'd worked there full-time since I was fourteen.

The pixies are about halfway down the path when Ralph—Story's mate—meets them.

"Papa, Tru battled an alien monster!" cries Page excitedly as she runs towards him and grabs his hand, twirling underneath his arm.

"Did she now?" He hugs her and kisses her on the forehead.

"Yeah, and Tru dangled a hunter by his throat."

I groan, cringe, and knock my forehead against the roof. "Thanks, Jeff," I grumble under my breath.

"Mum shouted at a mean witch," Novel adds, dancing ahead of them.

"Really?" Ralph raises an eyebrow, and Story shrugs as she holds his other hand and nestles into his side. "You didn't mention that in your text," he says into her hair as he kisses her cheek.

"You know I don't like bullies. I would have stabbed the hunter in the eye if Tru had given me a chance."

I chuckle as Jeff dramatically re-enacts the alien octopus

battle with Novel and Page playing along. Much to my amusement—even full of popcorn—he does a commando-style roll to avoid Novel's *tentacle*.

The troupe of pixies goes inside, and with a nod and a wave from Ralph, the door clicks closed.

Even from here, I feel the steady, reassuring hum of the burrow's ward.

All safe.

My tummy flips, and I sigh as I stare at the tiny door. I've seen the design plans, but I'll never see inside their new home as I'm not six inches tall. It's a shame, but what can you do? It's just one of those big-creature things, I guess.

I'm glad Story has made steps towards focusing on her traditional needs, and I love that the troupe has a proper home of their own. I tap the roof of the Defender. I'm not sad... it's just a slight life adjustment, that's all.

*It's silly as they are right there—next door.*

I push off the car and spin on my toes. I miss them. And it's crazy 'cause I don't even like people. Blah, kids. I mock shudder and then touch my still-wet cheek. Who am I kidding? I adore the little monsters.

I miss Justin and Morris too. They both stayed in the flat because it's closer to work; unlike the rest of us, they didn't want to live so rurally. I can't understand that. Who doesn't want to see the stars and hear the birds? They were both so excited before I got my new job. I think... I think me being the local executioner frightens Justin. He's been off for the past few months. I have no idea how to broach the subject with him. What if I'm making a lot of fuss over nothing?

I haven't got many friends, and my heart can't take the loss of even one. So of course instead, I give them space.

Another bout of sadness creeps in. My friend relationships

are changing; we're growing apart.

I don't like it.

While everyone around me seems to be doing grown-up things like having babies and moving forward with their relationships, I'm just the same as I've always been.

*My life is stuck, and I'm alone.*

Frowning, I mentally pull myself out of my funk and look at the house. The farmhouse has a long way to go compared to the finished burrow. I scrub my face. There is still so much work to be done, and I wanted to do it myself, but of course I haven't got enough time to do everything I want.

At least on the outside, the house is perfect. I allow myself a small, proud grin. When we first purchased the home, the walls were rendered a dirty white, and the plaster had crumbled and cracked in places, spreading mould and dampness inside. I didn't want *white*.

I swallow as a memory tries to invade my mind, and I push it back down. I stuff those sharp shards into the same dark hole where I stuff everything. They claw and bite on the way down.

I had the render stripped back, and a team of stone masons —dwarfs—clad the outside in a dark grey stone. I also replaced the roof tiles and the old rotten wood sash windows. The windows' like-for-like equivalent cost me a mini fortune, and were painted purple to match the front door; they are so worth it. Grey and purple. I nod. And for a genuine modern touch, the entire back of the house is glass.

The floor-to-ceiling windows are coated with an expensive spell so the occupants have an uninterrupted view of the surrounding fields. But with the spell, no one can see inside. Twenty-three acres of organic grassland wrap around the house, and I'm negotiating another forty acres of woodland along the western boundary.

Yeah, I love the outside of the house.

The inside of the house is still a building site, but it's getting there. My beloved home is coming together. It seems slowly, but after all, it's only been three months. We have at least finished the main bedroom—well, more of a suite, with an attached bathroom and an epic weapons room.

I kick a chunk of stone, and it skitters across the overgrown driveway—which will be the last thing on my list to fix. A ginger blur tears around the side of the house and, on almost silent paws, pounces on the stone.

Dexter.

His claws dig into the ground, and his teeth flash as he cautiously lifts a paw and peaks underneath. With abject disgust, he meows and batters the stone away. Scowling, he pads towards me.

"Reow." He forcibly butts his head against my leg in his custom kitty greeting.

"Hi, Dex." My insides flip. Ah, and there it is; the adorable monster cat reminds me yet again I'm not alone. Not one bit.

I bend and scratch behind his ears. He rubs against me, and I watch, fascinated, as every loose ginger hair on his body seems to jump and stick onto my jumper.

*No, I'm not alone.* I'm being silly, and I've had a bad day.

I peek at the scar on my hand, a perfect rendition of Kleric's lips. If I'm lucky, I might never be alone again.

I don't like change, that's all.

"Reow."

"Yes."

"Berrrt."

"Yesss." I have no idea what he's saying. "Yes. You are such a good boy," I coo. "You pounced beautifully on that naughty stone."

He narrows his eyes and then wiggles so my hand drifts down his spine, and he raises his bottom for an extra scratch and flicks his tail so it wraps around my wrist.

"Mert?" He drops his head to sniff at my boots and sneezes. They must have traces of scent on them as I had to walk back through the crime scene to get to the Land Rover.

"Yes. I missed you too, and tonight you missed all the fun. I battled an alien octopus and almost got my face melted off, not once, but twice, and then a vampire hunter tried to stab me."

*So much fun.*

"Breow," he chirrups as he dances around my feet.

"I'm useless without you watching my back, Dex." I shoulder my kit—I can't leave it in the car—and the pretty purple front door opens on silent hinges as we shuffle inside.

I stand on the threshold, rub my face, and mumble into my hand. "I messed up bad, Dex," I confess. "This girl, Caitlyn, came out of nowhere and *saved me*. A human girl killed a bad witch with a frying pan. Boinked him on the head. It's not a scientific conclusion, but I'm pretty sure his brains leaked out of his nose. He was dead before he hit the pavement from a single hit. It's a bad day when someone saves you with a frying pan." I let out a laugh.

Even to my own ears, it sounds sad.

The front door clicks closed, and Dexter nudges my leg. "I'll order her a new frying pan in the morning. The hunters took away the gooey one." I flick the lights and... nothing.

*Huh. Did the builders mess up?*

I squint into the blackness.

The ward of the house hums at my back, but it's hardly reassuring as Dexter growls—and what feels like foul magic pulses from the darkness.

# CHAPTER SIX

THE DARKNESS of the house mugs me. Unlike a proper pureblood vampire or even a bitten, I have no night sight. I'm plagued with human vision in this form. So I wait, breathing quiet and slow, letting my eyes adjust to the gloom.

Knife in hand.

Silence and darkness.

I stretch out my senses. Yep. Greasy, rotten, evil magic. And not just magic. I take a deep breath; above the smell of the building work is the scent of rot—and not vampire rot.

That's *dead*-dead body rot.

*Not this again.* The taste of bile fills my mouth as stomach acid burns up my throat and I have to work to swallow to avoid throwing up. It's a natural reaction to the smell—my body telling me *don't eat* that.

*Yeah, no shit. Thanks for the advice.*

This reek is beyond revolting, and that's saying something. This is the night for gross smells. I hold my breath, but the stink sticks; I'll no doubt be able to smell it in my hair.

Speaking of hair, the baby hairs on the back of my neck stand on end, goosebumps pepper my skin, and fear trickles down my spine.

I twist the fear into something else. *I'm so excited,* I tell myself until my body begins to believe it. A smile tugs at my lips as wrath tugs at my soul.

*How dare they come into my home.*

I can be a patient hunter.

No. No need to go hunting. They will come to us if they are still in the house, and I need to present myself as a juicy target. How better than to stand here in the dark?

Moments tick by and no one comes to greet us.

*Perhaps we need a better lure?*

"Hi, honey. I'm home!" Just to be extra weird, I open the front door. "I need a healing potion. My leg is sore!"

Dexter turns his ginger head and gives me a look as if to ask, *What the heck are you doing?* I shrug and close the door with an extra-hard slam.

"Hello!"

Nothing.

No sound troubles the silence, and no one comes to greet us. Shame. "I'm pretty sure the intruder or intruders are long gone." *That doesn't mean the house isn't crawling with foreign magic and technology though.*

The knife still in one hand, with the other, I slide the kit from my shoulder, rest it on my thigh, and root around for a light spell.

Good thing I keep this bag organised; the light magic glows a pale yellow in the dark, which helps. I bring the spell to my lips and under my breath whisper the incantation for gradual light. The last thing I need is to blind myself.

The marble warms and the spell softly glows in all directions, spilling through my fingers. I open my hand and blink as my eyes adjust while the light forms into a ball and rises into the air.

The warm, growing light chases away the darkness and touches the hallway walls—the new wainscoting wall panelling looks lovely, primed and ready to be painted, and... the light highlights the glint of metal on the stairs.

I tilt my head.

The lingering tiredness in my bones washes away with the spike of adrenaline that floods my blood.

"Well, I didn't install that art feature. *How thoughtful.*" I take in the old, stripped-down staircase—prepped for the carpenter to do his thing—now with dozens of blades buried into the wood.

Knives of different sizes, some old, some new.

Some of them buried to the hilt, and others just balancing on their tips and barely in. They glisten in the spell's light.

It is a terrifying sight, and most people would freak out. I let out a low chuckle. *I find the display fascinating.*

"How nice to leave me so many weapons. I wonder how many I can stick in the intruder before they bleed out?"

I know I need to check my house over with a fine-tooth comb. I don't want any extra surprises. I've already been jumped once tonight. With a sigh, I dig back into my kit and throw a handful of micro-cameras into the air to record this mess.

*No more mistakes, Tru.* With that thought, I pull out a fancy plastic capsule and a bag of mixed herbs. Rattling around inside the capsule is a See Magic spell.

Professionals only use this super-duper-special magic on important crime scenes, the death-of-a-world-leader level of a case, not an 'oops, someone broke into my home' situation.

I shouldn't use it.

Not for this, but... Eff it. They came into my house.

The capsule has three seals. I need both hands, so I slide the blade away, my kit goes back on my shoulder, and I put the bag of herbs between my knees for safekeeping.

To open the capsule is like a Rubik's Cube level of difficulty. Finally, I pop off the plastic lid, and... Huh. It's a tad anticlimactic. For all the effort, I expect a dramatic puff of smoke, a *wah* sound effect or something. I tug out the potion and peer inside the glass vial, and the clear liquid looks like water.

The See Magic spell should highlight everything that has happened in this house in the past few hours.

It should illuminate residual magic as a sickly green. Any creature, alive or dead, will be highlighted in red and technology in blue.

It's so sensitive that if a fly farted, the magic should pick it up. Or that's the theory.

I tip the bag of mixed herbs into my palm and add the potion. Another singsong incantation, this time no whispering needed.

The herbs burst into flames. I let out a squeak and jerk out of the way as the blue fire engulfs my hand and almost gets my face. It takes everything in me not to drop the flaming mess on the floor.

Then—thank fate—the flame goes out, and the ash in my palm disappears with a puff of smoke. With a thick, nose-hair-burning smoky aroma, the See Magic spell activates. It whooshes through the house, blowing the loose pieces of my hair away from my face, and the spell's heat dries my eyes.

Tiny spots of blue zip about taking data and readings—the micro-cameras. It's working. I have this weird gut feeling that I need to do something extra. I shake my head and ignore that inner voice.

Dark smudges smear the floor.

*Hmm. Black?*

I lean forward to eye a thick patch in the middle of the hallway. Perhaps it's a dark green? I spin the container and squint at the label. It gives me a colour chart in teeny-tiny writing. I groan. Hopefully, the cameras will get this on film, and I'll study the fine details later. The spell isn't going to last all night, and I need to find out what the hell they were doing in my house.

I spin and see that the black stuff goes up the stairs. Magic bleeds from whoever's been here. Rotten, disgusting magic leaking so much I can make out faint footprints on the floor. No red, at least, so there's nobody up there.

My gaze follows the black splodges in the hallway, enormous feet with a deeper imprint on the left leg, a slight drag on the right, and a small set leading to the cupboard underneath the stairs where the electric box lives.

I make sure I don't touch any of the magic residues as I tiptoe to the warped cupboard door. The old door—white glossed to within an inch of its life and soon to be replaced—creaks.

I peer inside. The ball of light bobs above my shoulder and highlights the new fuse box. I flick the main switch, and the house lights up with a click and a buzzing hum.

Every working light.

The hallway, the upstairs landing, the empty home office on my right, and the sitting room on the left. It all lights up as if someone turned on every working light in the house just for funsies.

"It's like bloody Blackpool illuminations," I mumble, quoting my grandad's favourite line whenever he used to deem I had too many lights on as a kid—it's a Northern English thing.

I stare back at the smudges, and something inside me, that same nagging gut feeling, an instinct, urges me to add some of my magic to the See Magic spell. *My magic?* That's not something I've ever done before. It's not something I've ever tried, and it's a stupid idea.

My magic is a messed-up unicorn version of vampire compulsion. It's mental manipulation. I can't just flick it about willy-nilly. I'm not a witch. But something tells me to give it a go. Magic, after all, is instinctive. I huff. *Go big or go home, right? What's the worst that can happen?*

Famous last words.

The ball of magic I keep locked in my chest quivers, and with an almost careless toss and a too-late wince of regret, I throw a tiny bit of my magic into the active spell. Cerise pink power zaps out from the tip of my index finger. It feels right. The hybrid magic zips into the air, joins the See Magic spell, and... cannibalises it.

*Uh-oh.*

I watch, horrified, as the magic colours swirl around us, seem to condense and blacken, then turn into shadows. Dexter bumps against my leg in silent support. The magic-made shadows get thicker and almost corporal.

Next to the front door, one familiar-shaped shadow is tall and thin with a rainbow shimmer blending into an oil-slick mass of colour around the edges. The smaller one is cat-shaped, and the edges glow blue. Is that Dexter and me? Wow. Now that's kind of cool.

"Oh crap." I change my mind when the shadows *move*.

# CHAPTER SEVEN

SUPERFAST, the shadow that is mine whips out a knife—I'm impressed at its speed. My heart rate evens when Shadow Me mimes opening the front door. *Phew.* I haven't created shadow monsters of Dexter and myself, and they'll not be taking over the world anytime soon. No, the shadows are re-enacting the moments when we first entered the house. I've given the See Magic spell volume and animation, I guess.

After a few uneventful minutes, the shadows fade. Okay, this is good. I roll my shoulders and neck, feeling a little freaked out and stiff. Cautiously I gather more of the magic from my chest, then push the power into the nearest black splodge.

This time it's more complicated. The black residue is older

and stubborn. It doesn't want to behave. I grit my teeth wrangling the magic, and sweat beads on my brow as I feed it a little more of my power—a bit of pink, a dash of pale blue—the magic sparks.

A few seconds. Nothing happens. Then, with an internal *bong* in my head, the spell beckons me to the back of the house. Dexter must have heard the same call. The fur along his back fluffs up, and he lets out an angry hiss as he meanders down the hall.

I follow his fluffy butt.

Moonlight and the solar lights from the garden spill into the room, highlighting the bare wires hanging from the newly plaster-boarded walls. The light fittings still need to be installed, and tins of paint and building equipment are neatly stacked in the far corner. Through the double-height windows, there is a view of endless fields and the corner of the oblong outbuilding that's been converted into a state-of-the-art gym and guest accommodation.

In the middle of the floor is a black pool of rotten magic.

*Now that is not good.*

As we approach, I notice the See Magic spell is dormant. Broken? No—it comes to life when we move closer. The tension on the surface of the pool breaks, the water ripples, and the shadow movie begins to play out again as if the magic was waiting for our presence. *Creepy.*

The shadow intruders snap into existence with a wave of smelly magic—a fate-awful rotten stench. The smell is so strong that I stumble back and slap my hand over my mouth and nose in a poor attempt to block out the smell.

Dexter sneezes.

I narrow my watering eyes. Where the heck did they come from? My head spins with possibilities as the shadows condense. Shadow Me mimed using the door; these shadows came out of thin air.

I blink, realising they used a portal. A ley line tear must be hidden underneath all that black goo. *Portals again.* Oh no no no. That's not good. A cold shiver trickles down my spine. My gaze flits around the room. You can't portal into the middle of an active ward—a ward like the one wrapped around the house.

It shouldn't be possible.

But... but magic is tricky, and just when you think you know the rules, it changes the game. Look at me. I'm forever doing freaky things. Or it could be demons again? My stomach flips. Kleric can do the whole smoke thing, but I think that's magic between mates of the royal line and not an ordinary demon thing. I shake my head and put it in the back of my mind for now. I'm not going to jump to any conclusions. I need to process the facts.

I lean forward, watching the home invaders, two shadowy creatures, one a great lumbering beast and the other a smaller person. Instead of different colours edging their shadows, they are black on black. Perhaps... I narrow my eyes; the shadows have a hint of dark green at the edges.

Death seems to waft off them like dry ice.

The big lumbering shadow shuffles across the room, and as the creature moves, the right leg drags. Ah, that confirms my suspicion about the black splodgy tracks I had seen in the hallway. Go me. I was right with the enormous feet and the slight drag on the right leg.

The smaller shadow, in comparison, moves light on their feet, and they touch everything. I growl low in my throat when the nosy shadow mimes opening my fridge! I bet if I had more furniture, they would open every drawer.

The See Magic spell doesn't pick up anything malicious left in the small shadow's wake, but that's not the point. I scowl. I don't want them touching my things.

Dexter stalks both shadows back into the hall, and after going through my sitting room and home office, the nosy shadow heads up the stairs.

I start to follow and grind to a halt—the bloody knives. I can't go that way unless I want to lose a toe. I drum my fingers against my thigh in frustration. I don't know if I can do this magic again or how long the current spell will last. I don't know if the micro-cameras will pick up this strange magic, and I need to watch with my own eyes. I need to check my bedroom.

I gaze up at the gap between the first floor and the stairs. Doable. A quick assessment of the length of the hallway, and my idea just might work. I drop the kit bag at my feet, crouch, and spring into the air.

As my feet leave the ground, my wings snap out.

With the space I have to work with, they can't fully extend, and a single weak flap is all I have time to do before they must disappear. My wings dissipate, but the momentum is enough to shoot me into the narrow gap between the ceiling and the stairs. My hands grab hold of the wooden bannister.

Below me, Dexter yowls.

"Give me one sec!" I yell through gritted teeth as I pull myself up. The old wood makes a dreaded crunching sound. It creaks and crumbles away underneath my hands. "Don't come up the stairs, Dexter. You'll hurt yourself." I tighten my hold and haul myself over the old rail before the bannister can break.

My heart is pounding when my feet hit the landing as the small shadow reaches the top of the stairs. I ignore the shadowy creature nosily exploring the empty guest bedroom and instead turn my attention to my bedroom door. The damaged ward sparks and sputters. Hairline cracks dash through spider webbing from the centre, and the hurt magic booms inside my head.

"Well, that's weird. When did magic become so vocal?" I wince and rub my temple. I feel a bit sick. I must be somehow connected to the ward through the See Magic spell.

I sigh. The ward is damaged but still intact. A flash of ruby ripples through the magic barrier, and then it shimmers with an angry crimson. The nosy intruder didn't get into my room. I'm so glad I put up an expensive temporary ward. It was mainly a precaution to ensure no one could enter my personal space, what with the builders coming in and out of the house all day.

"Reow." Dexter admonishes me. He sits at the bottom of the stairs, eyeing the blades. His tail twitches back and forth, and then he backs up to the front door. His ginger bottom wiggles.

"Dexter," I warn him.

He bolts, leaps, clears half the treads, and with impressive kitty agility, his paws land on top of the creaking bannister. With perfect balance, he runs across the top of the rail, and within seconds, he lands at my feet.

"Mert."

I drop my hands that had been half covering my face. "Show off." Thank fate he's okay. I blow out a breath of exasperation like a whale. Dexter licks a paw, and my attention returns to the nosy shadow. We both watch the magical past unfold as the intruder attempts to smash the ward to pieces.

The shadow hammers at the ward, throwing spell after spell. It's a useless and sickeningly expensive endeavour. This goes on for a good ten minutes until, finally, the nosy shadow gives up and moves back down the stairs, and we watch as the big lumbering shadow creature then installs the bladed-art feature.

I jump over the bannister, avoiding the stairs, and watch the shadows finish up. After leaving all the lights on, the nosy one turns off the fuse box, and they both return into the back room and disappear, fading into nothing.

I sag. The magic in my chest is still there, but it feels drained, so I stop feeding the spell, and immediately it reverts to the original See Magic spell.

I slowly, methodically check the house.

A lone feather lies on the hall floor. I scoop it up and drag it between my fingers, tilting it to catch the light.

Drinking Xander's angel blood gave me pure white wings, but after months of Kleric's blood, they've turned blue. Various shades of pretty blue. Dark blue at the tip and fading to an ombré effect of pale blue towards the hollow shaft of the calamus. I have no idea what the colour change means. I stuff the feather in the back pocket of my ratty jeans.

I grab a bright yellow builder's bucket from the back room; crusty bits of plaster coat the rim and the bottom. I stuff a plastic evidence bag into it and grab some thick anti-magic safety gloves—in case the knives on the stairs have anything nasty on them, like poison. The bucket bounces against my thigh as I head to the stairs and begin the weird task of pulling the knives from the treads. They clink and clack into the bottom of the bucket as I ascend. *I was right. The blades are crap.* I freeze in my tracks when I get halfway up the stairs.

*Is that...*

I huff out a laugh. "Now I'm delighted I wore gloves," I tell Dexter, who's watching from the upstairs landing.

*Is that a finger?*

Yes. Yes, it is. Next to the severed finger is a wickedly sharp knife. It's probably the only good blade. It goes into the bucket with all the rest. I finish clearing the stairs, and finally, the finger sits all alone on its wooden tread.

I stare at it. The finger has zero blood, and it looks a little gooey. I poke it, and when it doesn't suddenly spring to life, I pick it up and squish the digit between my gloved fingers.

*Ew.*

It's equally squishy and crumbly. This here might be where the residual stink is coming from. My nostrils twitch. *Necromantic magic.* Mr Draggy Right Leg was a bloody zombie. I look at all the splodges of rotten magic with extra horror. *Zombie.* I shudder.

No one wants to see Great-Aunt Dorothy stumbling towards them with her best dress rotting off her animated corpse. As an assassin, I've put many people into the ground. The dead getting up and mindlessly shambling around doesn't sit right with me.

I find it extra creepy that a zombie oozed his awful self all over the house and left a body part on my stairs.

I need to brush up on creature theory in case I meet the zombie face-to-face. They do tend to bite if not appropriately controlled.

From what I can remember, the good news is the zombie shouldn't be contagious, but who in their right mind would want dead rotten teeth chomping at them? Plus magic is always doing strange stuff. No way do I want to be bitten.

I feel itchy. I need to use purifying spells for the house, Dexter, and myself. You can't be too careful when it comes to zombies. Reanimating the dead is the worst. It is strange magic. Necromancers have control of the dead—zombies, spirits, ghosts, ghouls, and if the fearmongers are to be believed, vampires.

Yeah. You can guess the vampires love that.

The touch of death within a bitten vampire could be enough for a strong necromancer to grab hold of to use said vampire like a zombie. But as there is zero documented history of that ever happening, it remains a scary story.

The rumour persists, I guess because nobody outside the necromancer community knows what a strong necromancer can do, not really. So it's extra concerning that someone with a pet zombie portaled into my house.

*What the heck did I do to piss off a necromancer?*

I realise I'm squishing the zombie finger like a freaky stress ball. Yuck. "Tru, that is minging," I tell myself as I hurry down the stairs. I need to put this thing in an anti-magic evidence bag pronto.

I also need to fix the ley line tear in my floor. The portal's size is smaller than the one under the bridge that almost swallowed the Land Rover, so it should be an easy fix with a small chalk circle and a potion I have, avoiding the need for a witch visit. Then I need an extra strong Clean Me spell and a massive handful of purifying balls.

I double bag the zombie finger and remove the protective gloves and bag them too while pondering what I don't get. I paid a witch a small fortune to protect the house, yet someone circumvented the ward and opened a portal into the active ward with a zombie.

That must mean that the nosy intruder is immensely powerful. But... the nosy necromancer wasn't powerful enough to get through the bedroom ward, so it's more likely an ordinary gateway witch opened the portal for the intruders, and if that's so, is it possible I was sold a duff ward? Yet that also doesn't seem right. I would have noticed if the barrier ward had been naff. And the ward around the house still feels substantial. An entire coven of witches would take hours, if not days, to get inside the house.

So if the ward isn't crap, the only thing I can think of is that the witch who created the ward on the house let them in.

*Witches again.*

I rub my face and groan.

Crikey, I feel so damn tired. Okay, before I do another thing, I need to redo all the wards.

I shuffle to my kit bag and grab all the magic I'll need.

Someone opened a portal underneath my car, putting the pixies at risk, and some nosy necromancer came and had a good look around my house with a pet zombie and, if that wasn't bad enough, left me a cute warning of knives on my stairs.

As if saying, "I can get to you anywhere."

I was wrong earlier when I hoped that things would return to normal with the male witch's death. Why did I say that? I know better than to tempt fate. I think they used Marcus, the witch, as a fall guy, and this mess didn't end with his death.

No, it's just the beginning.

# CHAPTER EIGHT

THERE'S a polite tap on the front door, and I dash down the hall with Dexter on my heels. I don't know what it is about someone knocking that gives me a mini panic attack. Every. Single. Time. I'm such a weirdo.

I either think, *Who the heck is knocking and do I really have to answer?* or convince myself they'll leave before I can reach the door.

I fling the door open and see a familiar face.

"Executioner, nice house," the lab technician mumbles.

"Thanks, Michael. I appreciate you coming out so late."

Tall and thin, with a dark comb-over and a bright smile, the lab technician from work is playing courier tonight. I arranged for an urgent collection. He awkwardly stands away from the spitting and flashing newly applied ward—I snuck out and redid the pixies' burrow to be safe. The wards are all temporary spells, the same brand as the one on my bedroom, which I also replaced.

I'll have to explain everything to Story in the morning. No doubt she will be upset that I didn't ask for her help with the break-in. She can help with the witch to visit tomorrow. We're going to have a friendly chat with Rose, the witch who set the house ward. I could go tonight, but I'm so stinking mad. I might do something rash.

Fun fact: creatures generally can't answer questions when you're strangling them.

"So you have some evidence for me?"

I nod at the two evidence bags propped against the garden wall, almost hidden behind a clump of grass growing wild in the driveway's old stone. I'm unwilling to have that zombie finger in the house, not after I used a Clean Me spell and purifying magic to eliminate the stinky smell.

"Great. Oh, and I have a package for you. It was on your desk. I know you don't like coming into the building, and it's been there for quite a while." Michael blushes, fidgets, pulls out a box tucked underneath his arm, and thrusts it in my direction.

I step outside the ward so that he can pass me the parcel. It's heavy. "Thanks, Michael. That's very kind."

Michael's cheeks grow redder, and he scoops both evidence bags up and moves the bag with the finger closer to his face. "Zombie?" he murmurs.

"Yeah. It's squishy." I awkwardly shrug when he looks back at me.

"Squishy." Michael shudders. "Well, it was nice seeing you. Have a good night. I'll send the results to your assistant as soon as they are ready." Tipping an imaginary hat, Michael hurries back to his silver Ford Fiesta and leaves.

As I watch him go, I give the box a shake. I never get parcels. I never get anything. *Unless this is a gift from Kleric!* I grin and dance inside. After I lock up, I run upstairs two at a time and take the box to my suite of rooms.

I tug my boots off outside the door.

The replaced ward crackles and hums as I step through. Dexter flops onto the bed, and his left paw claws the bee fabric of my favourite bedding. I drop the box next to him. I need to wash my hands. While I'm at it, I might as well get ready for bed.

Once I'm in my pyjamas, I bounce onto the bed, tear open the packaging—and gasp. Nestled within fancy black tissue paper are two black silk *sword boxes*. My hand trembles slightly as it hovers over the swords. I don't know which box to open first. I laugh.

Gosh, I feel a tad overwhelmed. I've never had anything like this.

I tilt my head at the tingle of magic, and almost of its own accord, my fingers drift to a delicate silk sword bag that had been all but hidden.

*Oh.*

I grasp it and tug.

The powerful magic, somehow familiar, bites at me.

I rotate the bag so I can read the label:

TINCTURES N TONICS - SPECIALISTS IN PORTABLE POTIONS.
*Congratulations on your discerning purchase.*
*This item has been custom made for the recipient, and a*

*drop of blood while reading the provided incantation is required to activate.*

*Please note: In terms of safety, security, and privacy, once the magic is primed, the item will only obey the user...*

Blah, blah, blah.

The words blur as my brain feels like it's going to explode. A magic bag! I can't believe it. A *magic* bag. The black bag isn't just any bag; it's a tiny pocket dimension, ridiculously rare and extortionately expensive.

My grandad's old red toolbox I keep at the end of the bed has similar magic—perhaps that's why the magic on the bag feels so familiar. But though I can store things inside it, the magic was primed to my grandad and trying to get things in and out is a nightmare. Plus lugging the rusty, heavy thing also has issues. It's not stealthy enough to be used every day.

This bag is way more sophisticated than the toolbox.

*Sorry, Grandad.*

"So silky." I reverently stroke the bag. "My precious." I can't help my goofy grin as I hug it to my chest.

*What was I saying about this being a nightmare night?* No, I take it back. This night is ending like a dream.

The possibility of storing a plethora of weapons—depending on how ample the dimension space is inside—makes me giddy, and then being able to fold the silk bag and put it into my pocket... the possibilities boggle my mind.

I might never be without a weapon ever again.

I carefully place the pocket dimension on my knee to prime it with my blood, but I'm wiggling like a puppy and take a deep breath in order to calm down; I don't want to make a mistake with the incantation.

After reading the simple incantation a few times for practice, I remove the attached hygienically sealed finger-prinking lancet from its packaging and take another deep breath. Calmer now, I prick my index finger and with my thumb squeeze out a single drop of blood. The blood drips, wetting the rim of the silky fabric. I chant to activate the magic and watch as my blood is absorbed.

The pocket dimension's magic hums, and the outside of the bag sparkles.

"Time to test."

On the bedside table is a knife. There are blades scattered around the house. I pick it up and place it inside the bag. It disappears. The weight and shape of the bag do not change.

Oh wow; when Kleric buys a gift, he goes all out.

I count to thirty, slip my hand inside, and picture the blade in my mind. The hilt slaps into my palm. I let out a little squeal, and the bed squeaks as I bounce up and down.

Dexter scrunches his face and prowls as far away from me as he can without getting off the bed.

"Sorry." I pull the knife out and place it back on the table.

Okay, so that worked. *This is amazing.* I wonder how big the pocket dimension is. I'd love to stick my head inside and have a look around—which I've done before with the toolbox, so I know I'd be fine. Well, unless the magic messes up and Story finds my body tomorrow without its head.

*Uh-huh.*

No one said I wasn't impulsive... And then there is the warning on the label. Yeah, perhaps it's not the best idea. I grin. Maybe I'll stick my head in there later. I put the bag down and grab the first of the silk sword boxes, and with bated breath and heart pounding in my ears, I open it.

I freeze.

It is a breathtakingly beautiful double-edged sword.

I don't think I've seen this style before—something inside my chest aches. I didn't learn as much as I should about weapons from my grandad. If I could go back in time, I would shake my younger self and perhaps smack her across the back of the head to make her listen to his wise words.

*To every word.*

My adoptive fae grandad would have loved this blade. The memory of his voice echoes in my mind, entrenched so deep it's almost as if he's standing beside me as I pull the sword out of the box. Gosh, so much detail. The round guard where the blade begins and the handle ends, there to protect the user's hands but also contribute to the weapon's balance, has a galloping pale pink unicorn. I peer closer—the rose gold or perhaps a titanium gold alloy doesn't interfere with the weapon's weight; the sword is light and beautifully balanced.

A gurgle escapes me when I notice the unicorn has *vampire fangs*. I giggle and shake my head. The detail is astonishing.

The hilt collar also has a fanged unicorn, and so does the pommel. The unicorn there is raised, and I can't help wondering, *If I hit someone in the face with the butt end, will it leave a unicorn mark?* I snort as I envision myself stamping someone on the forehead.

I can't wait to find out.

The handle is wrapped in elegant black leather and is the perfect length for my hand. I slide the scabbard off the blade, and the shine of polished steel is a feast for my eyes. This is the best weapon I've ever seen. The craftsmanship is exquisite. Kleric has outdone himself. I place the blade back in its box and spot the handwritten gift card.

I hum with pleasure. The black gift card—the cardboard is

velvety smooth between my fingers, only the best card stock. I read the swirled writing:

*To replace the sword you lost.*

*Love, Xander.*

The smile, so wide it hurts my cheeks, slides from my face. Zombie butterflies smash against my insides. I let go of the card, and it flutters back into the box.

*I feel sick.*

I slap both hands across my mouth, scramble off the bed and take a few steps back. To replace the sword I lost. The blade he cut in half more like it. *Dickhead.* Black swims in my vision as pure rage replaces the shock. I grind my teeth until my jaw aches, and my entire body shakes with anger.

What do you do when the man you used to love, a man you waited nine years to notice you, the guy who chucked you into a prison cell, sends you a gift?

I hate his guts, so now he decides it's the right time to hammer up the charm.

*Love, Xander.*

The words throb in my brain. How effing dare he! All I want to do is punch him in the face. Angry, hurt breaths rattle my chest, and I wipe a lone tear from my cheek.

*I'm not far enough away.* A scream slips from my lips, and I turn away and hotfoot it out of the room before both swords get launched through the brand-new plastered and painted walls.

*It's not the swords' fault the guy who commissioned them is a nobhead.*

Outside the room, my body sags, and I have to lean against the landing wall so I don't collapse.

I need Kleric. I need him like I need to breathe. I drop the shield in my mind. *Have you got a second to talk?* I beg.

*Of course.* His warm voice calms my rapid, angry heartbeats. I sink to the top step of the stairs, and as my bottom hits the first tread, I slump to the side.

Even in my brain, I can't form the words I need to say. I can't make the words work, so I go for the easiest option and show him the memory. I show him everything.

*I'm sorry. Are you okay?*

*No.* I growl, then close my eyes and take a deep breath. *I'm mad. I'm so pissed off. Why... Why does he have to be such a dick?* I press my cheek against the rough wall.

Wisely, the demon doesn't answer me.

I feel stupid for this moment of weakness. Kleric is going to think I'm out of my mind. Unable to sit still, I jump up, stomp back down the hall into my room and grab the cursed box and the silk bag pocket dimension off the bed.

With the box held away from my body as if it's going to explode, I march to my weapons room, yank open an empty drawer, drop the box inside, and slam it closed.

Out of sight, out of mind. Right?

I shove the silk bag on the top shelf. *I hate him.* I snarl. *How dare he send me such a beautiful gift!* I slap my palms against the cabinet and lean into the dark wood. I want to rip the room apart with my bare hands. But I know I'd only hurt myself, and I love this room.

It's been months since the angel chopped my sword in half. Months. He must have had them commissioned after that night. I can admit that he owes me a sword, but he didn't have to get exquisite blades with bloody vampire unicorns.

*Angel blades. That's why I didn't recognise the style*—I bet they're a matching pair, and the bloody things also have super-duper magic.

What on earth? How do I deal with this? I bet they are both the perfect weight in my hand.

*You thought they were from me,* Kleric says.

Yes.

*I'm sorry.*

*You have nothing to apologise for.* I scrunch my eyes closed. Now I feel like I've somehow betrayed him.

I miss his velvety soft black eyes. His kind smile, the way he looks at me as if I hung the moon. My stupid heart hurts. No one has ever looked at me the way he does. Like I'm his entire world. It's scary. What we feel is not real. But oh, how I want it to be. *You can't offer him anything but a magic-induced fate*, and there it is right on time; the little nasty inner voice pisses over everything. I give it a mental middle finger.

*I miss you*, I tell him.

*I miss you too, very much. I'm sorry he hurt you. If it makes you feel any better, I don't think he intended to. Not this time.*

I huff.

And there is Kleric, the voice of reason. The demon is patient and kind. Older than dirt, Xander is hot-headed, while Kleric is all ice.

*Not this time.* I reluctantly agree. I need to get a grip.

The swords stuffed in the drawer call to me the way an excellent weapon calls to a warrior. I stomp out of the weapons room and throw myself face-first onto the bed. If Xander sent me flowers, I could smash the bouquet over his fat head. But beautiful, perfectly made swords? I bury my head in the covers. It's a sneaky move.

Sneaky, conniving, nobhead angel.

I don't like this feeling. It makes me feel weird.

*Are you hungry?*

Before the intruders and Xander's gift, I was starving, but now not so much. *I could eat,* I grumble. Kleric doesn't mean regular food.

The sharp smell of sulphur fills the room. I lift my upper body from the bed as dark vapour swirls out of the ether, and with a shimmer, a glass tube appears within the smoky haze—demon takeaway. I pluck the vial out of the air.

The viscous fluid inside is dark green.

Kleric's blood.

My demon can get through any ward if I'm inside; the kiss on my hand is the key. Even a world away, the demon does not allow me to go hungry. My vampire side has never been so well-fed—though I'd prefer to wrap my arms around him, bury my face in his throat, and feel his warm, salty skin against my lips as I bite.

Glass instead of Kleric.

I appreciate his kindness. *Thank you; you are very kind.*

*You're welcome. It's the least I can do.* The grumble in his voice breaks my melancholy and makes me smile. My demon is pissed. He's just as angry as me. He's just better at hiding it. *I have something else for you.*

*Oh?* More dark vapour fills the room, and when the smoke clears, there is a plate of pizza. It smells divine. I stare at glorious cheesy goodness. *Um. Demon pizza?* Is it safe? *With demon cheese and demon tomatoes?* My stomach gurgles.

*It's a pizza. We do have pizza, you know.* Kleric chuckles. *Well, we have the ingredients for it. It's just something I rustled up for you after your fight with the alien.*

*You cooked for me? Thank you so much.* I grin. Can this man get any better or be more thoughtful?

*I can hear your stomach growling from a world away. Please eat before the animal inside there escapes and goes on a rampage. While you are eating, tell me about your evening. Tell me about the alien octopus and the frying pan.*

I snort, settle back into the cushions, and tell him about my evening.

# CHAPTER NINE

THE OBNOXIOUS SOUND of ringing drags me from my dreams. Groggy, I slap my hand onto the bedside table, catch the phone's edge, and it spins away from my questing fingers and clatters to the floor. The awkward sleepy smash and the phone's fall must have accepted the call as it has stopped ringing, and I hear a tinny voice underneath the bed.

"For eff's sake." I groan.

"Tru? Tru!"

"Yep, one sec," I grumble, then louder, I tell the mystery caller, "I dropped the phone." With another groan, I flop like a fish out from under the warm duvet and land awkwardly on my hands and knees.

With my eyes half-cracked, I slide across the carpet and

hunt down the damn handset. At least I'm now wide awake to take the call. *How on earth did it get so far underneath the bed?* Gosh, I need longer arms. I end up sticking my leg under and using my toes.

"Tru?" comes the urgent whisper as the mobile finally reaches my ear. "They are breaking into my house. The ward is not going to last."

"What? Who?" Who the heck is ringing me at—I glance at the screen—three a.m.? The witching hour, when magic is most potent. Great. I rub my face vigorously, hoping it will stimulate my brain. Then it clicks. The whispered voice—it's Caitlyn.

*Oh no.*

"The witches—"

There's a blast, and I must snatch the phone away from my ear. Otherwise, I'd lose an eardrum.

"Hello, Caitlyn?" I check the screen, and the call has disconnected. I call her back, but the magic blast must have fried her phone. "Well, crap."

With a few taps, I enter my work password, sending out a citywide red alert for emergency assistance at Caitlyn's address. Well, a citywide alert for everyone but Story. I might have set it to alert her in the morning. The pixie needs her sleep. It's not like I'll get immediate help from anyone else, but it's the process.

*Way to go, Tru.* I knew retaliation would come, but I didn't think it would come so quickly. I can't see into the future, and I certainly don't have a crystal ball stuck up my bottom. But I should have listened to my gut. I should have insisted and stashed her somewhere safe.

I quickly change into spell-resistant work clothes, rush to the weapons room, and start loading up. Dealing with the witches, I'm going to need a lot of spells. So many spells. I fill my trouser pockets. It's not ideal; if things get physical, I could break a vial.

Almost of their own accord, my eyes find the innocuous-looking silk bag I'd placed out of the way on the top shelf. I never had any intention of using it. My fingers drum on one of the lower shelves.

*I'll regret it.*

It's already primed with my blood, so it's not like I can give it back or return it. *I'm a weak woman.* I grab the pocket dimension and start throwing in the spells. I chuck in everything useful I can think of, all my weapons, a change of clothes, and I even roll up a couple of soft blankets. The pocket dimension takes it all.

*If I'm using part of his gift, why not use it all?* Fighting magic users like witches deserves magical swords. Right? I shake my head. *I'm so going to regret this.* I pull out the bottom drawer and yank out the still-packaged swords.

Once out of the boxes, I hold both blades to shove them into the dual crossbody scabbards so they will be easy to draw. I don't even have to adjust the harness; they fit perfectly. Foreign magic tingles up my arms, and it's like...

*Ow. Ouch.*

The blinking angel swords bite me! I try to drop them, and neither blade will let go! *I don't like this.* It almost feels like the swords are drinking my blood, which is ridiculous, but I'm part vampire; I understand blood drinking. I also understand the magic that blood contains.

Trust the angel to buy bloodthirsty swords.

The uncomfortable sensation ends, and a rainbow sheen flashes across both blades. I tilt my head and give the right sword a little flick. Magic rolls over the hilt, and within moments the entire blade goes black.

Huh, a stealth mode. Cool.

Another flick and the sword changes back. *I wonder what else they can do?* I've no time. *Come on, Tru, get a wiggle on.* Caitlyn said witches, plural, and the temporary ward I gave her won't last long against a full-on coven attack.

I slide each angel blade home, fold the pocket dimension into a tiny square, and tuck it into my pocket. You've got to love magic.

## CHAPTER TEN

Dexter doesn't notice me leaving as I creep like a thief through the house. I push the front door closed with just my fingertips so there is barely a click to be heard. Usually, I'd take him with me. But with the high possibility of a nasty confrontation and spells being thrown about willy-nilly, I don't want to risk him being caught in the cross fire, and the beithíoch hates flying.

I jog past the Defender, head around the back of the house, and grip the top rail of the wooden fence. I spring over. The frosty ground crunches beneath my boots as I move away and shift into a unicorn.

With no time to stretch—every second counts—I spin and gallop across the field. The frozen earth, unyielding in my human form, gives way underneath my hooves, and pieces of sod fly in my wake, thudding on the ground behind me.

The winter wind whips my mane and ruffles the feathers of my wings, which are now carefully tucked against my sides.

*Wait for it.*

I pick up speed.

My hindquarters burn as I push more power into my back legs, and my hooves dig into the ground as my stride lengthens and my entire body strains.

*Now.*

I let my wings out, angling them to catch the icy air and deflect it downwards. My front hooves rise. I jump, pushing off with my powerful hind legs, and my wings beat. The ground drops away as each flap pushes me higher and forward into the night sky.

When I contemplated flying, I imagined myself majestically cantering across the sky. How cool would that be? But no. If I'm not careful, my legs get in the way, and I have to tuck them underneath me so they don't cause drag.

I fly over the woods at the back of the house and turn my nose toward the sea. At least I know where I'm going. The bridge next to Caitlyn's house is a good landmark. The quiet homes and bright streetlights pass underneath as I increase my altitude to make the most of the wind speed. The strong tailwind gives me a boost.

As I get closer, I need to consider my approach. I don't want the witches to see me coming and give the game away or, worse, knock me out of the sky. The night is bright with almost a full moon, and I stick out like a sore thumb. Being up here makes me vulnerable—a target. I enjoy flying, but it does make me nervous. It only takes one idiot with a spell or a crossbow to try to shoot me out of the sky.

And I'm not exactly inconspicuous with my colouring, rainbow mane, tail, and bright white fur. The blue wings blend me in a little better than the angel white, but there's no way of disguising my fur and iridescent hooves. I'm like a beacon. Stealthy, I'm not.

Story joked she'd get me a full-body rug for night flying—she'd seen these rugs used to keep stabled show horses clean overnight—but the thought of anyone seeing me head to toe in a spandex rug is mortifying.

I have to suck it up and hope no one thinks to look up. I haven't got time to mess about driving. This way, it will take me minutes to arrive, and I need every second. My flying unicorn form might not be sneaky, but it is fast.

When I've been seen a few times, I've been called an alicorn. I snort. I'm not going there. I'm just a unicorn with angel wings. Thank you. Calling myself an alicorn, adding that little ditty to my CV, pushes it. It pushes me over the edge. I'll stick to unicorn-vampire hybrid; that's enough weird for anyone.

The air up here is freezing. Even my thick fur and the body-temperature magic from Kleric can't protect me from the frigid wind. I'll be glad to get down. Flying in winter is terrible but much better than in summer. A fly in the eye or up the nose is unpleasant, and I've swallowed some a few times.

I dip to the side and aim towards the cinema car park, the best place to land. The car park comes fast—it's incredible how quick getting somewhere can be when travelling straight. I drop behind the cinema. The enormous modern building offers me good coverage. As soon as my hooves scrape the tarmac, I shift to human and sprint across the car park.

The icy night seems to hold on to all the tension as magic saturates the air, and the atmosphere buzzes like an approaching thunderstorm. I feel the spells popping and fizzing just ahead. It's like a war zone. I taste the magic on my tongue and pray to the powers that be the witches are still on the outside and the ward has held.

The commercial buildings around me are silent this time of the morning, and the houses are quiet for a different reason as frightened people hunker down, worried their homes will be next.

My body jerks at an explosion. Bloody hell, if the witches aren't careful, they will damage more than Caitlyn's ward. What are they thinking?

They are not.

I can't believe the Hunters Guild isn't already here. They must have got so many calls. Cowards. And the Witch Council should really get a move on and gain control of this mess as this entire situation doesn't look good on them. Then there's the human police who won't intervene even when the area is packed with human families. They can't. They don't have the resources.

Of course what usually happens is everyone will turn up when the dust has settled.

A small part of me wishes I had some professional backup. Oh, I know I'll be fine. I've been in similar situations before, and I'm confident I can handle this. When it comes down to it, I'm just an antisocial creature, and I much prefer to work alone. I just wish I had a way to communicate. I shifted, so I couldn't bring any tech with me. No micro-cameras, datapad and no mobile phone. I almost feel naked.

I'm also kicking myself for not having the fortitude to leave some cameras outside Caitlyn's house. Recorded evidence of the witch's misdeeds would have made a better case.

I vault over a low-lying hedge, and my feet hit the pavement. The bridge next to Caitlyn's is just ahead. No sign of the portal or the chalk circle remains.

When I get to the bridge, I go up.

This time I can't use my wings. If I did, I might as well wave a banner and scream, "Woo-hoo, here I am!"

The bridge's architecture works for me. The concrete has been set into big blocks; where they meet each other are grooves that give convenient handholds. The sides are also at an angle, and with enough momentum, I should... reach the top.

I pump my arms and leap.

I scramble and claw my way up, far from elegant in my ascent, but eventually my fingers hit the bottom of the guardrail, and I do an impressive static chin-up. I'm glad I have good upper body strength. With a bit of déjà vu, I throw my leg over. *What is it about me climbing over rails?*

I'm also glad the overpass is deserted, and I don't scare the crap out of any unsuspecting drivers. I land on the road, drop into a crouch, and creep across the two lanes to the other side.

I peek between the mesh of the crash barrier. Being so high gives me an unencumbered view of the road, the row of houses, and the witches.

Crikey, the witches are mad.

I puff a sigh of relief though—I've made it in time. They've yet to breach the ward even with the continued chanting and battering of spells.

I bought those temporary wards from Jodie, my witch friend. I'll have to go to her shop and give her a hug of thanks and buy a boatload more. I also need to find out if the ward witch who made them can be commissioned for our permanent property wards as I need to get them fixed.

I watch the witches. Oh, surprise, surprise. The only witch I recognise down there is Rose. The witch who did the ward on the farmhouse and the burrow. The same wards that let a zombie inside. I chuckle and tap the frozen metal of the guardrail. Yeah, this right here is what is known as a big fat coincidence and a huge red flag. It looks as if Rose and I will be having our little chat earlier than I had planned. Unless she does something stupid and I have to kill her.

I finish the head count, and as I thought, it's an entire coven of thirteen, all women. This is typically the case with witches, as male witches are super rare. For them to lose a single male witch is a travesty. I can understand their anger. Their grief.

But in reality, they are trying to hurt the wrong person. If I'd been on the ball yesterday and stopped him before the frying pan did, this wouldn't be happening. If Ethel hadn't thrown the portal-closing magic at me, I wouldn't have made such a colossal mistake in the first place. I shoot those thoughts down as the what-ifs will drive me mad.

Marcus only had himself to blame. He would still be alive if he weren't running around opening portals and attacking me.

My full attention turns back to the witches. It's a relief to only recognise one witch out of the thirteen. They are dressed for the cold weather in various bright colours, bags and pockets bulging with spells. The way they move and waste their magic makes me fidget. I see spells falling short of their target, and one dark-haired lady in a red coat stands out for being particularly bad. Every time she chucks a potion, she closes her eyes.

These women aren't trained combatants.

I'll have to be very careful not to kill them.

At least they didn't bring any children. The oldest I estimate to be around 150, and a few look around my age. Witches age much slower than humans and regularly live to over three hundred.

Multiple scenarios flicker through my head of what will happen if I engage them now in the street versus waiting until they go inside the house.

Neither option is good, but the odds are better I'll be able to contain the fallout inside.

That decided, now I wait. The best time to go down there is when they enter, as they will be distracted.

I use a sticky spell to attach the pocket dimension to my left thigh. I practise putting my hands inside a few times, locking down the movement to muscle memory. Once happy, I reach into the silk bag, and an oddly shaped object slaps into my palm.

I bring the charm into the moonlight, feeling its smooth, cool surface against my skin. It's black and shaped like a cat, with mirrored eyes that hint at its magic. I rub the cat's head with my thumb and chant the incantation under my breath to activate its unique brand of magic.

A Reflect Me spell. The cat charm reflects magic back to the user. It is made by Gary Chappell, a famous witch. I'm not kidding when I say you'd have to sell organs to get hold of one. They are ridiculously expensive and only available to the extremely wealthy or law enforcement.

If the witches behave, it shouldn't be a problem. But if they hit me with any nasty spells... Let's put it this way: it won't be me rolling around in agony. A couple of days ago, I saved a female troll from a group of angry elves, and she gave it to me. I haven't had an opportunity to use it. It will be interesting to see how it does and if it lives up to the hype. I know it self-recharges, but I need to determine how many magic shots it will take before it stops working. Let's hope I don't find out.

I roll my shoulders and slip the cat charm into my sports bra so it will stay in place and keep in contact with my skin.

Then I pull out a handful of Restrain Me spells. I eye the witches. I hope I can take them down without having to kill them. I don't want to hurt an entire coven; that's an excellent way to end up dead.

The witches let out a joyous cry as, with a spark, the ward flashes crimson, and with a pop, it dies.

A heavyset witch marches to the front door and throws a spell. There's a bang. The door crashes off its hinges, and they all rush inside. I cringe. Gosh, they are so poorly organised that it doesn't look like they've left anyone outside to keep watch or guard the door.

It's a witch free-for-all.

My stomach flips. I tuck my concern for Caitlyn deep inside where it belongs. Worrying makes you reckless, and impatience will end up getting me dead. I much prefer the steady, sneaky approach. I need to do this quietly.

I go to that cold, calm place inside myself to get the job done, where creatures are objects and no longer people.

I jump over the guardrail and use the concrete side of the bridge to slow my descent. My feet sting as I hit the pavement, the pain makes everything sharper, and then it's a sprint to the broken front door. I flatten my back against the outside wall and wait a few seconds. When no one chucks a spell at me, I move.

I enter the house.

# CHAPTER ELEVEN

THE FIRST FOUR witches I encounter have their backs to the door as they clump nervously at the entrance while everyone else seems to be deeper inside the tiny house. My eyes flick upstairs. All sorts of yelling and thuds are coming from the increasingly angry witches up there.

It sounds like Caitlyn has locked herself into a safe room—something many homes have nowadays. Most are made just big enough for two people to squish themselves into. They are next to useless, with poor, mass-produced magic—she'll have perhaps five more minutes. Like a locked front door a simple spell can open, people need their comfortable lies. Whatever helps them sleep at night, I guess.

*I'm coming, Caitlyn. Just hold on a few more minutes until I clear downstairs.*

I concentrate on the first four witches. The frightened, huddling women would spark my empathy if not for the nasty melt-your-face-off spells they are clutching. Clearly, they are not here to knit, and that's incriminating enough for me.

I roll my own marble-sized spells in my palm. On the balls of my feet, I creep behind them. Adrenaline sloshes through my system, and I let myself grin. I love sneaking about.

Witches' entire lives are focused on magic, so it's very rare—not impossible, but rare—for them to be fighters. Anything that takes them away from their magical art is seriously frowned upon. But their blinkered magic focus means they're next to useless in a fight if they can't throw spells, draw runes, or chant.

So the rules for dealing with them are simple: get hold of their arms, keep them from speaking, and they are pretty much out of the game.

Quick as a whip, like skimming a flat stone across a lake, I chuck the Restrain Me spells. One after another, each ball smashes into a witch's unprotected back, and the magic stuns her. They all freeze in place and don't make a peep as the spell snakes around, wrapping them up nice and tight.

I pluck the nasty spells from their inert hands and rifle through their pockets, popping everything for safekeeping into a spelled evidence bag. I finish just in the nick of time as each tendril hardens into a head-to-foot beehive-shaped shell of a full-body restraint.

They now look like weird giant ornaments. I tilt my head... or alien babies.

I nudge the first of the witch cocoons out of the way. It slides easily across the thin grey carpet, and I push it past the blue two-seater sofa, then prop it next to the old television sitting pride of place on a wonky cabinet.

The chaos upstairs does an excellent job of disguising any sounds. I shove the other three witches quickly and lean them against the plain magnolia wall that's crying out for a splash of paint. I arrange them until all four are stuffed into the far corner, out of sight from the kitchen and upstairs.

Grabbing a temporary ward, I chuck it at the wounded gap created by the downed front door. I can't afford for anyone to sneak in behind me or sneak out. I can't be bothered with having to chase any of these ladies down.

As the magic seals across the front of the house, the spell swells in the magic-soaked air and pops into place with a ping.

*Uh-oh.* I cringe. *Did anyone feel that?* Anyone sensitive, say a house full of angry witches? Well, if it's all going to kick off, I'd rather contain the spells to the inside of the house. I'm amazed that the homes around aren't piles of rubble. The witches are behaving wildly. Grief does that. I'm sorry they've lost a loved one, even if he did try to kill me.

I creep towards rustling sounds at the back of the house. Two more witches are ransacking the kitchen.

"Have you found anything yet?" says the lady on the left. Her brown-and-white jumper has an adorable pattern of puppies.

"No, it must be upstairs."

"It better be in this house. We've looked everywhere." As fate will have it, puppy jumper turns to search the cabinet behind her. Her brown eyes widen, and she gasps. "What—"

I flick my wrist and send a restraint spell flying. It stuns and wraps around her just before the other witch is on me. She doesn't throw a spell. Instead, she tackles me like a rugby player. Her arms wrap around my waist, and her shoulder slams into my stomach. *Oof.* I feel like I've been run over as she hits me with the force of a double-decker bus. The witch has game.

The Restrain Me ball in my hand goes flying, uselessly smashing against a kitchen cabinet.

I block her attack, keep my feet, and sweep her legs from underneath her. As she falls, her flailing arms shove me. I stumble out of the kitchen and into the living room.

She hits the tiled floor with a crack, and on her hands and knees, she lifts her head and bellows, "Intruder!"

All sound from upstairs stops.

*Great.*

I've lost the element of surprise, so I might as well identify myself. "I'm the executioner!" I yell into the shocked silence. I even go so far as to hold up my empty hands. "I'm not here to hurt you, but I will if you don't come quietly." When no one says anything, I cautiously continue. "This vigilante hunt is over; no one needs to get hurt."

The floorboards upstairs creak with movement.

*Okay?*

I catch a streak of yellow out the corner of my eye, and there's a thud of impact just underneath my collarbone. A spell has smashed into me. Nasty yellow liquid splashes underneath my chin and dribbles in globby rivulets down my chest.

"For fuck's sake," I grumble.

The reflection charm burns against my chest, I feel the magic barely brush against me, and then it slingshots back to the witch who threw the spell.

A scream comes from upstairs, there is a thud, and a witch dramatically takes a tumble down the stairs. I wince as she falls. She awkwardly hits her head on the bannister and the wall before crashing into a moaning heap at the bottom.

*Ouch. That had to hurt.*

Her moans of pain are grating, and guilt eats at me. I move a little closer and watch her skin break into tiny bumps that turn into hives. *That's not so bad.* The hives bloom into scary-looking purple boils.

*Oh.*

The skin bubbles and then bursts open, weeping yellow puss with a custard-like consistency.

*Ew.*

I back away. That spell was aimed at me. *Thanks, Gary.* I give the cat charm a gentle pat of appreciation.

None of the witches say anything, but I feel angry eyes flicking between me and the still-moaning woman. I guess I can provide them with an explanation if they haven't already worked it out. "I have a Gary Chappell Reflect Me charm," I shout. It might help if they know they are out spelled. I must try to convince them to give up this madness and try my best to resolve this peacefully.

"The Gary charm won't last forever," someone mutters.

Well, until it does, they might choose their spells wisely. "If you give up now, I'll ensure the guilds take it easy on you. Now you've only committed a few crimes. Breaking and entering and the excessive use of dangerous magic. If you kill me, it's the death penalty for all of you." I let that sink in.

I'd like to say more, but it'd be a mistake. Putting my foot in my mouth is an exceptional talent of mine and the last thing I want to do.

Four years. The hunters and the human police get four years of training to do their jobs. I got a manual. A shitty manual. If that doesn't scream that they don't expect me to live long in my role as an executioner, I don't know what does. I'm not worth the training. And that makes me an idiot for taking the job. I should have let the demon thing with Xander play out and let the world burn. At least then I'd still be asleep in bed.

"I want you where I can see you. Please come out with your hands in the air, and for your safety, keep your mouths shut." There's a beat or two of contemplation, and I almost fool myself into thinking they'll comply and give up.

Then all hell breaks loose.

*Bloody hell.*

The entire front room comes alive with zipping spells thrown every *witch* way. I lean just enough for one to whistle past my face and dodge behind the kitchen wall.

*Oh hello.* The kitchen rugby witch takes the opportunity to jump me again. She grabs hold of the top of my head, and her nails dig into my scalp and hair.

*Ouch.*

I hammer a punch to her elbow, and she lets go. I duck and move from her grabby, hair-pulling, clawing hands. She makes a weird roaring noise in her throat, drops her head, and tries to charge me again. I slip to the side, and she runs past me, bounces off the wall, turns, and comes again.

I sigh. It's strange fighting someone untrained. Their moves make zero sense. The flailing of limbs... The weird screams... It's all so unpredictable. The scratching and the biting...

"No," I growl and bop her on the nose before her teeth can land. "Bad witch."

After recently having a zombie invade my house, I have a severe aversion to chomping. Fancy that.

The only good thing is that she tires quickly, her chest heaves, and she drops her hands, giving me just the time I need to grab another restraint spell from the silk bag and... There.

She's all nicely wrapped up, and her potions go into the evidence bag.

I peek out of the kitchen.

The spells are still raining down from upstairs. They aren't even trying to aim. "What a shit show," I mumble, rolling my eyes. "These witches have money to burn and no bloody common sense."

Seven witches down, six more to go. I rub my face. Over halfway through. Not bad.

The lady at the bottom of the stairs is silent. Uh-oh. Not a good sign. I hope she didn't get hit with any of the rogue spells.

Carefully I lean out and throw a healing potion at her. I miss. "Crap." I've yet to learn how to bend things around corners. I need to move her. If she stays there, she will die from the boil-custard-making spell or get hit by something horrible. And dead is still dead, even if the witches did the deed. No one will believe it isn't my fault.

But I can't afford to get hit; if another nasty spell hits the reflection charm, it might kill the next witch.

I pull out the new angel blades. Not to hurt the witches but to batter any rogue spells away. Most magic needs some kind of body contact. If the attacks can't touch me, they shouldn't be able to do much damage—unless they want to blow me up, but that's a whole other problem.

And yes, I shouldn't be using these fancy-arse angel swords as bats, but what can I do? You must use what you've got. Plus seeing me with swords might frighten the witches enough for them to call it a night.

I twist one sword in a close-to-the-body clockwise pattern, and the other I spin in the opposite direction. Each blade rotates and turns to ensure that I'll be protected if I keep my back tight to the wall. There isn't enough room to twirl myself and them.

I move out of the kitchen, swords spinning. They feel perfect in my hands until... both swords *hum*. I frown as heat trickles from my chest down the blades, and they vibrate in my palms.

*That's strange. They better not bite me again.*

The air around both swords shimmers, and with a mix of rainbow colours, magic fans out of them. The shock would have left me stumbling if I weren't so light on my feet.

The blades' magic creates some kind of bubble, a shield?

Instinctively, it doesn't feel as strong as a ward, but this bubble is somehow better and more flexible.

*Wow, this is so strange.*

I keep the blades swirling, and the translucent, flexible shield stays in place as I creep across the living room. It's only a few strides. A single spell pings off the shield. Followed closely by a hail of them.

I grin.

When I get to the witch, she's in a right state. My stomach rolls when I look at her. I've got to move her. But I haven't got three hands. I can't rotate both swords while pulling her out of harm's way.

"Let me help her," I beg. "She's in so much pain. Can't we do a cease-fire until I move her somewhere safe?"

The witches' spell-throwing doesn't pause. I can feel their fear saturating the air almost as much as their magic.

*Eff it.*

I grit my teeth, get low to the ground, sheath my left sword, and grab hold of her ankle. With a sharp tug, I drag boil witch away from the stairs. I rotate the single blade above my head and kick the unbroken spells out of the way.

Thank fate, the carpet is so thin it makes this easier, and the bubble shield, although smaller, stays in place. Huh. The sword's magic might work on intent. Now that's a freaky idea. I grin. Perhaps they objected to playing bat the spell?

Then it hits me. *Oh no, I'm going to have to say thank you to the angel.* What a horrible thought.

It's only a few more feet, but it feels like miles. Finally, I pull boil witch onto the kitchen tiles. I sheath the sword and immediately splash her with a healing potion. It takes a few seconds, but her breathing is less laboured. I use a medical-grade sleeping spell and then another healing potion.

I grab a clean towel from a basket of laundry and fill a mug from a shelf with water. Using the towel to protect her airway and eyes, I rinse her exposed skin, washing away the pus and any spell splatter. That's as much as I can do. I turn her onto her side in a recovery position and face her away from the pool of yucky water.

The kitchen is getting crowded.

"Go home," comes a reed-thin voice from upstairs. The other witches up there shush her, but she ploughs on. "This is coven business, Executioner. It has nothing to do with you."

"That's where you're wrong. Caitlyn is a witness to a crime, and she's under my protection. I won't let you hurt her. She's an innocent human—"

Another witch lets out a snorting peal of laughter. "Is that what she told you? Human? Look, we all know your kind likes to stick together."

*My kind?*

"She owes us a debt. Just leave here, and we will pretend this never happened."

"I can't do that."

I glare at the stairs. Their height advantage needs to be

fixed. It's like shooting fish in a barrel, and I'm the fish. I need to get on the same level without killing anyone. The sword shield won't work—the space is way too tight to swing about in—but a temporary ward to the top of the stairs should give me enough cover to breach. Or I could...

I sprint into the living room, dodge two spells, and another, a blue one, hits my arm. The reflection spell heats, the blue spell boomerangs, and there is a corresponding thud from upstairs.

Five witches to go. *Come on, Gary, don't let me down,* I mentally mumble as I bolt up the stairs.

# CHAPTER TWELVE

THE PALE GREY carpet feels thin underneath my boots as I zoom up the stairs three at a time. I think my bolt upward shocks them as much as it does me. *What are you doing?* I mentally scream to myself.

No one attacks.

My heart is pounding when I reach the narrow landing, a sword nestled within my grip, ready to swing. The space is very tight, and I've more chance of hitting the walls.

I don't want to hurt them, especially the dark-haired lady still dressed in her red coat peeking out the bedroom door. She closes her eyes and, letting out a mousy squeak, dares to throw a spell at me.

I step to the side, and it goes over the rail.

Mousy opens one eye and then the other. She stares at me as if I'm going to eat her face. The other witch beside her immediately drops to the carpet to lay down her spells. Mousy does the same, and they both hold their shaking, empty hands above their heads.

"Is that everything?" I growl.

They nod.

"Okay. Go on and wait downstairs. Keep your hands up and stay silent." I stand in the bathroom so they can get past me.

As they rush downstairs, I hold my tongue though I want to tell them to watch their step and be careful with the terrible magic debris in the living room. But they *are* witches; they should know better than to go poking about down there.

That's three witches left and the one unconscious—from the blue spell dripping down my shoulder—her feet are sticking out of the bedroom.

"If we don't surrender, will you resort to cutting us into pieces?" asks the heavyset lady with a worried frown. She studies me intently, her eyes narrowing on the angel blade in my hand.

I remember she was the first to enter the house. Her voice is also familiar. She's the one that snorted and laughed at me.

*Of course not,* I want to scoff, but instead, I glare, ramping up the malice. I need these ladies to lay down their magic and go downstairs.

She sighs and dramatically puts her hands up.

"Okay, keep your mouths closed, place your spells carefully on the floor, and then head downstairs with your hands in the air."

The other two witches look to the talkative one for direction, and she nods. They all slowly lay down their spells and empty their pockets.

Back to the wall, I cross the landing to the bedroom, and as I watch them offload their pockets, I check on the unconscious witch. She looks like she's peacefully sleeping. Her breath comes out with a wheezing little snore at the end. I'm glad I don't have to look at any more boils. I splash a little healing potion on her neck just to make sure and sacrifice another sleeping spell. She's unconscious, and as with boil witch, I don't want to risk a restraint spell.

"You okay, Caitlyn?" I glance through the door into the bedroom. The bed is a mess of hastily thrown-off covers.

"Yes," comes a frightened voice from inside the tiny safe room tucked into the corner. It looks to be a little larger than a standard wardrobe.

I sag and close my eyes for a brief second with relief. "Do you need a healing potion?"

"I'm not hurt. I haven't got a scratch on me. Do you want me to come out?"

The talkative witch shifts her feet.

I narrow my eyes and point my left sword at her heart. "No." The word is for Talkative as well as Caitlyn. "Stay where you are for a few more minutes please." And in a lower tone, I growl at the witches. "Go. Downstairs. Now." They do.

Rose—who did my ward—is one of them. She gives me a dirty look as she passes. "Rose," I greet her.

"Don't," she snarls, holding up her hand. "Don't call me for another job. You're blacklisted."

I purse my lips and nod. "That's good to know." Though I don't think anyone will be calling Rose anytime soon. She needs a licence to do wards, and criminals don't get licenced, and when the Witches Council has dealt with her, a revoked licence will be the least of her troubles.

My lack of reaction vexes her. Her entire face scrunches up, and she looks at me like she wants to set me on fire.

"Oh, and Rose, while I have your attention. Do you by any chance know anything about the two creatures that broke into my house last night while the ward—your ward—was active? One was a zombie." I dust a piece of glass from my top. *Did you let them in?* is heavily implied.

She stumbles on the second step and grabs the rail. "That's not possible." Her knuckles go white.

"It happened."

Her freckled face reddens with anger. "No refunds."

"That's fine." I wave her away. "I'll add it to the official complaint. I'm sure whoever investigates will audit all your work. Oh, and I have irrefutable evidence you let them into my home. You'll be ostracised from the witch community and get at least ten years in prison."

"You wouldn't dare!" she snarls.

"I so would." I glare at her. "Who was it, Rose?"

Her nails dig into the wood. "Other witches from out of town," she mumbles. "One is a gateway witch, and my coven owed her a favour. She said they wanted access to pick something up. I was told you'd never know they'd been there."

"Names?"

"I don't have a name. I didn't speak to them. I just did as I was told."

I won't get anything further from her, and I have too much to deal with right now. I smirk, flip my blade in a salute, and turn my back before I do something stupidly petty like push her down the stairs.

I use a towel from the bathroom to scrub my face and clean the worst of the magic goop off my chest and arm.

Then I lift the unconscious, still-snoring witch off the bedroom floor and heft her over my shoulder in a classic fireman's carry. I take in the living room below as we descend the stairs.

*Ooh, it looks bad.*

It's a war zone.

Some of the magic casings are unbroken while other spells drip from the walls and ceiling, staining the carpet, making it crunchy in places and burned in others. The sofa is a mangled mess. Something purple, strange, and fuzzy is growing out of the far corner, and the television... I shake my head. It looks perfect. How did they miss that?

Rose pokes at a witch cocoon, and the other four witches awkwardly stand around, glass crunching underneath their feet. I hope they feel embarrassed. Appropriately used, the glass should vaporise when a spell's magic activates.

I poof out my cheeks. I can't safely hold these witches as they are while I wait for backup. If backup ever comes. I'm not trained for this shit, and I don't trust them to behave. This mess is a bit much for one person to deal with.

I hurry down the last of the stairs, and while the witch on my shoulder dangles, I dip my hand into the pocket dimension and chuck the Restrain Me balls. I restrain them all. Rose turns, opens her mouth, and a ball doinks her in the centre of her forehead. It looks like I made a perfect shot, but I was aiming for her mouth.

"We will chat later in holding," I tell her with a smile. Her stunned eyes glaze over, and the cocoon swallows her whole.

Eleven witch cocoons and two sleeping.

Not bad.

I offload the witch on my shoulder into the kitchen, and with some wrangling—it's like creature Tetris because the kitchen is so tiny—I plop her next to her now-boil-free friend.

I then plod back upstairs to get Caitlyn. Gingerly, I avoid the piles of unused magic. I could bag them, but I'll leave it for the professionals. I don't want to mess with any more spells.

"Okay, you can come out now. Slowly. Watch your feet." There's a click of a door, and a fully dressed Caitlyn rushes out of the safe room and throws herself into my arms. "Oh, erm, okay." I wrinkle my nose in horror as she does an impression of a spider monkey. I stiffly pat her back.

*This is weird.* I'm sure other people like this, but I'm not really a hugger. I allow her to continue the hug, offering comfort as I'm not a total nobhead.

"Tru, thank you! Thank you so much for coming!" She rubs her nose on my neck. *Oh crap, is that snot?* "Are they all dead?"

"Dead? No!" What does she think I am? Geez, my reputation must be shot if she thinks I can easily go around murdering people.

"Oh." She pulls away and ducks, dropping her chin to her chest to disguise her disappointment.

People say and do things they don't mean when they are shocked. Not everyone enjoys a fight. Caitlyn must be so frightened. I hurry to reassure her. "They are all wrapped up —" They look like alien eggs or the cocoons from Gremlins; I better not say that. "—and won't hurt you. For now, I promise you're perfectly safe." I rub her arm. The poor girl is traumatised. "Your living room and the stairs are in a bit of a mess. So be careful where you place your feet. The house isn't safe."

She scowls.

But I press on. Now is the time to chat about the off-world

pocket realm. I can't think of anywhere better. It is the perfect place for her to go. "The Sanctuary—"

"No."

"It will just be for a few days. Caitlyn, you can't stay here."

"You want me to go to the pocket realm? No. No way." She shakes her head.

I follow her down the stairs, and she stops to eye the witch cocoons and the magic-trashed living room.

"Yeah, it's bad," I grumble.

The purple fuzz in the corner is creeping towards cocoon Rose. I roll my eyes and shove Rose unceremoniously to the side and out of its path. The television wobbles. I stuff my hand into my super handy pocket dimension for a bag of salt and then circle the fuzz with a thick line. Magic doesn't like salt. I back up to check if I missed a spot, and there's a crash. I close my eyes.

It's the television.

"Sorry," I say with a wince. I hope the Witch Council and their magic cleaners get here soon.

"It's fine." Caitlyn picks her way to the front door and gives me a look of exasperation when the ward blocks her. "I want to go outside."

I huff and follow.

I hold out my hand, and she grips it. Almost rushing, she drags us both through the door. Once outside, she drops my hand. "Thanks for all your help. My phone is fried, so I'll be in touch when I get a replacement." Caitlyn randomly waves down the street, or I think it is random, until the sound of an ignition and a car's headlights flick on.

A green Ford Focus pulls up to the kerb, and after giving me a side hug while I try my best not to crawl out of my skin from being subjected to more invasion of my personal space, she opens the passenger door and slides inside.

*What?*

"Caitlyn, I really think—"

She slams the door in my face.

"—you should wait." I scratch my head and watch the car's taillights disappear under the bridge and out of sight. I turn and mournfully peek back into the dripping house. I shake my head at the mess and the creepy cocoons. When I renew my spells, I'll ask for a different type of restraint.

"Did that just happen?" I mumble. I can't believe that she just left. I should have stopped her. *Crap, I'm no good at this.*

My breath fogs the air. It's even more freezing out here after the house's heat, but at least I can breathe. The magic inside is stifling. I prowl up the street and walk to the edge of the pavement, wiggle the swords and knives out of the way, and plop down on the kerb. I pull my knees to my chest and mentally prepare to wait for the cavalry.

I hate waiting.

I take a deep breath of fresh air. It feels like the entire world is asleep and I'm the only one awake. I'm exhausted. I rub my face and huddle. Kleric's temperature magic is regulating me, so it's not that I'm cold. I'm just feeling out of sorts.

The urge to move, swing my new swords, and discover their secrets thrums through me. I'd love to see what they can really do. I wriggle and look up and down the road. This street has had enough excitement for one early morning, and me whipping out the dual angel blades and spinning them around in all my glory might not be the best idea.

Glumly I sit and wait.

## CHAPTER THIRTEEN

I STOMP down the narrow grey-on-grey corridor. Saturday mornings, these offices are usually a ghost town. Most workers will be back on Monday. Unfortunately for me, I don't get the luxury of weekends off. Jenny, one of my colleagues who does work the weekends, sees me coming. She sees my face, spins on her heel, and dives out of the way.

I'm— *Ahh.* I can't even think; I'm so pissed.

"What's up with you?" Story asks.

I let out an embarrassing little scream as she appears from nowhere. Her sapphire-blue form zips at my face and hovers millimetres from my nose. I'm sure my eyes go cross-eyed as I attempt to focus on her. I'm so bloody tired. If I'm involved in a wacky witch-and-necromancer conspiracy, they are doing a great job of trying to kill me with sleep deprivation.

"Caitlyn called in the early hours," I grumble.

"I know. I got your red alert this morning. Late, I might add. We'll discuss why you didn't ask me to go with you in a bit. So what's with the face? The witches?"

"Yeah."

"I heard it was a mess."

"You heard right."

"The girl, Caitlyn, she's okay?"

I nod and continue stomping to my office.

Story flies alongside me. "Mother Nature, Tru, this is like pulling fangs. Come on, tell me why are you so mad?"

"The Witch Council took my prisoners," I snarl through my teeth.

"Since when do you have prisoners?"

"Since I made them into witch cocoons after they chucked spells at my head. There were these custard-producing boils, and this purple magic fuzz was growing out of the walls and—"

"A witch what? A cocoon? You're not making any sense. Tru, did you hit your head?"

I groan. Well, it's more of a half groan, half growl.

We finally get to my allocated office. I fling open the door, and it thuds against the wall as I land behind the desk in the cheap chair. It rolls back with the force of my body and spins. To avoid looking at the boring grey walls, I tip my head back and stare at the boring grey ceiling.

I ask the universe for patience.

Story flies above my head, spinning with me. "So? What happened?" Her pretty face scrunches up in exasperation.

I lay the angel blades out on the desk and tell her everything, from the break-in with the zombie to the blades on the stairs, the gift of the angel swords, the three a.m. phone call, and the witch war zone. I end with me waiting for backup for three bloody hours. *Three hours!*

"So the Witch Council came, took over the scene. That's a good thing? Right?" She pokes the unicorn on the pommel of one of the blades.

"No," I whine. "They were my prisoners. Mine. I wanted to talk to them. I wanted to talk to Rose again."

Story struts across the desk. "Tru, you're not an investigator, and you already work too hard. I shouldn't have to say it, but you know. You know the witches deal with witches. That is the way of the world. What did you think they were going to do?"

My forehead thumps on the wood next to her feet. "I wanted a chance to sort this out." With my face smushed against the desk, my words come out muffled.

"Why?"

I lift my head a little. "They opened a portal underneath the car. They could have hurt you and the kids. Then they broke into my house. If Dexter hadn't been out hunting, they could have hurt him. Killed him. A necromancer brought their pet zombie into my house. They poked around my stuff and left a bloody zombie finger on my stairs!"

"You've got no evidence that it's these witches."

I shrug. "I know." My forehead thumps back onto the wood, and Story strokes my hair.

"We're fine. We are safe. Caitlyn, thanks to you, is also fine. You saved the day. Woo-hoo. Tru, you've got to leave it to the professionals."

"I'm a professional," I grumble into the wood.

"You're a professional pain in the bum. Please don't

pretend you don't know what I mean. Unless the witches officially want you to kill something, you can't interfere."

"It's personal," I tell her. I wince as Story tugs my hair. "Ow."

"Big baby."

"I know. Okay. I know. I was told if I keep my head down and my mouth shut, I might, if I'm lucky, get access to the files when they've done." I didn't even get a poxy *thanks* for stopping the coven from blowing up half the town. *Bloody witches.*

I'm not an investigator. That's been made clear. The witches don't care that I, on paper, outrank them. If I'd pushed it, they would have given me the runaround, and I'd have got nothing. I'll have to wait for the scraps of information they are willing to give.

"You can't keep poking at stuff, hoping some baddie will try to kill you. Not with this. That's not how real life works."

*Aha. Now that's a good idea.*

A bit of spit has pooled underneath my chin. That's gross. I'm gross. "Okay, you're right." I lift my head and surreptitiously wipe my mouth and the desk with my sleeve.

"Of course I'm right."

The desk phone rings. I turn my head and pretend I haven't heard it. I can't be bothered.

"Are you going to answer that?"

*No.* "Do I have to?"

Story rolls her eyes, her hands drop to her hips, and she stares from me to the phone and back. She taps her foot and gives me the mum's face she's perfected to wrangle the kids.

*For eff's sake.*

"'Ello."

"Executioner." Richard is on the other end. "The angel

ambassador is—" There's a mumbling of voices, and the phone crackles. "Excuse me, the angel Xander is here to see you."

*No.*

No. No. No. No!

I want to smack my head against the desk again. "Of course, Richard," I say through the enormous lump in my throat. It's so big I can hardly breathe. My lungs burn from the lack of oxygen.

"Perfect. Thank you, Executioner. I'll get someone to escort him."

"Thank you," I rasp as I place the handset gently in its cradle.

"What's up?" Story asks.

"Xander is coming."

"What? Here? Now?" she squeaks.

"Yes."

We share a look of horror, and Story's rose-gold wings bust out of her back. She flings herself into the air.

"Where the heck are you going?" I cry.

"I'm going to write your reports. I'll do the first draft, and you can check for continuity before I file. I believe I have all the info." She taps her temple and zooms out the door.

*Unbelievable.*

I haven't seen him in over three months, and I could go a lifetime not seeing him again. The urge to connect to Kleric for moral support is a living thing inside my brain. I wish the demon were here.

Gosh, I miss him.

In my heart, Xander was dead to me when he locked me in that prison. I have wished that I could hate him these past few months. Yet I've not got it in me. I've not got it in me to hate him, but that doesn't mean I want to talk to him.

*Nice one, Tru. He bought you a fancy gift, and now you've got to pay for accepting it.*

I fiddle with the swords on my desk while I wait for the inevitable. "It's your fault." I scowl down at them.

Are they really worth the pleasure of Xander's company?

## CHAPTER FOURTEEN

My door is open, but there's a light knock on the wooden doorframe. A nervous jitter runs through me. I puff out my cheeks and ready myself.

*Here we go.*

"Just in here, sir. I'm sorry about the walk. Executioner." The front-of-house security officer, Dina, greets me with a nod. "Story requested your car be collected. It's parked in your usual spot, and she asked for these belongings to be sent up." She hands over the Land Rover keys, phone, and datapad.

"Thank you. That's very kind." I focus solely on her and ignore the angel as he prowls into the room.

"You're welcome. Oh, and the beithíoch"—Dexter—"came in with the vehicle. He's in the lobby, as we have a youth group tour." Dina's lips twitch, and I return her smile. The monster cat will be in his element, getting kitty cuddles from all the kids. Dina waves and closes the door.

The almost silent click echoes in my ears like a shot. The office is suddenly an awful lot smaller. There's no air. I cough to clear my throat and give myself a second to scrape my frayed nerves together.

When I don't rise from my crappy office chair to greet him, Xander nods, acknowledging the slight. I'm not his puppet to play with anymore. I see him how he is, without the rose-coloured glasses.

I rudely check my phone. *Ooh, look at all those messages.* Besides, Caitlyn might have rung. I'm still worried about her. Nothing. Just a bunch of dull work stuff.

"You are using the pocket dimension?" Xander's voice is gruff.

The silk bag still attached to my leg suddenly feels like it weighs a tonne. I nod, eyes still fixed on my mobile. I make a murmuring sound of agreement under my breath.

*Where is he going with this?*

"You can put your technology inside when you shift. Your shifter magic won't affect the dimension, so anything you put inside the pocket storeroom is safe from outside influences."

"Oh," I say eloquently. It makes complete sense now that he's said it, and I feel a little daft that I didn't think of that myself. Then again, I wasn't firing on all cylinders at three a.m.

"Thank you." I push the words through my gritted teeth and, with my heart feeling like it's out of my chest, mobile and on the run, zipping around my body, I bite back my pride. *Let's get this over with so he can leave.* The least I can do is be polite. "Thank you for the gifts. I got them last night." I put the phone away and raise my eyes.

I blink.

He looks different, worn.

Xander's entire appearance is disconcerting. He's an immortal angel, yet he looks like he's aged. He's more brutal if that's even possible. His golden eyes have lost their sparkle, his complexion looks sallow, and his dark hair desperately needs a cut. He's also lost weight and has packed on more muscle.

Then there are his clothes.

When I was seventeen, he was my guardian, and I lived with him. So I have seen him casually dressed at home but not in public.

To see him like this... he's wearing jeans, for fate's sake. The tight top clings to his broad shoulders and highlights his tempered waist. His thick, muscled thigh nudges against the desk.

Grief. Losing his sister, Robin, has taken a toll on him.

I pity him but shut that feeling of empathy down before it can show on my face. I will not give him anything, not even compassion. He lost that right. Xander's actions towards me sloughed off a piece of my soul. He irreparably damaged me, and I must remind myself he's the enemy and a threat. As a reminder, I allow a tiny sliver of the past to crawl up from my subconscious's dark, rotten depths. My heart rate increases, but I plough on and allow the memory to fester into the forefront of my mind.

I remember...

I remember the white cell. The buzz of white noise fills my ears, and my breath dies in my throat. I see sparkling golden eyes, and the angel's voice joins the buzz of white as it repeatedly echoes inside my mind, calling me a psychopath. The white tries to drag me under, and the helplessness that grips me is overwhelming.

My vision goes hazy as all I can see is white.

The kiss on my hand burns, pulling me back from the edge, and I take a sweet, ragged breath. The taste of sulphur hits the back of my tongue, and I feel a familiar heat wrap around me. And then... Then there is a demon in my mind.

*Kleric.*

It's as if he cradles my soul, protecting it from harm, and his warm, solid, calm presence makes pushing the memories back easier. As they return to where they belong, each breath becomes less of a chore. I'm no longer there, locked in that white cell. I'm safe. I'm safe.

*Are you good?* he asks.

*I'm good. I'm okay. Thank you.*

*Nice one, Tru. That was a hell of a reminder.*

Kleric takes a second to see through my eyes, and he growls low in his throat. The sound reverberates down my spine. *What is he doing there?* he snarls.

It feels like he's standing beside me and not just in my head. *I don't know. Let's find out, shall we?*

Xander, with a golden, narrow-eyed stare, watches me. "Tru, you look well. You've gained back the weight you lost. I'm glad."

*Glad I no longer look like a starved and tortured prisoner, he means,* I grumble to Kleric. *What a suck-up.* A compliment from Xander—it freaks me out more than his randomly turning up to the office. I squint. *What does he want?* Thinking about it, his visit is probably not random at all.

*Yeah, it seems kind of sus. What do I say about coincidences? Iffy. It seems all a bit convenient that he turns up today. Oh, such perfect timing to visit after a thoughtful colleague dropped off his gift last night. Either he spelled the* gift box to let him know when it had been opened, or he set the entire situation up.

Ahh. I can't stand him. I'm looking well. Ha. After the crazy twenty-four hours I've had, I don't look "well." I look like shit. I'm a grotty mess and still covered in spell residue. The angel is full of shit.

I sink back into the chair and scratch the back of my head. *Okay, I'll play.* I don't offer him a seat. "Ambassador, what do you want?" I do my best to cut through his bullshit to the root of his visit—the heart of the problem.

"That is no longer my title," Xander says smoothly.

I tilt my head.

"I'm no longer the ambassador for the angels."

"What? Since when?" I almost slide out of my chair at the look of derision that crosses his face.

*I don't know what to say. What do I say?*

I can feel Kleric's cool calm as he assesses the situation. The demon wisely keeps silent. So I follow his lead.

I've heard nothing about Xander's problems. If I'm honest, I deliberately shut down and put my metaphysical fingers in my ears on anything related to him and the angels.

I know. I know I should watch him like a hawk just so I can anticipate if he makes a move to turn on me again. He's my enemy, after all. But I'd rather take the risk and not know anything about him. The man is toxic to my mental health.

Xander's expression twists as if he's about to say words that will physically hurt.

I brace myself.

"It haunts me, Tru. It haunts me what I did to you. I made so many mistakes. Many, many mistakes. I left..." He swallows and looks down at his hands. "I left my sister in that warehouse to rot, left her for strangers to find, to handle her body."

I'm frozen in my chair. I don't know where he's going with this. If tears roll down his cheeks, I'm done. Like the Roadrunner, I'll be out of here. *Meep-meep.*

"That day in the warehouse. In the warded room, I saw the bodies." His entire chest moves as he takes a deep shuddering breath. "And I decided they were someone else's problem." Xander rubs his mouth and shakes his head as if he's a dog with a flea in his ear or he's shaking away a memory that won't go away.

I already figured that out myself. He'd been in and out of the warehouse way too fast to do anything but take a quick look. At the time, I was glad. The entire building was unstable after a dragon had chewed it, and it could have collapsed at any moment.

Also, if he'd found the murdered angels that day, Xander would have killed me—especially the old me who wouldn't have lifted a finger to stop him. I was too loved up to protect myself then.

"It was easy to convince myself there was no way an angel could be in that mess. Within that pile of bodies." He lifts his chin, and his honey eyes bleed with pain and sadness. "Do you know how difficult it is to kill an angel?" Xander then laughs. It's a horrible sound. "We are almost indestructible, impossible to kill—"

*Well, I don't know about that.*

"—and my sister was so... so strong." His face and eyes are full of grief.

He's really milking whatever this is. *Listening to this, to him, isn't worth the swords,* I say to Kleric. I glance at the office door. *I wonder if Xander will notice if I leave.* The man is so self-absorbed I bet he wouldn't for at least ten minutes.

*You don't have to say anything. Just listen to what he has to say,* Kleric tells me.

*Okay... Okay, I can be kind and listen.* I gnaw on my thumbnail.

"She was the best of us. Strong, brave, a pain in my arse." He huffs that grating laugh again. It makes me seriously uncomfortable. I wiggle in my seat. "It never even occurred to me she was a victim, that she could be a victim and be dead. *Missing* I could handle. I was used to dealing with Robin's mess. I didn't check the bodies; they were the Hunters Guild's problem. It never even entered my head that three of my angels, angels I was responsible for, were dead and dumped there."

His eyes meet mine. "I was looking for something to pin on you."

And there we have it.

*He better not start throwing around accusations again. It wasn't my fault.*

"I saw what I expected, and I blamed you."

My insides twist. This is all good, but Xander still hasn't explained why he suddenly decided one morning to throw away nine years of... friendship? Love? Love, at least from my end. What a silly fool I was. The office chair squeaks as I lean forward. He may answer some questions while upset and vulnerable, boohooing about his sister.

But... do I care enough to know? I don't trust him as far as I can throw him, and taking in his cut, muscled frame, that wouldn't be very far.

I shake my head. You know what? It doesn't matter. I've said everything I need to say to this man. He can't tell me anything new to fix this, and I will not repeat myself. A broken bond, a damaged soul, is enough for anyone.

No way I'm going to rip open that wound.

I also think he's trying to manipulate me, which makes me realise he has never known me at all. Xander has had his strikes, and I'm way too black-and-white for whatever shit he's pulling. Whatever this little speech is working up to, I will not help him. If that makes me a bad person, I don't care.

I don't care.

Just like he didn't care when he sent me to prison to rot.

"It haunts me," Xander continues. Yep, he really likes that word. "My sister haunts me, and the other angels who died follow me around in my head. My arrogance. My incompetence—" He closes his eyes and bites his lip. "I lost my position as ambassador. They asked me to step down. I'm technically on a sabbatical so that I can grieve. I shamed myself and my family's name. The angels who were in my command can't even look at me. I'm lucky they didn't charge me with their deaths. It's only what I deserve."

*Karma, right?*

I wiggle again in the chair. I have to slam my compassion down. The office is full of his pain. It rolls around us like an ocean, making my mouth so dry I can't swallow. I don't know what to say. I don't understand why he's telling me all this.

*What is he leading up to?* He can try to buy me off and give me fancy gifts to soften me up and alleviate his guilt. I'm not that cheap and far too stubborn to forget what he did.

I should be happy with this display of pain, but I'm not. It just makes me feel sad. It's not like I can help him. I can't fix his mess. We are not friends.

"I can't go back to my world. My reputation is in utter shambles."

*What the heck does he want me to do?*

He holds up a hand to stop me from speaking. "Please, don't apologise."

*I wasn't going to,* I mentally groan. *Is he trying to play me?* And he dared to call *me* nuts. The angel is working up to a BAFTA performance.

"I don't deserve it. I wanted to let you know I'm here for you. I appreciate what you did and how you fought for and against me."

I wince.

Oh, I fought him all right. But not properly. It was more like he was humouring me rather than us having an actual fight. He cut my sword in half with a single fiery swipe of his angel blade.

*Dickhead.*

Even when I'm pumped full of Kleric's superstrong demon blood, I can't take the angel.

I rub the spot between my eyes. My eyeballs are hurting 'cause I've been rolling them so much. I need to set this mess straight and get him out of my office. Pronto. *Do regular people believe this crap?*

"Xander," I say in a no-nonsense tone. I lean forward and rest my arms on the desk. "Your choices have nothing to do with me, and please, I want no more fancy gifts or half-hearted explanations; we are far beyond that. Let me be clear. Are you listening?" I cup my ear with my hand.

His golden eyes flash.

Oh, he doesn't like that. It's hard to hold in my smile. "Kleric and I went to your house to deal with the demons for my own selfish revenge. I didn't do it for you. Now, if you would be so kind, please get to the point. I'm busy. What do you want?"

*I'm done with his games.*

"How is your demon?"

I stare at him. My head spins. Oh okay. That is a heck of a subject change.

"How are you doing with the long-distance relationship? It must be hard with him being off-world."

What the fuck? This is the week that keeps on giving, and it gets better and better. I can't help it. I laugh.

Xander frowns.

Kleric growls.

My laughter dies, and I dramatically sigh. "Xander, my relationship with Kleric is none of your business. I didn't realise that you needed to hear it, but we—" I wave a floppy hand between us as I grin at him. "We aren't friends."

It's the angel's turn to lean his hands on the desk. He's a little too close to the swords for comfort. Instead of grabbing them and chopping his head off, I lean back in the chair, cross my arms underneath my chest, and shoot him my best death glare.

*How are you doing with the long-distance relationship?* His words swirl in my brain, and now I'm troubled by the thought that the angel, despite not having an ambassador status, is somehow keeping Kleric and me apart and making the already tricky demon situation even worse.

"Are you keeping Kleric and me apart?"

The angel smirks.

It's only a ghost twist of his lips before his mask snaps back into place, but I can't unsee it. And as if the atmospheric, emotional switch is flicked, the sadness and pain rolling off him dissipates like magic.

*The manipulative bastard.*

His golden eyes spark with fire as he looks down his nose at me. "You asked me what I want?"

I hold a hand up to stop him. "No." I point my finger at his face.

Of course he completely ignores me. "I forbid it," he snarls.

"Pardon?" I wince. *Kleric, will you stop growling? I almost can't hear him.*

"I. Forbid. It." Xander says each word slowly. "Your relationship. You're too innocent to be associated with this demon. If you are going to be with anyone, it should be with me."

*Oh, for fuck's sake.*

## CHAPTER FIFTEEN

It's incredible how fast you can get someone out of your office when you have a livid demon roaring in your head. I was worried there for a second that Kleric would use his smoky magic to come through from his home world and beat Xander into a bloody pulp. My lips twitch. Now that is something I'd love to see. Not that I couldn't beat the living daylights out of the angel myself.

Or at least try my best.

I have Kleric mind blocked again. I can't think straight with all his growling. I shake my head. Xander wants me. I chuckle as I prowl the warren of grey-on-grey corridors to get to the front of the building to collect Dexter. It's a joke of epic proportions.

What is it with me and my luck? The angel was never interested in me when I panted after him for nine years. For nine years! He didn't even notice. At the first opportunity, he locked me in an off-world prison just to get rid of me.

But as soon as I stop, as soon as I hate his guts, he's all "I want to look after you. I care about you." I say the words in a low voice, sounding distinctively like a poor imitation of Arnold Schwarzenegger.

It was naive of me to think things with Xander were over. I should have prepared myself better after what he said that night at his house. What was it again? I stop my endless trudging, tilt my head, and roll the memories around. It's not like I'd forget. We were heading towards his front door. The demon Cynthia was out cold, heavy across my shoulder, and I remember the rain...

*"You have really grown into a beautiful and strong woman, Tru," Xander says, following us out of the orangery and into the hall.*

*I grind my teeth. He can stuff his words up his arse. The angel is seven weeks and a prison stay too late. I pick up the pace to the front door.*

*"We are bonded, after all."*

*I stumble and turn so fast—oops; Cynthia's head bounces off the wall—I stare at the determined angel with exasperation.*

*Gorgeous honey eyes with their sprinkles of gold framed with thick, black lashes look into me like he is reading my soul. He smiles at me, and with the hallway light shining behind him, he looks like a golden god.*

*My eyes flick to the massive blue demon who stands watching me with his gentle, kind eyes. Kleric nods, opens the door, and steps into the rain.*

*Dexter runs out after him.*

*The demon kiss pulses on my hand.*

*I huff, turn, and continue walking down the hall, and with a wave of my hand, I say,* "Sorry, Xander. I'm way too busy. I have a prisoner to interrogate and a portal to close. Demons to hunt." *I click my fingers.* "Oh, and please forget about the silly adolescent bond. Kleric is my mate." *I grin and step into the rain.*

*Xander's honey eyes narrow with utter confusion as the door slams closed in his face.*

Uh-oh.

I get it. I turned him down and set a challenge. For three months, Xander has allowed me to wallow, to get over my little incarceration issue while he has dealt with the ramifications of Robin's death. Now he thinks he can sweep in, white knight it, and I'll run into his arms.

I continue to walk, my boots stomping with each step. The angel has lost his purpose, and he's grabbing at straws. I'm the bendy one in his grasp. Now he's the most hated angel in his circle; he feels it's okay to slum it with me. And that's what he'll be doing, slumming.

I'm not stupid. I rub at the sharp pain in my chest. I can see it in his eyes. He looks at me as if I'm some strange bug that he squished on the bottom of his boot. No. It's worse. I'm the bug that got away, and he's decided he must step on me. *I'm not a bloody bug.*

The idea that all his focus will be on convincing me we should be together while dragging Kleric and me apart is horrifying. It's also something I can't ignore. Xander isn't just hurting Kleric—other creatures are caught up in this mess. We could go to war with the demons, a world where even a lower-level monster like Cynthia can cause absolute havoc. Carnage.

They can look like anyone. It's a war we can't win. They would annihilate us.

Xander can't be that stupid.

Story says I tend to go off the deep end with my thinking, and she says I go on a wild tangent without evidence. James Bonding, she calls it, as she thinks I make villain motives up in my head. I don't... I roll my eyes and huff, blowing the loose hairs off my face. Okay, I do, but with good reason in this case. The angel is a menace.

As I finally get to the lobby, the floor underneath my feet changes into fancy marble slabs. I immediately spot Dexter in his massive monster cat form. He's lying on his back, legs akimbo, and half a dozen schoolchildren are giggling around him.

"He's so soft."

"Touch him again."

I chuckle under my breath. I can hear his rumbling purr from over here. I adore that cat.

A lady I recognise, a regular human customer at the café where I used to work, catches my eye. She gives me a small wave and walks towards me. Her hair is a mix of grey and brown, and she moves as if her joints ache. Frowning, I move to meet her halfway.

I don't envy humans; growing old must be challenging, to feel young on the inside, yet you see a stranger reflected at you in the mirror. It must be sad.

As a shifter, shifting is on a cellular level, so anything wrong with the cells is instantly replaced. Our cells don't grow old. We stay in our physical prime until something horrible happens and we die. We are less destined to live an immortal life and more to suffer a horrific death. Good times. Each race has its quirks, I guess.

I suffer the opposite of the human condition. Inside, I feel ancient. All those souls I've dispatched weigh me down if I dare to stop and think about it.

When we are almost level, the lady shoves her phone in my face. I blink and do my best to focus on the screen.

"They said you wouldn't help, but I came anyway. I've been waiting all morning. I would have waited forever. This is my granddaughter, Petra. She's missing. The vampires have taken her."

The girl in the photo has light brown hair and cornflower-blue eyes. She sits on a sofa, her skinny arms wrapped around a fluffy black-and-white cat. She beams a smile at the camera. She can't be any older than nine.

"She's eight," the lady says.

I take out my mobile, click a few buttons, and snap a photo of the screen. "When? Where? Give me all the information you have." I guide the lady from the busy thoroughfare of creatures entering the building and into a quiet corner.

Her hands shake, and her human heart pounds. She's petrified, terrified of me. It makes my own heart hurt. It's understandable. It's been bad since people found out about my hybrid status, but being the feared executioner is a hundred times worse. Her voice though remains steady. She's determined to give me all the information that she can.

Her name is Mrs Hardy, and she tells me in excellent detail about what has been happening in the South Shore area of town.

The vampires have been actively hunting, Mrs Hardy insists, and she believes their nest is around the corner from her home.

"I'll look into it."

I shouldn't. It's not my job, but she came to me to ask for help, which means something.

I plan what I need to do in my head, starting with a friendly chat with Atticus, the vampire leader. I need some type of formal permission. Nothing gets past him. He might know what's going on, and his vampires kidnapping little girls off the street is something he needs to know about if he doesn't already.

He also might know if Xander is up to something as well as more detail about the rogue coven. Perhaps my fixing a vampire issue might make him more agreeable with information.

"Today?" Mrs Hardy interrupts my musings. Her voice is desperate, and her eyes plead with me to do something. Anything. "She's all I've got left. Please will you try to get Petra home?"

I rock from foot to foot. "I'm not going to lie and give you false promises. If it is vampires and they've had your granddaughter for over twenty-four hours, her survival rate drops significantly." I don't know if she's still alive. It's a horrible world we live in.

"You will try?"

I don't think she heard anything I said about Petra's survival rate. I swallow and nod. "I'll try."

"Thank you." Mrs Hardy takes hold of my hand. Inwardly, I wince as she grips me so tight that the mobile digs into my bones. But I ignore the slight discomfort. "Please try to bring our Petra home."

I gently pull away. I have Mrs Hardy's contact details and everything I need. "I'll be in touch."

She nods, and all at once the fight seems to go out of her. She wobbles. I take hold of her elbow to steady her. *Oh no, please don't faint.*

Without being asked, Dina, the security guard, comes towards us with a chair. Mrs Hardy sits. "I'll get the lady some water," she says kindly.

"Dina, would it be possible to get someone to see Mrs Hardy home?" She doesn't look good.

"Of course, Executioner. I'll take care of her."

"Thank you."

# CHAPTER SIXTEEN

We climb into the Defender, and I drive from the Creature Council building. I had intended to see my gargoyle friends today to try out the angel blades. Frank is a sword specialist, and Stanley and Jonathan are my fighting buddies. I enjoy sparring with them as I can whack on them with all my strength and at my leisure. It's refreshing to go all out, and they like it because I'm a smaller opponent and sneaky. Our impromptu training sessions are a win-win for all four of us.

I shake my head and rest my elbow on the lip of the window while I loosely hold the steering wheel. The little girl takes priority, and this afternoon I'll be fighting for real instead.

I can't get the image of Petra and her cat—her sweet, innocent, smiling face—out of my head. I dig my fingers into my hair and groan. The hardest thing to learn is patience. I thought I had that down pat as a kid, but I was wrong. It's tough fighting the emotional voice that is nagging at you. Demanding you to do something, do anything to rescue them. It has to be the most challenging thing to ignore.

"How do you fancy hunting vampires?" I ask Dexter, who is sitting in the passenger seat beside me.

"Reow," he answers, which I take as complete agreement.

I drive far enough away from work so we won't be disturbed and then pull over to make the call. Nerves twist in my stomach as I dial Atticus's mobile number and pop him on speaker.

It rings three times before he picks up. Atticus's refined voice fills the car. "I heard about what happened with the witches on Rigby Road."

Ah. I settle back into the seat. He means business. It looks like today I don't even warrant a hello. It's not like him, the illustrious vampire leader, to be rude and forget common niceties.

I ready myself with a roll of my shoulders. "Good afternoon, sir. How are you on this fine day?"

Atticus, of course, ignores my poorly veiled sarcasm.

"You tend to solve all problems with extreme violence." *I can't disagree with that.* "Not in this instance though. From all accounts, you handled yourself well. No deaths. I don't know anyone who could have pulled that off. Fighting over a dozen witches, a full coven of thirteen?" He hums with appreciation. "They should commend you for the excellent work. They condemned the house; did you know that? I'm told magical hazmat will have to purify everything and rip the entire section of terraced houses down. The Witch Council is frightfully embarrassed."

I'd pay good money to see Carol Larson's face when she got that bill.

"Yeah, it was a mess." I clamp my mouth closed to stop myself from telling him about the crawling purple fuzz. I need to stay on track. "So the reason I'm calling you is—"

"Excellent. I need a favour; I have a vampire nest that needs clearing, and it must be done today."

*What are the odds?* Two vampire nests. Well, now that sounds like a Saturday public service to me.

"Okay." I grab the datapad from where I chucked it in the footwell, and my fingers hover above my note-taking app, ready to type. I've found if I take notes, I'm less likely to put my boot in my mouth. "Where, how many vampires, and what have they been doing?"

"Bond Street."

Huh. And there we have it. It's my lucky day.

My cheeks burn from my smile. Bitten vampires are territorial, so there's no chance another nest could be in the area, least of all on the same street Petra was abducted and where she's still supposedly being held.

There is only one Bond Street in town, and to top it off, Atticus is asking for a favour. Win-win. Still smiling, I drop the datapad into my lap and tap a happy tune on the steering wheel.

"They've been getting a little ambiguous with consent," Atticus continues. "You know human blood has gone up again?"

I hadn't. I murmur a sort of acknowledgement. I do not want to lie outright or for Atticus to think I'm ill-informed. It's something Story monitors, and an email will undoubtedly be hidden in my inbox, never to be seen again.

Creatures everywhere are doing all manner of things, and I

haven't got time to know everything—and, as Story keeps telling me, it isn't my job.

I get blood from Kleric, and the demon has been determined to make sure I'm fed and fed well. My smile turns goofy. I'm spoiled. With my freaky unicorn DNA, my body can't digest human blood. If it was up to me and there was a guarantee that I wouldn't turn feral, I'd skip blood entirely.

I can almost stomach the cheap artificial stuff, but I get the shakes and become ill if it's all I drink. When I was younger, thanks to a certain angel, I discovered that the best blood for me contains magic.

Fortunately, other vampires, pureblood and bitten, don't share my dietary needs, and they can sustain themselves perfectly well on the artificial stuff. Their survival doesn't depend on human or creature blood. Some bad eggs don't want to, and they have a hard time accepting the word *no*.

"You cleaned out the blood rings a little too well—not that I'm complaining," he hurries to add. "What you managed to do in three months is remarkable. Blood crime is at an all-time low. Unfortunately, a nest has got a little bit rambunctious with the real blood movement. They need to be immediately brought back into line."

*A little bit rambunctious. Yeah, right.*

"How far in line?" I grip the steering wheel. *Please say dead.*

"Kill them. Kill them all. I'll send you everything I have on them." The datapad on my lap pings. "I want to send a message, and whatever you want that message to be, I'll leave it at your discretion. There are around eight to ten members, all bitten and newly dead, with an older master who could be a challenge—but not for you, I'm betting." Atticus chuckles.

"According to sources, they have a meeting this afternoon at two o'clock."

*An hour and a half to plan. It's going to be tight.*

"Will I have any backup?"

"No."

I stare out the window at two seagulls fighting over a sugar doughnut. Story would seriously disapprove of this mission. I grin and rub my hands. I prefer to work with Dexter anyway, and this is just what I need, a job to work out my angel frustrations.

You'd think being the executioner, that wouldn't be the case, and I'd be mad busy. Nope. Being an executioner isn't all die, die, die. Stab, stab, stab. No, it's politics and pissing powerful creatures off. I shrug. I'm a pro at pissing people off, so there's that.

When it comes to doing my actual job, justice around here moves slowly, and my kind of justice is less appreciated than you'd think.

I've been silent way too long, and Atticus clears his throat. "If you do this for me, Tru, I'll get you information on the Rigby Road situation."

Look at that, straight to the point. He's heard. Everyone has heard I've been sniffing around and that the witches are blocking everything from me. I wiggle in the seat, and the old leather underneath me creaks. I also need to know what Xander is up to.

Both are important, so I need to play this just right.

"I dunno, sir, I had a busy night." I pause and fake a yawn. "I'm still covered in spell residue. If I drop everything for this, clean up your vampire mess... I'll need something else from you."

"Go on."

"Information. The ex-angel ambassador, Xander: is he causing issues resolving the demon conflict?"

Atticus sucks the air between his fangs, and he pauses to *um* and *ah* under his breath before saying, "That's a serious allegation. I know you two have a lot of history." That's putting it mildly. "Because of his connection to the demons and the unfortunate death of his angels, he has been barred from all negotiations. I can say that if he's influencing anything, it's not directly." He pauses for a second. "I'll have a look into it."

"Okay, great." I keep my voice light. I don't want him to know how vital his poking around will be. To Kleric. To me. "Let me just check what you've sent me."

I flick through the files on the datapad. Atticus's people have been very thorough. There are floor plans, details about the vampires, and all the relevant documentation including warrants. I sign everything and send it all back with a flick of a button.

An almost silent ping of him receiving the documents comes from his end. "Excellent. Call me if you need anything. The usual vampire clean-up team is on standby. Happy hunting, Executioner."

He hangs up before I can reply.

"Right, well, bye then." I shrug at the phone's home screen and then turn my attention to Dexter.

Stripes of winter sun shine through the window, and he's twisted himself at an awkward angle to get into the optimal sunbathing position. His ginger-and-white spotty belly gleams under the stream of light. Aw, the little guy is all tuckered out. I lean across and tickle his tummy—the static in his fur prickles against my skin.

"Must be hard being a cat."

One eye cracks open. "Purrrt," he chirps as his front paws grab and direct my hand to where he wants me to stroke.

I glance down at the datapad and, one-handed, send everything to Story. With my phone on silent, I pore over the information from the vampire leader, analysing every word with the meticulousness of an assassin.

The hour passes quickly. Satisfied, I key the ignition, check over my shoulder, pull the Defender back into traffic, and head for the sea.

Bond Street is just off the promenade.

Breaking into the local vampire nest is sure to get the adrenaline pumping. This will differ from last night's rescue mission. It's more in my wheelhouse. Not being able to kill is a lot harder than restraining potion-wielding maniacs. And doing this on their home turf, they won't be on high alert. Relaxed big fish in a little blood pond.

Easy.

What can possibly go wrong?

# CHAPTER SEVENTEEN

SITUATED on the corner of Bond and Rawcliffe Street, the vampire nest is a dilapidated commercial building shaped like a wedge. The decoratively carved datestone at the top of the building declares the build date to be 1889. I bet it was lovely in its time.

The Land Rover shouldn't attract attention in the busy area, so I take a gamble and drive past.

As I approach, I get another bit of luck. A car a few vehicles ahead of me begins the horror-filled dance of parallel parking. The Defender rolls to a stop next to the front door. With poorly veiled impatience as I eye the place, I make a show of flapping my hands and tapping the steering wheel—nothing to see here.

South Shore Printing is plastered across the signage, along with a website and a phone number. According to the information pack, the vampires sell ink and all types of printing equipment. I presume they're making a rip-roaring trade online as the shop itself is as inhospitable as you can get.

The rusty blue shutters on the windows are all down and padlocked. The front door is still accessible, but a handwritten sign reads: CLOSED FOR STOCKTAKE.

All the shops along the street are a little worse for wear. Any metal is rusty, and most of the painted fascias are peeling. The pubs though are in better condition, using more natural materials like stone.

I guess it doesn't help to be so close to the sea. The salt and sand in the air eats away and degrades the buildings. I bet the maintenance costs alone are eye-watering.

Magic they might use to add a layer of protection is expensive and will also quickly decay. It also doesn't like salty air. Magic users living on the coast have it hard or, I guess, have a guaranteed income from the repeated business as spells must be renewed more frequently than the ones inland.

We park on a side road nearby. I bite the bullet and ring Story.

"You need help?" she grumbles. I know like me she has already read all the information I sent her.

"Yes. Please."

Story adorably lets out a little growl.

In normal circumstances, we'd have a communication spell, but both of us must be in the same vicinity for the magic to activate, so we shall go old school for this mission. From within the glove box, I dig out an earpiece, connect it to the phone, and slip the tiny device into my ear. I then grab a handful of micro-cameras so we can record what's going on.

"You know this is a stupid idea, especially after what happened with the witches. Why are you helping Atticus?"

I haven't got time to go into detail about Xander, and I'm sure as heck not telling her about wanting to get more information on the witch case.

"Is this about that dickhead's visit? What did Xander do?" she snarls.

I groan. Ever since Story got her mum card, I'm positive she gained some mother superpower of foresight.

"They abducted a little girl." I pause to let her absorb my words. "Her grandma accosted me in the lobby. The little girl is eight years old, and her name is Petra."

"Oh, Mother Nature," Story whispers. Then she barks into my ear in a stronger voice, "Well, what are you waiting for? Go. Go. Kick their arses and get her back, Tru."

DEXTER AND I circle the street and hoof it down the alleyway at the back of the building. The business behind is a car mechanic. The radio is playing, and a pair of overall-clad legs are sticking out underneath a black Vauxhall Corsa. The mechanic's left boot taps to the rhythm of the song.

With a wiggle of his bum and a flick of his tail, Dexter scrambles over the six-foot brick wall. I roll my eyes as I go to the wooden gate. I'm not climbing unless it's the last resort. I jiggle the gate's handle, snap the rusty catch with a twist of my wrist, and meander inside the small concrete yard.

A well-placed red brick, probably there to prop the gate open, makes an excellent gate stop. I wedge it underneath the wood. It should keep the broken gate shut unless the wind picks up.

I listen for a few seconds waiting for any sign of alarm, but when none is forthcoming, I creep across the space and peek through the glass back door.

Empty.

I use a spell to pick the lock, and we slip inside.

Entering the vampire nest, I first notice the smell of unwashed bodies, vampire rot and the tang of blood that permeates the air. It makes my teeth burn with anger, and I have trouble keeping my fangs in place with that awful thick copper smell. That much blood isn't a good sign.

The empty room is an old kitchen that hasn't been used for that purpose for some time. Untouched dust is thick on all the surfaces, and the fridge is open and unplugged.

I move to the door that leads to a hallway and open it a crack. Dexter tries to force himself through and glares at me when I don't let him.

*Wait*, I mouth at him.

I again stand and listen, letting the cameras and Story do their thing. When the hall beyond proves empty, we get the all clear. I open the door wider. Dexter struts through, giving me a look over his shoulder that screams, "I told you so."

Knife in my hand, we both silently pad through the building. I allow Dexter to take the lead as he won't be as easily spotted. His tail flicks from side to side, and his eyes are impossibly wide as he hunts for the vampires.

"Shop area is clear," Story says softly through the earpiece.

The equipment nearby catches my attention. Without overthinking, I swipe a black ink cartridge from the stack on the shelf and dig my thumbnail into the plastic, popping the cap off. A familiar burst of fragrance stings my nostrils, and I stare at it like a live snake. A spell must have blocked its smell and kept the contents fresh—it isn't ink inside.

No, it's human blood.

I puff out my cheeks as a shiver of absolute disgust trickles down my spine. "Human blood in the ink cartridges," I murmur under my breath to Story.

Looks as if vampires will store blood in anything.

I bite my back teeth and grab on to the dead calm inside me, twirling it around like a shield and weapon. I let the horror of the blood cartridge fade away and get into the headspace of killing.

These vampires need to die.

I keep moving.

"Single target ahead, first door on the right," Story says.

Dexter pauses. He turns to get my attention and then fixes his eyes on the same door.

I nod. *Good boy.*

The door is open, and there's the tinny sound of cheap speakers. I turn sideways and peek inside. A dark-haired vampire is sitting behind a big, solid wooden desk. He laughs, flashing his fangs as he watches a video on his phone—the source of the sound. There is the telltale sign, a crust of blood in the corner of his mouth and a dark splodge on the chest of his blue top, the hallmark of a messy eater.

And his meal... the crumpled form of a little boy tossed aside in the corner like a discarded food wrapper that missed the bin.

I don't know if the child is unconscious or dead.

I close the door, and the cheap lock slides into place with a distinctive click. As the vampire lifts his head at the sound, I leap on his desk and stomp across his paperwork. Pens and paper go flying. He jumps to his feet and slashes at me—

there's a blade in his hand. I lean back and kick him in the face.

As soon as my boot connects, I realise I should have pulled the power in my kick as his head snaps back, it flops weirdly to the side, and he drops to the floor like a rag doll.

*Damn it. I broke his neck.*

I wanted to question him. If I leave him like this, he'll heal but not for another few hours. *It's a bloody shame.*

I put the knife away, jump off the desk and grab one of the angel blades from its crossbody holster. I kick him so he's flat on his back, plant my boot on his chest, and swing the sword at his neck. The blade cuts clean, severing the vampire's head from the torso.

It takes me a second to gather my courage. I dig deep to find the strength. Then I square my shoulders and move towards the child. *Please don't be dead.*

Dexter is sitting next to the kid, and he opens his mouth in a silent cry.

*I know, kitty cat.*

Deep breath in, lock my feelings down tight. I can do this. I kneel next to the child. The rattle of the kid's breath is a horrible sound, but it's also the best thing I've ever heard. I use a healing potion—it should keep the little mite asleep—and tug a soft, warm blanket out from the pocket dimension and wrap it around him. Gingerly I pick him up—*gosh, he's so light*—and tuck him underneath the desk out of sight. To keep him safe, I temporarily ward the area.

"We'll be back as soon as we can," I whisper. *Okay. Next.* I nod to Dexter, unlock the door, and we leave the room.

"From what I'm picking up on the micro-cameras, the door to your left has a Don't Hear Me Now spell. Tru, there are hostages in there. No vampires."

I don't ask if she's seen Petra. I need to maintain dead calm. I ward the door and keep moving.

"The door farther up the corridor will take you upstairs, where twelve vampires are preparing to have their meeting."

*Only eight vampires,* he told me. *Bloody hell, Atticus.* With the one guy I've already dispatched, it looks like it's thirteen baddies once again.

"Eight vampires are in the room at the end and three in a side room on the right. Those in the side room have a... a child."

*And vampire number twelve?*

"One male incoming." Heavy footsteps creak above my head, and the treads on the stairs to the first floor groan.

The vampire must have stopped halfway down to yell, "Phil, come on, man. We're waiting to start! We need those snacks. Bring a few of the little ones upstairs."

*Oh, well, if you want snacks...* My lip twitches with a silent snarl. *You can snack on this.* I rotate the knife in my hand. I move and flatten my back against the wall, then wait.

The heavy feet slap down the stairs when he doesn't get a reply. "Phil!" The door flings open, brushes against my torso, and a bald, stocky vampire stomps past me. "Phil, why do you have to be such a wanker!" He grinds to a halt when he spots Dexter.

Dexter sits in the absolute centre of the hall. His tail wraps around his back legs as he casually licks his front left paw.

"When did we get a cat? Can I eat him?" Stocky vampire says with a happy laugh.

I shift my weight onto my toes, bring the knife up in line with the front of his throat, and firmly stab him in the centre of his neck, severing the trachea so he can't make a sound. I wouldn't want his screaming to give the game away.

Dexter bolts between our legs so he doesn't get caught in the spray of blood. I free the blade with a brutal twist and drag it across the soft bit underneath the vampire's chin, severing the carotid and jugular with one precise stroke. Arterial spray coats the hallway wall in a rainbow of red. With my icy rage, I almost saw his head clean off.

I guide his body to the floor and use the sword to finish him. I take the time to clean my right hand and both blades. Chopping off heads or removing their hearts is the only sure way to kill a vampire. He could heal even with his throat cut and no blood left.

This makes sure he can't.

I leave him, and we make our way upstairs.

Sure enough, loud, excited voices drift from the room at the end. "The three vampires, the door on your right," Story whispers.

I want to save the kid. I want to save the child so much, but I make the impossible decision to deal with the larger group first. I haven't got a choice. I can't fight them all in this hallway. There is no room, and we'd be quickly overwhelmed.

We can only win this if we surprise the bigger group first.

I prowl past the door—the weight of the decision heavy on my shoulders—and throw a ward to the floor to keep the three vampires inside contained.

Dexter shifts into his larger monster cat form.

I pull out the spells I need and get ready with the sword. Fighting vampires is fast, dirty work, and from experience, I've found you haven't got time to throw spells. If you pause for a second, someone gets hold of you... well, it's a painful lesson, and you're in trouble as they're strong enough to start ripping off your limbs.

To cause the most panic and confusion and to mess with

the vampires' heightened senses and to also stop them from working together, I boot open the door and lob in a smoke spell.

We rush through the doorway, and I throw the last spell, a temporary ward, over my shoulder to seal the door behind us so there is no escape. That frees up my left hand to draw the other angel sword. The twin hilts feel warm and right in my grip.

Blinded by smoke, the eight vampires scream and shout, wasting a few valuable seconds. The smoke makes me just as blind to what's about to go down in this room, so I close my eyes, centre myself, and let my other senses take over as chaos ensues.

Then they attack, and I dance.

Such a beautiful dance of blood, steel, and pain. Their pain. I twist my swords, my breaths even out, and I fit myself into the moment, the sweeping of my blades. I picture the fan of blood as it flings into the smoke and rains down.

Blood clings to my face and closed lashes, but everything around me is crystal clear to my senses, and each moment, each second, feels like it lasts a lifetime.

In reality, it is so-so fast.

This is where I'm at my best, when nothing can touch me. I equally love and hate this part of myself. The loss of life hurts something inside me even though I know they are bad people. I'm not too ignorant to admit I was born to do this. As the vampires fall, Dexter pounces, finishing them.

When no one is left standing, with a wave of my hand, the smoke clears, and I see all eight dead-dead. For these vampires, there's no coming back. I turn to the door, finally ready to deal with the last three vampires, and... a massive vampire crashes through the internal wall.

A chunk of plasterboard hits my face, and a long piece of stud-work timber smashes against my right shoulder, knocking the right sword out of my hand. The blade clatters to the floor, buried underneath big pieces of wall.

*Whoa, that's one way to get around a basic ward, I guess.*

This must be the master vampire. His blade fans my face. I let him get close and hammer a punch into the side of his nose. Let's see how he does with getting dizzy. He shakes his head and grins at me.

I toss the sword to my stronger right and motion a "come on" gesture with my other hand. *Whee! This is going to be fun.* Let's see how this monster deals with somebody who can fight back.

"Tru! Dexter, no!" Story cries, followed by Dexter's howl of pain.

Unwisely, I peek. What has me freezing is not just seeing a knife buried to the hilt in my monster cat. *No, no, no, that can't be right.* It's the vampire standing over his bleeding body.

"Justin?" I whisper.

## CHAPTER EIGHTEEN

WITH THE SHOCK of seeing Dexter down and bleeding with Justin ominously standing over him, I make a mistake. The master vampire takes full advantage of my distraction, and instead of taking a swing at me, which is what I'm anticipating, he tackles me to the ground.

I crack the back of my head as I hit the floor and see stars. Thank fate for muscle memory as I hold him off with a palm to his chest, and I'm quick enough to get the other arm up to brace my forearm against his throat, keeping his fangs away from my neck.

I have never had a creature drink my blood, and I don't want to start now as I've no idea what it will do to a vampire.

"Oi, nobhead, this is seriously undignified." I attempt to shake him loose.

He hisses.

I get a face full of stinky, blood-rotten breath and wrinkle my nose. "Mint?" I mumble. I don't enjoy being trapped, and Stinky Breath is heavy. But I can do this all night as long as he doesn't keep breathing on me. "What is it with all the vampires lately not brushing their teeth?"

The stinky breath vampire ignores my complaint, laser-focused on the throbbing, juicy veins in my neck.

And then, out the corner of my eye, I catch movement.

*Oh. Well, crap.* What I can't do in this position is deal with her.

The petite blonde slinks over the debris and comes towards us with slow, calculated movements. "Master." She greets the vampire lying on me and dazzles me with a smile.

"Once you stop Dexter's bleeding, I need your help over here please, Justin," I singsong. *You're in a little bit of a pickle, aren't you, Tru?*

Blondie bends closer and sniffs me. "What do we have here? A shifter snack?" she purrs, licking her lips.

"I wouldn't snack on me if I were you."

She grabs my dusty hair and yanks my head to the side, exposing my throat. All I can do is grit my teeth and keep bracing Stinky Breath, who watches intently and excitedly snaps his fangs.

*This is great.* "Justin." I try again. I can't see him. Gosh, I hope they are both okay. I can't do a thing to help them. Not yet, anyway.

The blonde spits on my throat.

*Oh, now that is gross. What a disgusting, filthy person to spit on me.*

Then she uses a snow-white tissue to clean my neck. She scrubs so hard I'm sure she's trying to remove a layer of skin.

Lifting her head, she grins at me. "Plaster dust, and you've got blood..." She wrinkles her nose and wiggles her fingers to encompass my face and neck. "Everywhere. The vampire blood will ruin the flavour. You sure are a messy killer. I'll enjoy this; I've never had a unicorn."

"I wouldn't—"

She strikes. My skin pops under her ministrations, and the cow noisily gulps down my blood like a milkshake. My strange, powerful, hybrid blood. The hybrid blood with a splash of angel and a bucket load of demon. I'm not sure what that mix will do, and dimly I wonder if she'll hulk out.

Blondie groans against my throat as if she's having a wonderful time. *Okay, that's not good.* I need to risk dropping an arm to go for the closest knife.

"Save some for me," Stinky Breath growls.

"Yes, Mast—" Then she gurgles, coughs, and pulls away. Frantically, she rubs her throat. Her face has gone a funny shade of green.

I narrow my eyes. No, not green... blue. Demon blue. My eyes widen. *Oh heck, that can't be good.*

"Rachel?" Stinky Breath says. "Are you all right?"

The blonde vampire, Rachel, lets out a blood-curdling scream loud enough to rattle the windows, and then her head explodes.

"What! Rachel!" Stinky Breath bellows.

Bone fragments splat around us, and her headless body teeters, weirdly defying gravity as blood fountains out of her shattered neck.

*Oh, so that's what happens. Good to know.* I nod. My abs strain as I angrily shove at the shocked master vampire. Stinky

Breath doesn't move an inch, so I lean forward and headbutt him in my rage.

As our foreheads connect, I shift a single part of me.

My horn.

The sharp horn slices through Stinky Breath's head like a spear through a melon; blood and porridgey grey brain matter drips down his neck. I smile as I keep eye contact and watch the light leave his eyes.

"Try to heal that, dickhead."

My shifter magic zips through my cells, and the heavy horn disappears. I lift my hips and roll the master vampire's dead body off me. It flops to the side. I then drag my sore, abused carcass to my feet.

I teeter for a split second and then grab the closest sword, my angel blade. With a grunt, I use my hands and body weight to drive the sword into his chest. When I reach the heart, I twist the blade to pulverise the organ. Then, for good measure, I take the master vampire's head.

Out of breath, I wobble. I slide the sword away, grab a healing spell, and rush over to Dexter. My knees crunch as I drop to the floor beside him and brush bits of fallen plaster away from his fur. "It's okay, Dex, I've got you. It's okay," I coo.

For a second, my hands flutter as I stare at the weapon. *Oh no, it's iron! Iron is poisonous to the fae.* What the heck do I do? Okay, iron isn't as bad as silver is to shifters if I can get it out right now.

"It's an iron knife, Dex. I'm going to pull it out, but you have to lie still." I take a deep breath, grip the hilt, and ever so carefully pull the blade from his body. I do my best to keep the dagger at the same angle as it went in.

I throw the cursed thing across the room and then pull out

from the pocket dimension an iron-extracting spell. I pour it into the wound. Nasty black blood gushes out. My hand hovers as I wait for the right moment to use the healing potion.

*Come on, come on.*

The black blood slowly, slowly turns blue.

*Wait for it.*

The blood finally lightens, and I drip the healing silver liquid onto the wound. The bleeding slows, and the horrid wound seals, leaving missing fur and a nasty red scar. But it's healed. We caught it just in time. A minute longer, and Dexter would have died.

I close my eyes and rest my head next to Dexter's. His ginger fur and spiky whiskers tickle against my face.

My monster cat lets out a tiny meow.

"You are okay. You're okay, Dexter. I've got you." I stroke his bloody fur. My heart almost explodes with love when his chest vibrates with a purr. His eyes close, and his magic reacts, returning him to his house-cat size. I observe his sleeping form. "He's okay." I don't know whether I'm telling Story, Justin, or myself.

I sit back on my heels and lift my eyes. "Justin, what are you doing here?"

The vampire stands in the gap of the damaged wall. He twists his hands and avoids eye contact. Trembling, his gaze is fixed on the bodies.

*He's in shock.*

"Justin, are you hurt?" I need to check him over for any damage. I get up and move towards him.

"Tru," Story croaks a warning.

As soon as I get near to him, with a scowl, Justin knocks my fluttering hands away. Hurt and still reeling from Dexter's brush with death, I lean away from him. Justin is trembling,

trembling with rage. His eyes scream with vitriol, and what I'm seeing doesn't make a lick of sense. It takes me a few more seconds, and then it clicks. My instinct was right the first time. I just didn't listen to my gut.

Justin isn't a captive. He's... No. I can't find the words.

"Go on then," Justin snarls and holds his shaking hands out from his body. "Aren't you going to kill me too? That's what you do, isn't it, Executioner? You kill vampires."

*Yeah, that's what I thought.*

Dexter wasn't stabbed by an enemy. No. He was stabbed by a friend.

There's this massive ball, a lump in my throat, and I can't seem to swallow. My heart hurts. Justin is my family. We've all been friends for almost ten years.

Until the move to the farmhouse, we all lived in the same tiny flat since I rescued him from a horrific situation. A vampire had turned him against his will, and when he didn't conform, she sold him. She sold him to a witch who starved him, making him easier to control, and then the witch used Justin as spell ingredients.

His blood, his hair, his skin, his bones.

The horror he had suffered made him scared of everything. I thought we'd got him the help he needed. As the years progressed, I was sure what happened to him gave him a deep empathy—a beautiful kindness.

How wrong could I be? Is everyone I love not who I think they are? What the heck is wrong with me that I don't see through their lies? And it keeps happening—I'm so bloody naive.

*It's not about you. Don't be so bloody selfish.* Good point. *He stabbed Dexter.* But there must be a reason, right?

"Why?" I croak. I brace myself for Justin's villain speech.

"You will never understand," he sneers.

Just like the other vampires, Justin's breath is rancid. Is he sick?

"You're not an actual vampire," he continues, "and you're not a real shifter. You're a freak, and I'm sick of your mightier-than-everyone attitude."

My tongue brushes across my fangs.

A part of me wishes he was a demon in disguise. I blink. Now, that would make sense. In seconds, I whip out a bloodstone that's been prepped with Kleric's blood. I thrust it towards Justin and wait.

*Glow green please, please glow green.*

It doesn't change colour, not at all, and Justin lets out a pain-filled laugh. "I'm not a demon, Tru. Is it too hard to believe that I can't fucking stand you?"

I feel sick.

"Why? Why this?" I wave my hand at the dead vampires.

"I woke up one morning, and everything inside me changed. This felt right. At first it was just catch and release. We'd hunt, pick someone, and let them go when we were done. They were weak, but nothing some orange juice and a biscuit wouldn't fix." Justin callously shrugs.

I nod my head instead of slapping him and lock my face down, schooling my expression into an encouraging one. I need to know everything.

"I didn't see the harm. The master..." He nods at the headless corpse at our feet. "He had an excellent compulsion. The humans, they didn't remember a thing."

*That doesn't explain the kids or the people imprisoned downstairs.*

"How long?"

"Three months." This all happened around the time I got

out of prison and took the executioner job. As if reading my mind, Justin continues, "It was all your fault. The press, the pressure of social media, the pressure of being your friend. Every arsehole and their dog had an opinion of you. They started protesting outside our home. Did you know that? No. Of course you didn't. They threw stones at us in the fucking street. They broke Morris's glasses, and he had cuts and bruises all over his face."

Justin clenches his jaw and grinds his teeth. "I needed an escape. I needed for once in my life not to be scared. Have you any idea what it does to a man to hide behind a creature like you? I'm not a coward. I'm not a victim, yet you made me into one. One day I woke up, and the blood comforted me. I felt free from constraints for the first time in my life. I've never felt healthier, stronger, or more powerful."

"Did you know they were targeting children?"

"This is not my fault!" There's a slight whine in his voice.

"Did. You. Know. They. Were. Targeting. Children?" I pronounce each word slowly to get through his poor-me rant.

Justin nods his head. He *nods* his effing head. "They taste so sweet." He rubs his mouth as if trying to put the words back in.

I fist my hands and lock my emotions down. When I've finished this, then I can fall apart. "Morris, did he know?"

Justin scoffs. "If he'd known what I was doing, Morris would have come to you. I haven't seen him in over two months. He left me."

Neither of them told me. I had no idea. I've been a terrible friend.

"He isn't what I want, not anymore." Justin becomes agitated and begins to pace. I block him from moving closer to Dexter, and he moves the other way. "Besides, he's human, a walking blood bag. I need to be with my kind. I'm a vampire, Tru, even if I didn't choose to be one. I'm a vampire, and humans are my prey, my food. I'm better than what you made me into. With all your stupid rules. I'm my own man." He thumps his chest as he rants.

"Yes, you are." I swallow. I can't deal with this stranger anymore. This man isn't my Justin. It's like his soul is dead. I force myself to stay on track and cough to clear my throat. "I'm looking for a little girl. Have you seen her? Her name is Petra. She's eight years old, has brown hair, blue eyes..."

I reach for my phone to show him the photo, but Justin twitches and his eyes flick to the office behind him.

# CHAPTER NINETEEN

"No, you shouldn't go in there." Justin moves to stop me.

Without thinking, I push past him. "Petra!" I yell. My boots crunch as I scramble over bits of board, plaster, and chunks of wood. "Story, can you see her?" No answer. Crap, did my phone get turned off in the scuffle? I enter the room, and my eyes scan for the little girl. "She should be here. Petra, sweetheart, your grandma sent me."

I see the edge of a purple trainer, and my heart misses a beat. The child is lying on the dirty carpet, wedged between two stuffed chairs. I dive across the room and shove one chair out of the way.

It is her. It's her!

Petra is so pale that her skin looks see-through. Three sets of bite marks mar her tiny neck—recent bites.

The bite radius of each mark is slightly different, indicating three different assailants. Three vampires. I measure the bite on my throat with my fingers. Yes, it's a rough match. That's Rachel's bite. With shaking hands, I drag another soft blanket out of the pocket dimension and, being ever so careful, wrap the little girl, tuck the blanket underneath her chin, and smooth her brown hair behind her left ear.

"The micro-cameras took samples. Petra was dead before you entered the building. She was gone before you met her grandma," Story says through the earpiece. Her voice is a scratchy monotone.

The cameras see everything, and Story had known.

I don't envy her job. Staying silent is way worse than being patient. So much worse. Story knew and had to help me anyway. She didn't say a word. She couldn't, as she didn't want to distract me.

"This isn't your fault," she whispers.

I pull the earpiece out and drop it into my trouser pocket. I can't right now. My dirty fingers grip the chair, and I dig my nails into the cushion, clawing at the fabric to pull myself up. I get my shaky legs underneath me so I can stumble to my feet.

When I turn, Justin is just standing there, staring. Dexter is where I left him, surrounded by the dead and still in his healing sleep. I flinch. What I have just done and what could have happened slams into me.

*I left my vulnerable and unconscious friend alone with the person who hurt him.* I can't fathom it—my stupidity. I feel so bloody ashamed. I tug at my hair. *It's hard to wrap my head around the fact that Justin is now an enemy.*

"Sweetheart, I'll be right back," I tell Petra.

Tears drip off my chin as I move away from her in a

lurching walk. My heart pounds, my jaw aches, and the demon kiss on my hand burns. Each step I take towards Justin feels like a mile. I use my shirt sleeve to wipe the sorrow away, unconcerned that I'm spreading vampire blood even more across my face.

Without much thought, the angel blade is in my grip.

Justin must see the exact moment I lock myself down and the dangerous creature I am shows herself. *Tru isn't home right now.*

"I-I have the information you will need," he cries as he stumbles back, holding his hands to ward me off. "The printing company. I have information about the company; it's a front."

I prowl past him and kick a dead vampire's leg and some plasterboard out of the way, uncovering the missing blade. *I'll need both swords for this.* I pick it up and spin on my toes to face the vampire.

"Go on," I say.

My head tilts to the side as I wait, and when I don't immediately move towards him. Justin's entire demeanour changes. He straightens and puffs out his chest and juts his chin in self-satisfaction. *Cocky.*

"The printer cartridges have blood in them. I set that up," he says, poking his chest. "I did that."

"You set that up. With the human's generous donations, did they all get orange juice too?"

Justin shakes his head, and pure exasperation washes across his face. "You don't understand. I'm the mastermind behind the business. I set everything in motion. We are going to expand countrywide, and thanks to you, the competition is almost nonexistent." Justin pokes his chest again, and a smug, fevered light sparkles in his eyes. "Vampires will never go hungry again, and we will never have to drink that artificial swill."

I adjust my stance. "I already know about the blood cartridges, Justin." I rotate the swords to warm up my wrists. In the back of my head, I note my left forearm aches.

Justin's eyes widen when he realises he has lost my interest. He backs away, his movement stilted. He almost zombie shuffles as he moves closer to the window to escape. "I know more. I know what's coming for you next. I can help. We can work together. You need me, Tru, and I know you won't hurt me. We're family. I know I've made mistakes, but I'm willing to learn from them. I'm willing to change. I'll go back to the counsellor and apologise to Dexter..."

With three quick strides, I'm face-to-face with him. With precision, I cross my forearms and thrust the crossed blades on either side of his neck, and then violently, brutally snap my arms apart. The swords scissor, slicing through the vampire's neck, cleanly separating the head from his body.

On autopilot, I turn away so I don't have to watch his body as it crumples. Robotically I methodically clean both weapons. Once clean, I slide them away and stand for a few more seconds, and then my legs go out from under me.

I hit the floor. I rock backwards and forwards, crying silently into my knees.

I don't see the smoky vapour, but I go willingly when I'm gathered into familiar muscular arms. I climb into his lap and melt.

"I'm here. I'm here," Kleric tells me as he holds me tight. One massive pale blue hand threads through my hair, and the other rubs my back as he makes soft, comforting sounds in the back of his throat.

He holds me while I fall apart.

# Chapter Twenty

There are moments in your life that define who you are. These are the moments that will change you forever. – Tru Dennison

Kleric continues to hug me, lending me the strength I need to get up off this body-strewn floor and move. I have a job to do. I just need a few more seconds, and then I'll get up.

We sit together in the middle of the carnage—the room is a tad full, and the stink of the dead makes breathing difficult.

Atticus did say he wanted a mess. I'd given him that all right.

I don't have to explain to Kleric or put into words what has happened here today. I allow him into my mind, and it is an open book. I'm so grateful for our connection. Kleric's steadfast emotions bolster my own. It's as if he's cradling my mind with our mate bond, helping to numb my racing thoughts so I can function.

I have a job to do, and there's a sleeping boy downstairs who needs to get back to his parents. I need to get up and finish this.

"It's dangerous for you to be here," I mumble as I rise.

Kleric doesn't answer.

We both know he can't stay long, or he'll risk the peace talks. If they have a mind reader ask Kleric if he's been on Earth or has seen me, he'll have to answer truthfully, and they won't care about the circumstances. To them, there is no excuse. Kleric would have broken the rules and ruined his reputation.

"Thank you for coming."

"Always." He stands, towering over me. He leans into me and kisses my forehead. "I wish I could stay," he mutters. His blue arms hang at his sides in defeat. "If you would like, before I leave for my world, I can take Dexter home. I can take him back to the farmhouse to finish healing. I'm sure Story will watch over him."

"Please." My voice cracks. Kleric once again offers me a gift, a gift to alleviate the worry of keeping Dexter safe while I deal with the authorities. It's going to be a circus in here very soon.

Dexter is soft and warm in my hands as I scoop him up off the floor and hand him over to Kleric. "Tell, Story..." *Tell Story what? Sorry, I killed our friend. Our family. I'll be lucky if she ever speaks to me again.*

My lips tremble. I press them together and look up. Unfortunately for me, no answers are written on the popcorn ceiling. Story, Ralph, the kids, Morris. What are they going to think of me?

I'm a monster.

A monster who killed a friend.

What was that Friedrich Nietzsche quote I love? *Die a hero or live long enough to become a villain?* Well, that's me. I'm a cliché of self-fulfilling prophecy. I've never felt so villainous in my entire life.

When I don't say anything further, Kleric nods and brushes his blue thumb against my cheek. "Come on, beautiful chimera. Before I leave, I want you out of this room." Kleric's blue tail wraps around my wrist and gives me a tug towards the door.

I don't want to leave Petra, but I know Kleric is right, so I force my feet to move. So they don't impede the investigation, I remove the wards. Kleric leads me down the stairs and into the room with the desk.

I check the boy, and he's just how I left him, safe and fast asleep.

"I'll be back as soon as I'm able." Kleric taps his head and smiles. "I'm always here if you need me." He doesn't give me empty platitudes or try to make me feel better, which I appreciate. He knows as well as I do that with Justin... I did what I had to do. His eyes shine with love and understanding.

With a final nod, my demon disappears with Dexter in a cloud of smoky vapour.

I stand alone in the room, and for ages, all I can do is look at my trembling hands, lost on what I need to do first. I pull out my mobile. I guess I need to request the vampire clean-up crew Atticus has on standby and request extra help for the victims. They'll need medical.

My mobile screen flashes with an incoming call. It's Story. *Great.* Guilt eats at me. I bite my bottom lip. Okay, I'll have to dig deep inside myself. It's a special kind of bravery to face someone when all you want to do is run and hide.

When I answer, the handset bounces in my shaking hand.

"I love you," Story says in a thick, emotion-choked voice.

I close my eyes. "I love you too," I whisper.

Story clears her throat. "The vampires and the human police are on their way. With Ava's help, we have already compiled a full situation report with DNA evidence and the footage. Ava took the liberty of removing a certain demon. Dexter is safe and asleep on your bed. I've spoken to the fishmonger, and he's delivering a salmon. You really need to shift before you touch the boy, as you are covered in blood. Please pop your earpiece back in after you get cleaned up."

"Okay."

"I've informed Petra's family."

My entire body tenses, and my palms shoot out to the desk to hold myself upright when the strength leeches out of my limbs.

Wow, Story has been busy, busy protecting me.

"I explained the timeline, that you were too late to save Petra, but you got justice. I also told Mrs Hardy you managed to save the other humans, including the boy under the desk. His name is Matthew, Matthew Reeves, and he's ten years old."

My eyes fall to the boy. *Hello, Matthew.*

"Story, I'm sorr—"

"No. Don't you dare!" she snarls. Softer, she says, "You have nothing to apologise for. We will talk about this when you are ready." Her voice cracks. "Now get cleaned up before the cavalry confuses you with a zombie or Matthew wakes up and sees you. Don't you dare frighten that little boy with your gore." The phone clicks, and she's gone.

I put all the electronics on the desk within easy reach and

shuffle into the hallway. *If I do this wrong, it will be a tight squeeze.*

As I did with my hand—was that only yesterday?—I shift and immediately snap back to human.

Huh. It's a breeze. The trick, I guess, is not to try too hard.

## CHAPTER TWENTY ONE

DRIVING, I think about everything but the cause of the elephant on my chest. My insides feel like they are in a blender and on a constant spin. It went okay, and the victims were healed, all on their way home to their families.

As I pull up to a set of traffic lights, something nags at me. Marcus, the frying pan witch, pops into my head. I pull up the memory of rifling through his belongings, and I remember catching a brief glimpse of his identification. His address is... I nod. I narrow my eyes on the house numbers. Yeah, that's it. It should be up here on the right.

*Should I?* My fingers drum on the steering wheel.

I need to keep busy.

Dexter is still sleeping, and the builders are at the farmhouse working. Drilling. I rub my collarbone. I don't have it in me to be sociable or pleasant and nice. "Would you like a cup of tea?" Yeah, I'm more likely to smash the cup over some poor sod's head.

I feel so bloody angry. I'm not safe.

The lights change, and as I drive down the road, I make a quick decision and pull over into a handy parking spot. I might as well have a nosy while I'm nearby. *What will be the harm?* It's not like I'm looking to pick a fight. Well, not much of one anyway.

And I did say my standard modus operandi is to rattle a few cages and make the baddies angry. Get them to stick their head above the parapet again as they try to kill me. My lips twitch. The thought almost makes me smile.

I grab a box of micro-cameras from the handy cubby between the Defender's front seats. Before I get out, I set the micro-cameras up, and with a press of a button, I attach the feeds from the dozens of tiny cameras to the app on the phone. I make sure to leave a handful watching the street and the dead pan witch's door.

Marcus lives in a modern apartment block. Three flats to each red brick building, and as his place is on the ground floor, it has its own entrance. A waist-height brick wall encloses a small garden. I prowl through the gate and down the path that snakes between scraggly patches of frozen lawn. As I get to the entrance, I grab some latex gloves, shove them on and then, with an unlock spell, open the blue front door.

They have replaced the building ward with a crime scene one that should—I take a deep breath—let me in. The ward crackles harmlessly against my skin, and with a relieved sigh, I slip inside. Being in the law enforcement bracket for this kind of thing is handy. Being the executioner gives me clearance for almost everything.

I turn on the lights. His flat is small, clean, and organised. A black leather sofa with red cushions dominates the front room. It has a bachelor pad aesthetic. Marcus wasn't hurting for cash. This is an okay building, and he has nice stuff.

I don't know what I'm doing or what I'm looking for. It's not like there's a magic arrow with a fluorescent sign saying: VILLAINOUS PLAN, LOOK HERE!

I inspect the place. At first glance, the flat lacks personal things, photos, and favourite books. Marcus was a witch, and books are a big thing. So the lack of them is odd.

The hunters didn't toss the place either. I've seen searches where they destroy everything. But this time, I can follow where in the kitchen and bedrooms the hunters have been, with the slightly opened drawers hinting at a half-hearted search.

I ignore the obvious places for now and head for the kitchen. I turn out the bin—the rubbish tumbles to the kitchen floor. I use a fork from the sink to poke about—the gloves will only protect me so far, and I can't be too careful in a witch's home. I'm glad the guy recycles, and his compost isn't in with general waste. Marcus sure likes sweets, his favourite being strawberry Starbursts.

Disappointed at finding nothing, I shove the rubbish back, and as an added baddie headfuck, I leave my business card on the worktop.

I don't care if it rattles the witches, knowing I've been here without permission. That's a good thing; I want them to be pissed.

Why the hell should I play by the rules when nobody else does?

The flat has a tiny box room that must be Marcus's spell room. All the shelves have been cleared, and I can see patches of dust and clean spots, as if the dust had settled between bottles.

I'm unsure if the witches or hunters took away his magical items or if his friends—the same ones who broke into my house—took it all when they found out he was dead. I make a mental note to check the files if Atticus comes through with the information.

I wander into the bedroom and peek into his drawers and the wardrobe; they're packed to the brim. But the only personal items are his clothing. The space is tight as I move next to the window on the other side of the bed. I scan the floor for anything that might have fallen... I see a sliver of something.

Tilting my head to the side, I frown. "What do we have here? It looks like somebody's missed something." I lean forward.

Trapped between the bedside cabinet and the heavy leather bed is a photograph. It's lodged in pretty tight. I wiggle it to get it unstuck. When I get it out, I see it's a light, handmade wooden photo frame with a photo of Marcus, the dead pan witch, and he's kissing a girl.

Unfortunately, the candid snap is a selfie, and as they are kissing, their faces are smushed together. His face hides her entire profile. All I get is pale skin and long dark hair.

Human or witch, I do not know.

"Who are you?" I ask her, moving the frame closer to my face. I shrug and snap a picture with my phone.

*Perhaps Ava could find out more information.* I groan. But no, she won't, as she has refused to help in this part of the investigation. My tongue pushes against my cheek. She's been adamant about not stepping on any toes. She says she can't. It's frustrating, but I respect her decision.

I hold the photo frame and again contemplate the room. I don't think the mystery woman stayed here that often as there is no apparent space for her things. The wardrobe and drawers are all full.

But the photo is special enough to be framed and placed next to the bed. Marcus cared about her, so she's important.

I recheck the bathroom. All masculine products—no cream, no expensive hair stuff, no lip balm, and no change of clothes. Nothing but the photo. The mystery girl has left nothing behind. I return to the kitchen and place the photo frame in pride of place on the worktop right next to my business card.

Almost done. I grab my mobile and with a press of a button, set the internal micro-cameras, sending a camera into the top corner of each room. To save the battery life, these will remain inert unless somebody comes inside, and then they will record and ping alerts to my phone. I smile with satisfaction.

Yeah, I could do a proper search while I'm here, turn the flat upside down, rip the cushions apart, overturn the bed—hell, I've got all this nightmare rage burning in my chest. A little bit of destruction might help me cope. If only for a minute.

But I'm hoping my visit here will be enough to encourage them to investigate. The internal guilty nagging voice will ask, "What did she want? What did she find?" and it will bring them here, and if anything is hidden, they'll go straight to it to check if it's still there.

And I'll see it all on the camera feeds. I grin. Work smarter, not harder. I have to be smarter. My volatile hybrid emotions can't control me.

I give the living room a last glance, turn off the lights and then slip outside. I'm glad when the door locks behind me and I don't have to use another spell. As I trundle down the path, I take out my phone to check the time. I still have an hour to waste before the builders are officially gone. Maybe I'll go to the gargoyles and see if they want to spar as I'll need to be practically dead on my feet to get any sleep again in this lifetime. I sigh, and my stomach flips.

A potion comes out of nowhere and smashes into the centre of my chest. Surprised, I glance down. *Oh, that was an excellent shot.* "Red, a red spell is bad." I brace myself for the nasty spell to kick in. *Dying today has a nice poetic touch. Kind of karmic.* Story is going to be mad, and Kleric...

Oh crap. *My demon, I'm so sorry.*

# CHAPTER TWENTY TWO

INSTEAD OF HORRENDOUS PAIN, the skin on my left breast burns. *Ow.* I frown. That's when I remember I still have the Gary Chappell Reflect Me charm tucked in my sports bra. It's been in there this entire time.

With more heat scorching the skin on my chest, the charm forces the potion's power to bounce back. Then a violent wave of magic reflects at the person who threw the spell. It isn't long before a piercing scream from behind the garden wall disrupts the silence.

Ah, there they are.

A woman I don't recognise with short, mousy-blonde hair stumbles from her hiding place and into the road. Under the streetlight, the visible skin on her face, throat, and hands begins to smoke. Her long dark coat flaps as, in a panic, she waves her arms in the air. With a cry of agony, she throws her head back and screams. And screams.

*Uh-oh.*

With an audible puff, the spell ignites, and the smoke transforms with a roar into a flame. It dances across her skin, and with a whoosh, it spreads to her coat. She lights up, illuminating the evening like a living candle.

*Oh no.*

I wince as she continues to scream. In desperation, she throws herself to the ground and attempts to roll on the pavement to snuff out the flames. But her frantic movements do nothing, and the magical flames get worse.

Whoever she is and what she's done doesn't matter as I move to help her, but the flames beat me back. I can't get close enough to save her or put her out of her misery. The flames are too hot, and I can't do anything but watch. *Perhaps I could use a throwing knife?*

There's another whoosh. For a few moments, I don't know what's happening—and then with horror, I get it. The heat and the magic are causing all the spells on her person to ignite.

*Oh, bloody hell.*

The spells react badly. They implode! I duck behind the garden wall in time to avoid a raging cloud of magic. It whips into the air and scorches the ground where I was standing.

I hug my knees to my chest and cover my head with my arms. The ground shakes, and the windows of all the unwarded houses down the street shatter. After ten minutes, she's stopped screaming and the magic has calmed enough for the ground to be stable. I get to my feet.

The entire area is in chaos. It feels very much like a disaster zone. Alarms are blaring. In a house a few doors down, I hear a baby wailing and people shouting and crying with fear. I wince. I know I wanted a baddie reaction, but this... crikey.

Even for me, this is extreme.

I do what I can to help as I send out a red alert text for backup and magically cordon off the area. I pull out my trusty bag of salt and circle the unrecognisable charcoal husk of the woman with a thick line. The magic now seems inert, but the spell stuff she carried was wildly powerful, and I don't want to mess around.

Then I wait for the Witch Council representatives, hunters, and magical hazmat to arrive. All I can think is that it should have been me. My thoughts are so nasty that I know I'm really messed up.

I check the live feed, and I can't believe the micro-cameras outside survived, as did the Land Rover's windows. Not a single mark mars me or the Defender.

As a precaution, I send the attack footage to Story with a brief explanation so she can pass it on to the powers that be. She will also do her best to find out who the witch was and who she was working for.

The first of the backup arrives. The hazmat team piles out of their van and, with highly trained efficiency, deal with the scene. Seconds later, a single hunter gets out of his vehicle and heads towards me.

"Salt?" one hazmat guy shouts as he points at the thing that used to be a woman and the white stuff circling her.

"Yes."

He nods his thanks, and I move farther out of their way. The hunter gets closer. No, not a hunter. This guy moves differently, more predatory. Hunters always look like they're trying too hard, while this guy, a shifter, moves like an elite soldier.

Hellhound.

Hellhounds are old, powerful shifters with fire magic. As a fighting force, they are exceptional. One hellhound can accomplish what an entire department of hunters can only dream of.

*What is he doing here?*

The massive guy with his shaven head marches towards me as if I'm a suspect and he will gladly stab me to death. This is all I need. He gets so close the toes of our boots knock together, and as he stares down at me, his green eyes flash with contempt.

"Name," he snarls.

I square my shoulders and lift my chin. I've seen this shifter before. His short hair, big build, and those mean green eyes are easy to remember. Plus it's not every day you meet a hellhound, and I know his sister, Forrest. This guy is a wolf shifter; if I remember rightly, his name is John.

"Tru Dennison. I'm the local executioner. It's nice to see you again, John."

His eyes narrow, and after a few seconds, his chin lifts with recognition. "Ah, the hybrid—the unicorn shifter with fangs who got herself locked up. Yeah, I remember you. We met in court. You're my sister's friend." If my being a friend of his sister was a good thing, the disgust in his voice says otherwise.

"Yes, that's right." I'm not elaborating.

John rubs his chin, and for a second, his lips twitch with mirth. "You also have a soul bond with Xander."

"No, I don't!" I yell, then blink. I had forgotten he was a friend of the angel. "Well, not anymore after he threw me into that off-world prison. I have nothing to do with him," I finish with a scowl. The hellhound thinks he's funny, huh? I also don't care that his expression screams that he doesn't believe me.

"Right, sure," he grunts. "What's the narrative here, Executioner? Please enlighten me. You have an execution order for this mess?"

"No order. The woman attacked me, and I didn't touch or get to speak to her before she went on the offensive. I have footage of what went down if you're interested."

I expect him to refuse, but he surprises me by nodding. He continues his narrow-eyed glare that would make an ordinary person shit themselves. Not me. I wiggle my toes so our boots scrape together, narrow my eyes, and glare back.

After a few more seconds of our comical standoff—well, it would be funny if the hellhound wasn't so bloody dangerous —John shakes his head and drops his gaze. Yay, I won the stare-off.

"Send it to this datapad." He pulls the device from a wide side pocket on his thigh.

I flick the footage in his datapad's direction, and he pulls up the file and watches silently. He doesn't even wince when the witch screams. It's as if he's watching paint dry. After ten minutes, he stops the recording and looks up at me.

"You handled yourself well."

I blink at him.

He waves the datapad, tapping it against his palm. "This is enough evidence to clear you. You can go."

"Whoa, not so fast. She's coming with me," screeches a woman. We both turn to watch her. Black bobbed hair and bright red lips. She gets out of a black car and slips through the cordon. Her sky-high heels click on the tarmac as she scurries across the road. "A witch was killed, and this murderer is not going anywhere."

John growls under his breath. The sound raises the little hairs on the back of my neck. "Your witch killed herself by being an idiot," he snarls. "The executioner didn't lay a finger on her."

"Do you want to see the footage?" I ask helpfully. I waggle the mobile at her with a false smile. *Who the hell is this?* I surreptitiously snap her picture when she doesn't answer but continues to speak with John.

"I'll take this menace into custody."

"Not happening." John gives her his thousand-yard stare, the same scary one he aimed at me a few minutes ago.

"So you don't want to see the footage?" I pipe up again.

"No, I do not want to see the footage," she eventually answers with a sniff. She drops her gaze from the hellhound's and picks imaginary lint off her dress. "I've already seen it on the drive over."

*Go, Story. My pixie could give Ava a run for her money.*

"What I want to see is the magic you used. The magic that reflected that spell." She points at my chest and the red spell residue.

*Good luck with that.* I'm not about to go digging in my sports bra in public. I'm also not about to hand over a life-saving charm. It's mine. "No," I say firmly and throw in a smirk for good measure. I'm done with being polite.

Uh-oh, she doesn't like that.

The still-pointing finger drifts up and prods in my face. "Look here, missy. You might be willing to kill our witches and expect no repercussions. And"—she scoffs—"if you are willing to kill your dear vampire friend, a creature you claimed to be family, it's obvious you have no morals."

I flinch. My heart skips a beat, and on autopilot, my hand drifts towards the closest weapon, which happens to be a dagger strapped to my right thigh. *How bloody dare she! A blade in the eye would make the perfect accessory for this cow.*

It's only been a few hours, and of course they are already using Justin's death to get at me. It has to be the lowest of low blows.

The hellhound moves between us, blocking me from getting close. John snarls. "Oi. Listen here, witch. This is my crime scene, and until we have the race of the suspect, it will remain mine. I have jurisdiction. I don't even know who the hell you are. The executioner has answered all my questions, and I have cleared her.

"As you have just mentioned, she's had a long day. And you will be respectful of a creature that outranks you and hold your tongue." His head tilts to the side, and red flames erupt in his eyes. The orangey red overtakes the green. It's horrifying and even gives me pause. "Unless you have a great love for child killers?"

My mask is firmly in place, but it's the witch's turn to flinch, and she goes an unhealthy pale.

"No, of course not," she splutters. "I would never..."

Her words trail off as John leans closer, using his bulk to crowd her petite frame. "If you know my history, you will know I have an issue with anyone that dares to kill a child." His voice is a guttural growl.

The witch's entire body shakes, and I wouldn't be surprised if she peed a little. John is that scary intense.

"Good. I'm glad the executioner will have no further problems with your misinformed opinion. Keep that"—he makes a zipping motion against his lips—"shut. You're embarrassing yourself. Now get lost." He nods towards her car. "Now go on, off you pop."

She opens and closes her red mouth, glares at me, and then, without another word, clicks her way back to her vehicle.

*That was beautiful.*

"My mate is pregnant, so kids are a touchy subject," John explains as we watch her go. It's almost as if he's talking to himself. "For her, I'm trying to be a better man."

"Congratulations," I mumble.

"Is it? I don't know. I've never been so scared in my life." He huffs a sad laugh, shakes his head, and vigorously runs his nails through his short hair. "You may go."

"Thank you for your time."

From what I've seen and what Forrest has said about her brother, the wolf is a world-class dick. Our interaction has left me confused, but whatever I've done to get his help, I'll take it as a win.

I prowl back to the Defender. When I get inside, I recall all the outside micro-cameras. "That was interesting," I whisper as I put them back into their box. As I sit there, the magical hazmat team clears the scene. One technician goes house to house using spells to clean the debris and repair all the blown-out windows, and another heals anyone that needs it—from what I can see, just some bruises and cuts remain. They finish, and within fifteen minutes, they're packed and ready to go. Their speed in getting things done is shocking. John gives them a thumbs-up to drop the cordon and open the road. Yeah, just like that, the mess is scraped up, all good as new. I guess it's time for me to go home before anything else can go wrong.

## CHAPTER TWENTY THREE

I shut off the Defender, and as the engine ticks, I gaze at my house. I'm hesitant to go inside to see Dexter because I'm the reason he got hurt and almost died. I don't want to look Story in the eye when I could have done more to save our friend instead of killing him.

I'm so ashamed.

If I hadn't focused on my selfish needs, I might have seen the signs that something was wrong with Justin. And then there is this guilt, not just for his death but for feeling utter relief that there are no memories of him in this house. I shake my head. What kind of psycho thinks like that? Me. I'm such a twat.

As I open the front door, the perimeter ward weakly hums

under my hand. It's not fared well with the builders coming and going all day. I need to fix it. Especially now I've pissed everybody off.

I haven't got another ward of that calibre. I gave my last two to Matthew's mum—the mum of the boy we rescued—she was so scared. I couldn't help myself. It was worth it, helping the family feel safe. But I've messed up and will need to get a more permanent solution soon, within the next few days.

I blow a frustrated breath through my nose as I prowl through the hallway. I'm going to struggle to get a witch to come out. There's no doubt I've been banned, blacklisted, and declared persona non grata.

Never mind. I'll find a way.

Instead of rushing upstairs to check on my friends, like a coward I put off seeing them for a few more minutes. I'm working up to it. I wander to the back of the house. My gut twists, and I hunch into myself as the weight of upstairs and what I have to face is crushing. My boots kick up little bits of plaster dust.

The builders have made good progress. The kitchen area is finished and almost ready for installation. Everything has been plastered and is ready to paint. They have done an excellent job although... I pause. The mastic seal on a tucked-away window edge needs redoing. I make a quick note and leave it out for the foreman.

I shuffle back down the hall. The stairs look great. The carpenter has installed the new handrail with its supporting posts. When I touch the wood, my hand trembles. It feels glossy underneath my fingers. The design is just like the drawing, with a modern touch but still very traditional.

I climb. Each step is so damn hard. The toes of my boots scrape against each tread as if each foot weighs a tonne. When I get to my bedroom, I quietly remove my boots and slip through the ward. My socks sink into the carpet.

I take in the sight of the entire troupe of pixies on my bed, snuggled up with a still-sleeping Dexter.

Page is leaning against my monster cat's side reading a book, and Novel is lying on her stomach, legs kicked up behind her and a pencil between her teeth. She looks to be doing her homework which is propped up on Dexter's tail. Jeff is playing a game on his phone with headphones on, and Story is sitting between Dexter's front paws with Ralph, who gives me a friendly wave.

I wave back, and my attention goes back to Dexter. My eyes trace over him. He looks okay. "Is he okay?" I whisper.

Story gives me a relieved smile and nods. "He was awake before and had something to eat. The iron took a lot out of him."

Iron. How on earth did Justin get hold of an iron knife? One of many unanswered questions that will torture me for the rest of my life.

"Hi, Tru." Page beams a smile at me and blows me a kiss. I catch it and blow her one right back. She giggles, and her eyes drift back to her book. Something inside me relaxes. They didn't run away screaming. I'm with my family, and they are safe.

Jeff pulls off his headphones, puffs up his chest, and gives me a serious look. His pink face is so sweet and earnest when he says, "Tru, I'm sorry you had to cut Justin's head off. We still love him, but I'm sorry he was a baddie."

I jerk as if he slapped me. Blood rushes to my head, and I feel extraordinarily dizzy. "Um. What?" Horrified, I rapidly blink and turn to Story for help. How the hell do I reply to that?

"You've upset her," Novel says, kicking her brother.

"Ow!" Jeff wails.

Story shrugs and gets to her feet. "Don't kick," she reprimands Novel. "Jeff, you have to learn to be more tactful. Although your comment was well intended, it wasn't nice." On the way past, she ruffles her son's dark pink hair.

"Sorry," Jeff grumbles.

"I'll not lie to them. The world is hard, harder for us than most creatures. We do not have soft lives. Pixies have to grow up so quickly. We must. We are limited by our size, and a wrong step"—she says meaningfully—"and we are as good as dead."

I can't believe she told them, told them so bluntly. I pick at my thumbnail unconsciously as my heart pounds.

"I'm as honest as I can be with them. If I don't tell them the truth, who will? For us, the truth will ultimately keep us safe. Not telling opens the possibility for someone to use this against them. They loved Justin very much and still do. They need to understand that you can hate what somebody has done but still love them. Knowing about treachery is an important life lesson. I wanted to get ahead of this, as eventually they'd ask me where he is or why you're so sad. I regret not warning you or checking with you first. But this is our way."

When did Story get so wise? That damn lump in my throat is back. I nod and croak out, "Okay."

"Plus it's been on the news," says Ralph.

Oh no. I rub my face.

"Big news. You know how they get when it comes to you," Story finishes.

I know, and it is my fault I started my journey by using the media to get the Shifter Council to back off and leave me alone. Since then, I've always been newsworthy.

"Morris?" I ask.

"He knows. I rang him first before anyone. He doesn't blame you. He blames himself. He's still living in our old place. He said he will move out at the end of the month."

"He doesn't need to," I mumble.

"No, he doesn't need to, but he will, and then I think we should put it up for sale. I thought once we paid off the mortgage, we could use the proceeds to help the victims and perhaps in the meantime pay for Petra's funeral."

I nod. "That is a perfect idea, thank you."

"I'll handle everything with Ava. You need to eat. There is dinner in the fridge, but you'll need to heat it. Don't pull that face. No arguments. Oh, and we're staying with you tonight."

"Sleepover," Page whispers, her nose still in the book.

"You don't have to."

Story tuts, jumps into the air and flies across the room towards the en-suite. "Stop punishing yourself. You need to relax, eat, and spend time with us. I'm putting a bath on for you. We are all sleeping in here tonight, and Ralph has volunteered to stay up and watch over us."

A pixie sleepover. I drop my boots off in my dressing room, grab a change of clothes, and follow Story into the bathroom. She has already plugged the bath and has the taps on.

"I'm angry," Story says now she's out of earshot of little ears. She leans her forehead against a cool tile, and the steam from the bath weaves around her, dampening her beautiful wings. "So bloody angry."

I hunch, and she waves away whatever she sees on my face. "I'm not angry with you. I'm mad at Justin. He has caused so much pain. See those kids?" She points out the door. "They wouldn't exist without you, and they would have never been born without you saving my life. Maybe I would have survived that day and been blessed with children. Do you know how many pixies die? Not even five percent make it to adulthood. We are seen as bugs, not people. I have three beautiful, healthy children." Her sapphire eyes shine with tears. "All thanks to you and this beautiful life."

Story holds her hand to stop me before I can interject. "Justin fooled us all. What was he thinking? Playing silly vampire games. Instead of trusting you to do the right thing, get him help. He tried to kill our beithíoch. I watched him stab our Dexter with pure malice and hate. For no reason." She shakes her head. "Sometimes you save people, and sometimes they save you right back. Other times they are so broken inside it is madness to even try. He must have been so broken all these years." She nods at whatever expression is on my face and tips some bubble bath into the running water.

I rush to help. The bottle is bigger than her.

She flies towards me and pats me on the cheek. "Now, stinky, you smell like barbecued witch. Get in the bathtub."

"Ew," I chuckle. "That's just gross. I was hungry, but now I won't eat for a week with that image in my head." I scratch my scalp, and little pieces of dirt rain onto the tiles. Story has a point. "Thank you, Story."

"Always." She smiles sadly and flits out of the bathroom.

I turn off the taps and remove the Stick It spell from my leg and peel the pocket dimension away from my thigh. I then remove all my weapons, putting them inside the silk bag. I'll need to clean everything later.

Like a heartbeat, the demon kiss on my hand gently throbs. It's been a constant comfort since Kleric left the print shop and reminds me I'm not alone. That my demon has been silently watching over me all this time.

*Did you see everything?* I unplait my heavy rainbow hair.

*Yes.* His voice is a gentle, warm gruffness in my mind. *The hellhound was right. You handled everything well. For a moment there, I thought I'd lost you.*

*I'm sorry.*

*Please don't take risks with your life again. Listen to Story. You know she makes sense. The world is a better place with you in it. My world is better; I can't lose you, Tru.* His voice drops to a pain-filled whisper.

*I hurt you. I was... I'm really messed up.*

*You don't have to explain. I understand. I understand you.*

I haven't known him long, but I believe him. The demon does understand me. He has spent a lot of time in my head, seeing through my eyes, hearing my wacky internal monologues. It must be the mate bond forcing him to hang around, as there is no way anyone could like me after being privy to all that.

*Can we talk later?*

*I'm here when you need me.*

I strip off my filthy work clothes. *No peeking,* I tell him, and he groans. Red-faced, I chuckle and force myself to wrap the shell once again around my mind, blocking my demon from my inner thoughts and soon-to-be nakedness.

I pull the Gary Chappell charm from its safe spot, give the black cat an affectionate rub, and then pop it into the pocket dimension to keep it safe. I place the silk bag on the closest shelf and shimmy out of my underwear.

Then, with my own groan, I slide into the hot bath.

Crap, how did things go so wrong? Before, I at least trusted myself and my judgement, and now I doubt everything. I'm not a good judge of character. Most of the time, I hate everyone, so it hasn't been much of a problem. I've never got close to anyone, and before Story, I never made friends. At first I was playing human and was too scared to let anyone in. Worried opening up and having friends, I'd get myself killed.

Then when the world knew of my heritage, my hybrid nature... It's hard to make friends when everyone you meet sees you as a freak. I missed out on the necessary skills to make friends; as I get older, it gets harder and more complicated. Now I have to ask myself, am I too trusting? Or too suspicious?

The way things are going, I have a massive urge to scoop up the pixies and emigrate to the demon world to live with Kleric. Would it save my sanity to leave this mess behind, or would I be running away from my problems? Running away from myself.

No. I can't take Story's troupe to the demon realm. From what I have seen out of Kleric's childhood window—the sanity wall he made for me in prison—it isn't a safe place.

I sink farther into the bath, and the water hits my chin. "Justin," I say into the universe. "I love you and am sorry I couldn't save you from yourself. I'm sorry I couldn't save you from me."

Did I do the right thing? If someone told me the entire situation and asked for my advice, I'd be the first to yell, "Kill him!" But maybe that's me. I've always been odd, bloodthirsty. It's not even the vampire; it's the unicorn side of me.

I slip underneath the water, my hair floats around me, and the bathwater bubbles as I scream out my pain.

I could spend a lifetime trying to understand his motivations, picking apart memories, and in the end, all it would come back to is what Justin did to Petra and Dexter.

What he did was wrong on so many levels.

I'll have to push what happened to the back of my mind. Otherwise, not knowing Justin's full motivations will drive me crazy. He didn't just wake up one day thinking he wanted the blood of a child. It was a gradual decline, perhaps meeting the wrong person, perhaps he was sick.

I didn't notice. I didn't see the signs, and that's on me.

When my chest burns from lack of oxygen, I surface with a gasp.

I lie in the water thinking about stuff. I need to eat, clean my weapons, and send a request in for spell replenishment.

When the bath begins to cool, I get out and jump into the shower to wash and condition my hair. Then I get changed into my comfy clothes.

In the bedroom, the pixies argue over what film we will watch. There's a loud meow and a moment of hush. "No, Dexter," Novel says primly. "You don't get a vote as you only ever want to watch *Finding Nemo*."

They all giggle.

I smile a little. I guess life moves on.

# CHAPTER TWENTY FOUR

Hulking grey creatures over eight feet tall and built like human tanks—tanks with tails, wings, horns, and talons the length of my throwing knives—tower over me. They resemble the gargoyle statues on buildings, only humongous, with mouthfuls of teeth that in comparison make my fangs look cute.

Fighting them is almost impossible, but they do have their vulnerabilities. Getting a knife through the eye, behind the ear, and into the brain will work. There is also a sweet spot at the back of their necks.

All three grin at me, showing their pretty teeth.

I grin back. "I have some new toys." I pull out my new

blades and lay them gently on Frank's weapons bench. "Xander gifted them to me. They are angel made."

The three gargoyles move as one, elbowing each other to get a closer look.

"They're kind of pink," says Jonathan, wrinkling his nose with disgust, and a claw-tipped finger pokes at one of the pale pink unicorns making the blade spin.

"Yeah, they aren't very stealthy," Stanley agrees.

What the heck do they know? I immediately want to pick the weapons up and hug them. I adore the designs on these swords.

"Why is the angel commissioning you swords with cute vampire unicorns on them?" Jonathan asks.

"He cut my blade in half. He owes me."

"The word is he owes you more than just a sword," Stanley says.

I mime zipping my lips.

"It's like that, is it, shorty? We get no gossip from the big bad executioner. You've gone boring since you started your new job," Jonathan teases me.

"Shorty? Who are you calling short? I'm six feet," I growl.

"Two feet shorter than me, little unicorn."

"I can shift, and you can see how little I am when I stomp on your face."

Jonathan grins. "I've no doubt. We've missed you. I'm so glad you're visiting today. Sunday is the perfect day for you to kick my arse."

Frank clears his throat and shakes his head. "Did Xander tell you about their history? I've never seen quite this style before." He picks up a blade. "They have the look of..."

And my eyes glaze over, and my brain checks out with utter

boredom as they list various types of swords—a bit of this, a dash of that. I yawn. It reminds me of how I used to feel when my grandad would get enthusiastic about a particular weapon. Boring.

As an assassin, I should have a passion for this kind of thing, tools of the trade and all that jazz. However, when I find something that works for me, I don't care what it's called, and I tend to keep with it. I don't like change. For me, it also seems easier to stick to what I know. You develop the best muscle memory that way.

I didn't replace the sword Xander cut in half because those twin swords had been with me since I was a kid. I tried using the remaining twin sword with a dagger, but it wasn't the same, and my reach was affected. I've been procrastinating on finding a replacement for months. And then, of course, Xander sweeps in.

I hate that I love these new weapons. They shouldn't feel so perfect in my hands, especially as they are a gift from the angel. I tune back into the conversation. Frank and Stanley are arguing about the design.

"Are we sparring or having tea and biscuits?" I lean between them and press a finger on the closest blade, sending a little pulse of my weird magic down the hilt. "The secrets of these swords won't find themselves. Will you help me test these babies out?" I laugh when the gargoyles all *ooh* and *ah* as the blade turns black.

"That's rock," Stanley says.

"That's so rock."

"Eh, what did you say again about my blades not being stealthy? Huh?" I grin at them.

"They use magic." Frank's humongous grey hands move

the black blade to catch the light. Not a twinkle. The blackest black that's dead flat. It's like a black hole sucking in the surrounding light. "Tru, why didn't you just ask the angel?"

"Pfft." I shake my head. "He's a dickhead."

"Well yeah, that's given." Jonathan returns my fist bump.

"What have you learned so far?" Frank asks, his grey eyes twinkling.

"I can make a shield."

"Show me."

We spar for hours. The gargoyles are having a great time as they take turns whaling on me and hammering at the bubble shield. I, on the other hand, am struggling to fight back. As the shield works both ways, I can't stab them through it. I have to drop it to strike.

Trying to keep it up, drop it, and wield two blades is way above my mental pay grade. I can't get the timing right. I'm slow with the swords and slow with the shield. It's a mess.

The death of a thousand cuts—well, not death, but I'm so bloody tired I could be dying, and I have slices in various stages of healing all over my body. I spar in boots and combats. I'm all for dressing in what I'd wear for real-world training, but I'll have to throw this entire outfit out when I finish today. Which never happens.

I might have let them beat on me a little more than I should have. Punishing myself. Sometimes when I hurt inside, I need to hurt on the outside to balance everything out. I know it's wrong and unhealthy.

"I can't do it," I eventually whine. It took me fifteen years of hard work to perfect fighting with two swords. I'm ambidextrous, which helps, but this... This is a new level of hell.

I keep the shield on the left blade small—the width of a

buckler—and slash the right at Jonathan's neck. He meets the strike and then angles his sword to wallop the shield. My grip is all wrong—my shoulder and elbow ache. My fists, feet, and shins—heck, my entire body—feels bruised and hums with exhaustion. The bloody sword is too long, and my boots slide under me with the impact.

"This isn't working." If I wasn't using the crappie shield, I would have kicked his stone arse hours ago. "The sword is the wrong tool for the job. It was never meant to be a stupid shield."

"Jonathan, stop hitting her for a second. Tru, keep your hands up," Frank yells.

I do as I'm told. I scowl as my arms tremble in the stress position and sweat runs into my eyes. Frank sticks his nose mere millimetres away from the shielded sword in my left hand. "The blades are just a conduit. It's you, not the blades, with the magic." He pats the gargoyle on his shoulder. "Okay, Jonathan, step back."

I drop my lead-filled arms with a groan and rotate both wrists. Gosh, the gargoyles pack a punch. "My magic doesn't work like that. You know I'm not a witch."

"It's not just witches who possess magical abilities. Fae magic is even more impressive by comparison. The things fae lords can do would amaze you, turn your hair white and while your rainbow magic may seem small in comparison, don't let that discourage you from trying. Don't limit yourself by assuming you can't do something just because you don't know how."

"You're like a bumblebee." Stanley dabs his face with a towel. We all turn to look at him, and he smiles sheepishly. "There's that myth that says bumblebees shouldn't be able to fly, as they aren't aerodynamic, but the bumblebee doesn't know that and flies anyway. It's not true. In reality, the science behind how they can fly involves how they move their wings and the generation of tiny hurricanes that lift them upwards."

Hurricanes? I didn't know that. I love bees, and what Stanley doesn't know is I might have a bee obsession. What with my bee bedding and mugs, plates, and glasses. So his comment hits home. It's the perfect thing to say.

"Evolution, baby." Jonathan nods sagely as he grabs a towel and vigorously rubs his sweaty grey head.

Stanley rolls his eyes. "As a hybrid, you've had nobody to help or guide you. You've got to think outside the box and try. You shouldn't be able to shift, and you do. You shouldn't have wings, but you have. Why can't you use the magic inside you to protect yourself?"

"So," Frank says, "if you can do a bubble shield, why not something smaller, easier, like a shield on your skin?"

"Like rainbow armour. Our magic makes our skin rock hard and impenetrable," Jonathan says with a slap on his bulging biceps and a toothy smile.

"Really? Shield my skin?" I stare at the gargoyles incredulously.

"I don't see why not if you push enough magic and learn to direct it. You could fight in your normal style then." Frank rubs a nasty darkening bruise on his chin. I got him good. "With practice and time, I bet you could refine it also to be a weapon."

"Ah, don't tell her that. I've been having so much fun," says Stanley. "It's rare that she's so easy to beat up."

Jonathan throws his towel to the side. "Let's do this," he bellows. "Leave the shielding for now and weapon it up. You're more of an offensive fighter anyway. You're shit at defence."

"Try a dagger," Frank suggests. "Just like with the swords, but instead of a shield, make the blade sharper."

I shrug, put the swords on the bench, and pull out a hardy-looking knife. I flip it, thinking about how many times I've wiped my blood off this weapon. It can't drink my blood like the angel blades, but it has been covered a time or two in my claret dripping from wounds on my arms, pooling into my palms, and making the blade sticky with my essence.

This weapon is mine.

I send a pulse of magic down the handle, and the rainbow magic flashes. I think about making the dagger sharper, like a laser. I swipe at a grinning Jonathan, and the blade cuts the skin on his forearm. I freeze, he freezes, and we all blink at the trickle of blood.

I made an impenetrable gargoyle bleed. Nobody moves.

Nobody even breathes.

"Shit," Stanley says.

"Sorry," I mumble.

"We don't say a word to anyone about this," Frank says, and we all nod.

I have enough of a target on my back. If anyone finds out I cut a gargoyle... we'll all be in trouble. I'm glad these guys have my back.

"Okay, try it without the dagger. Let's try the shield again. Roll the magic across one arm just like you do with the blades."

I put the knife away and with a mental push allow the magic to trickle onto my skin. It tingles. I stare at it. It's too thin; it doesn't feel right. I go with my gut and layer the rainbow, make it thicker with each pass and flexible like armour. Once satisfied, I turn to the gargoyles and give them a nod.

"Okay."

Stanley slashes his sword against my biceps, and the blade slides off. I'm unharmed. He does it a few more times. "Rock on." Awe tinges his voice. "Remind me not to fight you for real."

"What about pressure?" I prod my magic-coated arm.

Frank takes my hand and gives it a good old squeeze. All the tiny bones in my hand crunch and snap like chicken bones. The gargoyle winces. "Sorry, Tru."

"It's okay." Ow. Ow. "At least we know the armour is not infallible." I drop the rainbow armour and flash my shifter magic down my arm and into my broken hand. The entire limb dissipates and pops back good as new. The crippling pain is a distant memory.

Jonathan stares at my newly repaired hand. "Girl, you're so strong it's scary."

"Whoa, that was fantastic," Stanley murmurs.

Frank gently takes my hand and turns it over to check for lasting damage. "Make a fist. It's healed. It looks okay. So when did you learn to do that?"

"Yesterday—no, the day before. Friday evening." I rub my face. "It's been a long week. Yesterday I shifted my entire body and snapped back to human without doing the whole unicorn thing first."

Frank narrows his eyes. "Can you shift and, while you're snapping back, move?"

"I have no idea."

Another hour and we find I can't move from the spot where I shifted, but with that practice, it gets even easier to control the shift back to human until I can do it almost instantly without thinking. I guess trying to move will be a challenge for another day.

I shuffle across the gym to get a drink. My mobile rings, and I answer the private number. With my job, I tend to answer everything. "Hello," I snarl. I might answer, but no one said I have to be professional, and I'm tired.

"Tru? It's Caitlyn."

Oh heck, what now? Please be okay. "Hi, Caitlyn," I say softly, friendly-like. I don't want the poor girl to think I'm angry she called. "How are you doing? Are you safe?"

"I'm good, I'm good. Well, life is hard, but I'm alive. I've been staying with a couple of friends, sofa surfing, keeping my head down. I forgot I said I would check in, so, you know, this is me checking in." She laughs painfully, then makes a self-deprecating sound. "I was wondering if you're free sometime for a chat?"

I glance at the gargoyles. Stanley and Jonathan are fighting with axes. I grin at the power of Jonathan's technique. It's like he's chopping a tree. I shake my head when he roars, and Stanley laughs at him. I wave to Frank, point at the phone, and slip out of the room.

"I'm free now. What do you need?"

"Can we meet in person?" The phone crackles, and she laughs a sad sound. "Of course you're busy. Forget I asked."

"No. No, it's fine. I can make time. When and where would you like to meet?"

"Is tomorrow morning okay? Can we meet for coffee at, say, ten a.m. at the Lakeview Café?"

"Yes, I can do that."

Now that the new plaster has dried and all the woodwork has been done, I'll only be painting all day tomorrow. Work has given me a personal day. I want to finish the kitchen walls and ceiling before the floor tiles go down, and because the tiles run through the entire back of the house, I'll have to paint everything. Twice. I could use a spell, but I'm looking forward to the hard work of doing it myself—therapy painting. I also have a fancy spray gun to try.

"Brilliant. Thanks, Tru. I'll see you at ten." We say our goodbyes, and glugging my water, I go back inside the gym.

# CHAPTER TWENTY FIVE

It's one of those gorgeous mornings, freezing cold with no clouds in the bright blue sky. I'm looking forward to getting out of the house and checking on Caitlyn. Her safety has been nagging at me for the past two days. I feel responsible for the mess she's in, and I hope we can work out a plan to keep her safe.

As I'm a glutton for punishment, when I returned from training with the gargoyles, I began painting the house. I worked late into the night and resumed this morning. Thankfully, I've made significant progress.

Now I'm showered and dressed in comfortable jeans and a jumper. "Do you want to come?" I ask Dexter.

He butts his big, hard, ginger head against my leg. "Reow." His tone is one of disgust and censure.

"I'll take that as a no then." I grab my car keys, give him a final scratch behind his ear, and march down the hallway. "I love you. Oh, and Dexter, stay away from the walls. We do not need to scrub the paint off your fur or pick ginger hair from the beautiful paint."

"Purrrt," he meows pitifully as he flings himself to the floor and pads the air with his front paws.

"Yes, yes, kitty grabby hands are cute, and I don't care if you don't like the colour. Keep away from my walls." I poke the air with each word. "Let. The. Paint. Dry."

Okay, I'm ready to go. I want to arrive at least an hour before Caitlyn to scope the area and ensure it's safe. With only a few blades close to hand and tucked out of sight, I'm happy and secure knowing there is an armoury folded away in my jeans to rely on if things go to shit. I do so love the pocket dimension.

I frown at the front door when the temporary ward around the house fluctuates and expand my senses. My estimate of a few more days was wrong. We will be lucky if the magic lasts another hour.

My head thuds against the front door. "Crap," I mumble. I can't leave the house or Dexter unprotected, and if this ward has faded so fast, the burrow's ward won't last much longer either.

My gut churns, and intuition pricks at me. I nibble on my bottom lip as I think. I have magic inside me, and yesterday with the gargoyles, I channelled it to make armour on my skin. *Perhaps I can do it again and stick it to the walls?* Make a rainbow ward, and... yeah, that would be wild. An idea forms in my mind, but I quickly brush it away as nonsense. *A rainbow ward. Yeah, right.*

There is a big difference between shielding a sword and my skin and shielding an entire house.

*What if I use my blood?* I gasp, and my stomach flips at the idea. Blood has always been a factor in my particular magic, from gaining angel wings to demon strength. Maybe I need to make the house mine first. *Yeah, that's a great idea. Bleed on the house, Tru.*

I can try. My lips twitch. I like the idea of being a bee and embracing what makes me unique. I take out the folded pocket dimension, and a blood-taking lancet slaps into my palm. I undo the seal and stab my index finger, squeeze, and a spot of blood bubbles up. Now to add the special sauce. I close my eyes and give myself to the boiling, churning magic inside my chest.

*Come on. Do your thing.*

My hand with the bleeding digit moves without my consent. I relax further and don't pull back when my blood touches the wall. Inside I'm screaming, *ew-ew-ew, my blood is on the wall! The same blood that made the vampire's head explode.* It's not like it can't be scrubbed off if I've made a terrible mistake, and no, the house isn't going to explode. Walls aren't as complicated as a vampire's digestive system. Right?

As I concentrate, I feel a surge of power from my chest down to my bloody fingertip. I focus on my desires: to safeguard the house, burrow, and surrounding land, allowing invited creatures, animals, and insects to move freely without harm. An impenetrable ward against uninvited guests. I also envision a forceful defence against any entity that seeks to hurt us.

I want it to react violently.

In my mind's eye, I visualise a protective barrier around the perimeter that gradually increases in strength towards the house and burrow.

The magic needs to be set deep into the earth like the roots of a tree, stretching underneath the ground like a network of protection that wiggles like worms and regrows if severed—the foundation of a ward that will last generations.

I'm getting dizzy, and my heart rate slows. The pain in my chest becomes unbearable as I pour everything I have into the new boundary. *Okay, that's enough.* I try to pull away, but the magic won't let me. It won't let go.

The primitive part of me, my subconscious, yelps in terror. I drop the shield to Kleric and cry out for help.

He takes the situation in lightning-fast. *Let go, Tru,* Kleric demands.

*I can't.*

*You can. This is your magic, and you're in control. I will help you.*

The scent of sulphur fills my nose, and Kleric's demon smoke twists around my wrist. It tickles against my skin, running over the kiss on my hand and pushing between my throbbing finger and its connection to the house. The magic severs. A pop of pressure makes my ears ring, and my hand flops weakly to my side.

*Thank you.* What would I have done without him?

I open my eyes just as Dexter stabs a claw into my shin. I frown down at him. "Ow, Dexter."

He scowls at me and then trots off towards the kitchen.

I ignore my monster cat's poor rescue attempt with a shake of my head and turn to assess the damage I've done.

"Um." *How on earth did they get up there?* I take in the hallway and the blood runes all over the walls and ceiling. I don't know what magical language that is. It isn't demon or witch. Not that I'm an expert in runes or anything, but I think... I have a weird feeling that I've made up an entirely new language.

Uh-oh.

*What is this?* Kleric asks.

*Our new ward.* I hope. I cringe and scratch my neck.

*It's beautiful.*

*Beautiful?* My left eye begins to twitch. Can he not see the blood decorating the walls? It's dripping! I screw my eyes up tight and take a deep breath. Then I yank open the front door and stumble onto the driveway. Perhaps the view is less freaky outside?

The new barrier around the house caresses my skin. The old stone crunches underneath my boots as I march a few strides and turn.

*Oh wow.*

My head tilts back. Well, that's a ward, all right.

*Are you seeing this?*

*Yes, I don't know how you did it, but you've done an incredible job.*

The rainbow ward shimmers in the sunlight, and if I squint, I can see it wrapping itself around the boundary of the land. It's even protecting the trees.

*Do you think it's safe?*

*Beautiful chimera, it's your magic. Of course it is safe.*

Somewhat reassured, I peek into the hall, and the blood on the walls is beginning to fade. It's being absorbed. Within moments, it's gone. I rub my collarbone. The magic inside me feels depleted, and I ache like I've been kicked in the chest by an angry unicorn.

*I need to go. I'm meeting Caitlyn.*

*Be careful. Tru, wait. You have used a lot of power. Here.*

Kleric's smoky magic comes out of nowhere, and I can't help but nervously glance around at the use of demon magic outside. A vial of warm dark green blood lands in my hand.

*Thank you.*

*Have fun.*

*Fun.* I roll my eyes, down the blood with a shiver—I swear his blood tastes like chocolate—and hurry to get into the Defender. As I replace the shell between us, I quickly text Story to update her about our new rainbow security system. Life keeps on getting weirder.

# CHAPTER TWENTY SIX

THERE ARE ONLY three cars in the small car park designated for the lake. In summer, this area is crazy busy, and no way you'd find a parking spot, but on a Monday morning in winter, it's quiet. Real quiet.

I prowl in the opposite direction of the café. The sturdy tarmac footpath I'm on loops around the lake for several miles. The area is open, with sloping grass on either side of the path, and in the distance, apart from a few scraggly trees, you have uninterrupted views. Caitlyn is smart in choosing this place to meet, as the saltwater lake has minimal surveillance.

Perching on a bench overlooking the lake, the street, and the car park, I silently observe. It's been a long time since I've just sat and watched the world turn. There are a couple of dog walkers and a lone shifter who is running. His trainers are almost falling off his feet with wear. I see nothing or anyone that rings any alarm bells.

I haven't been here since I was a girl, when my grandad used to bring me here for a rare adventure. I smile. Mine wasn't a normal childhood, but my adoptive fae grandad sure did try. The boat house is all locked up today. But during the warmer months, the lake is bustling with small rowing, peddling, and motorboats available for rental. The motorboats are pretty old—they must be older than me—and when slowly chugging across the lake, they emit a unique putt-putt sound.

My grandad used to say a beautiful siren lived in the lake. I was gutted when I discovered the lake was only a metre deep, which is way too shallow for a siren.

I get up and make my way to the café.

The Lakeview Café boasts a charming white wood exterior with a grey slate roof and large arched windows that offer beautiful views. Surrounding the café are picnic tables, perfect for enjoying the scenery. And to the left is a children's playground fenced off with black railings.

The double glass front door is adorned with a dark blue awning. I pull open the door, and the bell above jingles. Just like the old boats, the dark wood tables and chairs are exactly the same as when I was last here. How nostalgic. I glance around for Caitlyn, but I'm early, and as I thought, she's yet to arrive.

There's a new stainless steel counter with those self-service glass food displays. They're currently empty, so I wander towards the main counter.

"Morning. What can I get you, love?" says the friendly apron-wearing troll behind the till.

I beam a smile at her. "Good morning. Please may I order a pot of tea and... oh, is that carrot cake?"

She nods. "As it's our off-season and we don't have many visitors, the carrot cake is homemade."

"Homemade carrot cake for breakfast. How can I resist? Along with the tea, a slice of that would be wonderful. Thank you." After years of working in the same job as this lady, I'm extra nice. I know what it's like when a customer is pleasant. It can make your day, and when they're horrible... inwardly I wince. Let's just say no wonder I went into the business of assassinations. Working in the service industry can drive you to murder.

The lady rings up my order, and I hand her a twenty-pound note. "I have a friend that is joining me. Would it be okay if you take her order out of that?"

"Sure, no problem, love. If you want to take a seat, I'll bring your drink and cake over."

I smile my thanks as she bustles to get my order ready and choose a table in the back between two big arched windows facing the lake and the tarmac path. The windows provide more exit options than the traditional route of the main door, and the solid wall between provides good cover. If anything were to happen, I could easily break a window and shove Caitlyn right out while I dealt with the problem.

The troll brings over a tray with a dark blue teapot, a matching cup and saucer, a milk jug, a sugar bowl, and a massive slice of cake. "This looks wonderful. Thank you." I remind myself I'll have to come here again as, according to the menu on the table, they do a special afternoon tea.

"Enjoy."

I allow the tea to steep for a few minutes and then pour.

With the warm cup in my hands, I stare out the window and nibble on the carrot cake. It isn't long after I finish eating that the bell above the door chimes.

Caitlyn looks around, and when she sees me, she waves. *Oh, the poor girl.* She's wearing the same outfit as when I saw her last. The cup clicks against the saucer as I set it down.

Caitlyn points at the counter, and I nod in acknowledgement and watch as she orders.

Then she nervously walks to the table, wringing her hands. "You didn't have to buy my drink. Thanks." Caitlyn looks tired. She's pale and has bags underneath her eyes.

"No problem," I mumble. "You can have something to eat if you want." I presume she's going to sit down. Before I can stop her, she stealthily sweeps in and hugs me. I stiffen. When she lets go, I do that fake smile thing to be polite and awkwardly roll the sleeves of my jumper up for something to do.

"Thank you for meeting me." She pulls the wooden chair out from the table. It noisily screeches against the floor, and then she flops into the seat. "It's a nice day." She looks out the window at the lake.

"It is." The lady returns with Caitlyn's fancy coffee, and when she tries to hand me my change. I shake my head. "Keep it." She smiles in thanks and hurries away.

Caitlyn gulps her coffee and makes a face at the taste. "Have you been painting?"

I tilt my head. Caitlyn points at my forearm. I swivel the limb to see a splash of pink paint. Oh. "Ah, I missed a spot." I scratch my thumbnail over the paint, and after a bit of persuasion, it flakes away.

"It's an interesting colour."

I smile. "It's brighter on the walls."

"Bedroom?"

"No, the living room and kitchen."

Her eyes widen. "You are painting the living room and kitchen walls a hot pink. Wow. That's a brave choice."

"I had a colour consultant work it all out," I explain. It would be a mess if I did the colour palette myself. "The house will still look like a unicorn threw up in it but in the best possible way."

"So have you got a problem with white?" Caitlyn says with a smile as she takes another sip of her drink.

I flinch. I glance down at the table, my hand darts out, and I fiddle with the teapot. "Yeah, something like that," I mumble as I pour another cup. "So you said on the phone you're staying with friends?"

"Yes, and I'm fine. No need for me to go to the Sanctuary before you start all that again. The reason I called and wanted to see you was to check if you know what's happening." Caitlyn leans her elbows on the table and drops her voice. "With the witches. You see, a friend of a friend told me they let them go, the witches who broke into my house and terrorised me." Her pretty brown eyes narrow. "Please tell me you didn't let them go, Tru."

Caitlyn's stare is direct over the brim of her coffee, and her eyes are full of anger and fear. It's the fear that gets to me. I take a mouthful of tea. Thinking of the best way to answer.

When I don't answer quickly enough, Caitlyn's cheeks blaze pink. "Please tell me you know what is happening. Did they really let that coven go?" She waits for a second. "They tried to kill me, Tru!" Her voice raises to an almost scream.

The lady at the counter looks over at us with concern. I wave her away with a soft smile. *Nothing to see here.*

Caitlyn shuffles in the chair and almost folds herself under the table to make herself as small as possible. My heart hurts to see her do that.

"I saved you," she hisses.

I rub my face. This is such a mess. "I know, and I'm grateful. I'm so sorry, Caitlyn, for what you are going through. It's awful. If you will allow me to help you, I can arrange a safe house and some new clothes."

"I don't need clothes, and I'm not sitting around waiting for some witch to kill me. Why should I trust you?" She sneers. "If you're grateful I saved your life, do something. Get me the information."

I must remain professional even though my natural response is to explain myself, beg for forgiveness, and rush to do anything to help this frightened girl. But what I can't forget is we are in public, and Caitlyn is a civilian, a witness. Unless I get permission, I can't tell her a thing.

Not that I know if these rumours are true. At this point, I don't know if they've let the witches go or if they are all still locked up. The Witch Council is that tight-lipped.

"I'll have a contact look into it," I say diplomatically.

"You have a contact," Caitlyn snarls. "What good are you, Executioner, if you don't know?" She throws her hands in the air in frustration. "Why didn't you kill them when you had the chance?"

I frown. "Caitlyn, I can't go around killing people. There are processes in place for a reason, and the Witch Council governs their people, not my office."

She sighs and shoves the coffee away. Her lower lip wobbles. "They will kill me for helping you. This is your fault."

I swallow down my guilt and narrow my eyes. I know she's

upset, but I won't be bullied or cajoled into talking about this. "Have they attacked you since?"

"Well, no." She pops her bottom lip.

"Do you need a place to stay?"

"I can look after myself. I just wanted some information." We stare at each other, and Caitlyn scowls. Then it's as if she flips a switch in her head, and she lets out a sad-sounding sigh. "I'm being horribly inappropriate, aren't I? I don't mean to be rude. I don't want you to kill anyone on my behalf. I'm sorry. I'm just frightened."

She pulls her coffee back, takes another sip, and smiles at me shyly.

"My fear is making me extra bitchy. I know you will do everything in your power to help me. It's wrong of me to sit here and take my frustration out on you. You're doing everything you can, right?" She pulls a sweet from her pocket, unwraps it, and pops it in her mouth.

"Right." I don't roll my eyes. Go me. Her mood swings are making me dizzy. Is this what humans are like? I remind myself she's going through a horrible ordeal and I need to be kind.

She finishes chewing. "Thank you for coming to see me. I better go. Is it okay if I ring you again if anything happens?"

"Yes, that's no problem."

"Great." She smiles at me and claps her hands. "Thanks for the coffee." Caitlyn jumps up, and the chair again scrapes across the floor behind her as she dives across the table and throws her skinny arms around me.

Again, another hug, ew. I grind my teeth and awkwardly pat her back. She smells of strawberry sweets and coffee. "Keep safe. Do you want me to walk you to your car or drop you off somewhere?"

"No. I'm good."

I watch as she hurries off. That was such a strange meeting. I press the app on my phone and send the entire interaction to Story to see what she thinks. I'm glad I recorded it.

# CHAPTER TWENTY SEVEN

I turn the Land Rover onto the private road to the farmhouse and catch a twinkle of rose-gold next to the fence. It's Story standing on the top of Dexter's head. Her arms are folded across her chest, and she's scowling. *What on earth?* And here was me thinking my chat with Caitlyn was strange. This has thrown the morning into another level of weirdness.

I pull over. The door creaks as I open it, and the seat belt digs into my neck as I lean to the side and stick my head out. "What are you two doing?"

Both of them are staring at something on the other side of the new rainbow ward. I bob about in my seat, trying to see what has got their attention, but I'm at the wrong angle.

Story waves for me to come over.

*Why me?* I bounce the back of my head on the headrest and groan. I have a bad feeling. I click the seat belt and get out. Oh heck, I hope the new ward hasn't done anything terrible. Nah, what harm could the magic have done? I've only been gone a few hours. I tap my fingers on my leg as I prowl towards them. Maybe I should have tested it before I rushed off to the lake.

The ward greets me as soon as I brush against it. Like a pet, a playful puppy. It feels... satisfied. What the eff? *When did magic have emotions? Uh-oh. What did I do?* The barrier is mine, and it almost feels as if I set it free, and it's doing what it was meant to.

The power inside me has always been different, and I have more than most creatures. I know it's unusual to feel the nuances of magic in the air. I speed up. "What's going on?" I crunch through the grass.

"We had some unexpected visitors." Story's use of past tense isn't lost on me.

"Visitors?" I ask.

"I think the wards were weak, not because of the activity of the builders, but because these idiots have been sneaking up and messing around with them." She points at whatever or whomever they are staring at. "And it looks as if they came prepared; they weren't expecting your new super-duper ward."

"Oh, look at that." I twist my head to the side to piece the bodies together. There are three witches and a vampire. All dead. The ward has neatly sliced them into pieces. No blood, no mess. It's like they lost an argument with a laser net.

*Ah.* I hum under my breath as I'm reminded of the dagger cutting Jonathan's impenetrable skin. It's like that but on a way bigger scale.

I guess I did stipulate when making the barrier that I

wanted it to act violently to threats. "The ward did its job then." I rub the back of my neck. My eyes trace the mess. This is all we need—an entire collection of dead creatures outside our house. For sure, the shit is going to hit the fan. I scowl at them. If they weren't already dead, I'd kill them again.

"What have you done so far?" I ask.

"I've reported in."

"Where are the kids?"

"They are still at school. Ralph is watching over them. I thought it best that they stay away until this mess is dealt with."

"That's a good idea." I look at the bodies and then at the Land Rover blocking the narrow road. "I better move the Defender. Do you think the ward is safe for other visitors?"

"I don't see why not. Perhaps we will keep them on the other side as a precaution. Oh, and you should know the ward gave a warning ripple before it zapped them."

"It did? The magic gave a warning?" I spin to gaze at the ward. It's doing what I asked it to, I guess.

"Yes, and Dexter felt the warning too. It also flashed red."

It flashed red. Cool.

"I'm sure we will find out if the ward can behave as they will arrive soon." She wiggles her phone. "I just got confirmation that the vampire leader is on his way for *him*." We both gaze at the dead vampire.

Atticus himself. "Interesting." The reclusive head of the Vampire Guild and the Vampire Council. I thought this would be way below his pay grade to come out on a personal visit. The dead vampire is packing some serious weapons.

An assassin team of four, made up mostly of non-combatants, the witches here to take down the wards. For a hit on me, they should have brought more creatures. This is sloppy. "I don't recognise anyone. What about you?"

"Yes." The word comes out hoarse. "I know those eight." Story swallows and hugs herself.

"What? Eight?" Story points, and I follow her finger and squint. It's then I notice the lumps, more bodies in the grass. "Shit, are those pixies?"

"Yes," she whispers.

"I'm so sorry." Pixies could have easily hidden and weakened the wards over the past few days, especially with the witches' help. "Are you okay?"

Story shakes her head.

The realisation begins to dawn, and I have a horrible feeling. "Story, what time did this all happen?"

"Just before ten."

My stomach flips. Ten a.m. was when I met Caitlyn. Shit. We've all had a few days of compassionate leave because of Justin's death. The kids didn't want to stay home from school today, and it was a last-minute decision for them to go. The team of assassins must have presumed everyone was home.

Everyone but me.

They weren't sloppy, as they were never targeting me in the first place. They waited until I left the house to come after my family. And to have pixies on the team... They came today with the sole purpose of getting assassins into the burrow to kill the entire troupe. I feel sick. The potential consequence if this attack hadn't failed hits me hard. If I hadn't done the ward this morning, Story and Dexter would have been murdered.

Red flashes over my vision, and with hands on my hips, I have to stare at the ground and take a few deep breaths.

*It's okay. It's okay. They are safe.*
*Safe for now.*

I wonder when I'll land on the wrong side of fate. I keep sliding past by the skin of my teeth—not unharmed, as parts of me are so broken and chipped I'm metaphysically glued and covered in duct tape.

I'm still moving. I'm too stubborn not to keep going. But this?

I can deal with my own pain and hurt. But to see the people I love the most suffer? To be targeted? I'd rather spend eternity being roasted in hellfire.

Who the heck is targeting me so hard that they are going after my family? My fists clench and unclench at my sides. The portal, the break-in with the zombie, the candle witch, and now this?

I'm going to find them and make them suffer.

"Do you need anything from the house?" I ask as, on numb legs, I stumble back to the Land Rover. I need to get away so I can deal with this rage.

"No, thank you. And Tru, the micro-cameras are up."

I nod. I better watch what I say and do then. Rein in the urge to burn down the world. Calm determination slithers inside me, coiling around the emotions that threaten to cripple me. I let the dark side take over, and the cold mask of a killer slides into place.

They are messing with the wrong person.

I get into the Defender, and as I drive through the barrier, for some bizarre reason, I say, "Good ward." The magic tingles against the skin on my face, my eyes almost pop out of my head as it, um, licks me.

I park in my usual spot and visually check the house. I can't believe those bastards got so close and I didn't know. It won't happen again. Slowly I meander back down the road. While I walk, I peel away the shell on my mind, and with a gentle mental nudge, I get Kleric's attention.

*Have you got time to talk?*

*Yes.* His beautiful voice fills my head.

It doesn't take me long to get him up to speed with what's happened as I show him my memories.

*They sent a murder squad! Okay, that's it. I'm done,* he growls.

*You're done?* Is he done with me? I knew it was too good to be true. I don't blame him. A gnawing lump forms in my throat as overwhelming sadness wrecks me.

*Yes. Fuck everyone who is keeping me away from you. I'm coming home.*

*Home?* Tears prick my eyes, and I blow out a breath. Oh, heck, he had me for a second there.

*Yes, to you. You're my home, beautiful chimera, and I'm returning for you. Try to be careful. I'll be with you in the morning.*

*You're coming home tomorrow?*

*Yes. I'll see you tomorrow morning.* Kleric disappears from my mind.

And then the blacked-out vehicles arrive.

## Chapter Twenty Eight

Dressed in his immaculate custom suit, with a short, clipped-to-the-scalp, no-nonsense haircut, shiny shoes, and wool coat. Handsome, if somewhat plastic-looking. He's so perfect he doesn't seem real. Atticus. The pureblood—born, not bitten—vampire leader eyes the rainbow ward and the bits of dead vampire scattered at his feet.

"How did they die?" he asks in his posh, cultured voice.

"The ward." My tone implies that he might lack intelligence. I know, I know. I'm being a bit salty to the vampire leader, but I'm rightfully pissed.

Atticus takes a big step back from the innocent-looking rainbow. It takes everything inside me not to laugh. "An interesting killer ward, made by someone very talented. Do I know the witch?"

"A witch didn't make it," I tell him as I cross my arms over my chest and watch the hunters lay out the body bags.

"Who did?"

I turn back to him. "That's confidential information, sir. The ward is safe. If your boy here hadn't wanted to harm, he wouldn't be dead. That goes for all twelve of them. You know my job and that I spent years as an assassin. These dead idiots came to my house. They have scent maskers and enough spells and equipment to kill half the town. You can't tell me they snuck over the fields with all that kit to be neighbourly."

Atticus ignores my little speech and continues. "The rainbow colour is fascinating," he says as he narrows his dark brown eyes.

*Ooh, scary.*

"It is not up for discussion."

"I see. Okay, well, we will investigate this failed attack. Miss Story said she has footage of the entire thing."

That's good to know. I didn't realise Story meant she had cameras up the entire time. With the new ward and me going out, it makes perfect sense. I love her foresight and common sense. This will make things easier with the investigation to come.

"Meanwhile, the council has convened and issued you a contract. You have a new target. The Grand Creature Council will need you to implement this with immediate effect. This is the highest level of importance, Miss Dennison. The target is classed as extremely high risk, so to assist you, the Hunters Guild will send the hellhounds."

"What, hellhounds? As in more than one?" I blink at him.

Atticus nods.

A team of hellhounds for one target? To assist me? What the bloody hell is going on? Are we going to war? The ward at my back grumbles a warning directly into my brain. It tickles. My head snaps to the right. "Hey!" I snarl at the bald guy, a hunter who is poking at it. "Don't touch. It doesn't like you." I watch as he drops his hand and moves away.

I'll remember him. Others have brushed against the ward, and it hasn't reacted. That guy is up to no good. I nod at Story, and she gives me a chin lift, letting me know she'll find out everything about him.

Atticus watches us. I don't like the intrigue in his eyes.

"Sorry, sir, you were saying?"

"I've sent the documents to your datapad. I want the confirmation of your acceptance of the execution order before I leave."

I eye him with suspicion and shake my head. I pull out the folded pocket dimension, and out of it comes my work datapad. "If you will excuse me for one moment." The pureblood vampire sees way too much, so I turn to find some privacy while I read.

"Another three witches," screeches a voice near the road. "You allow that abomination to kill five witches and do nothing!"

*Oh, here we go.*

I close my eyes in exasperation as a car door slams. The witch from the other night, the woman with the bobbed black hair and red lips—I still don't know her name—stomps towards me.

"If you want me to read the documents for this job, please deal with her," I say out the side of my mouth and walk in the opposite direction.

"Miss Peak," Atticus says, oozing charm as he neatly intercepts her. "The executioner is busy."

"Busy? She's busy murdering my witches!" She screams so loud everyone still on scene winces.

Her witches? Now that is interesting. "I didn't touch them," I mumble as I search the datapad for the documents the vampire has sent. Ah, there they are.

"No, you never do," she snarls. Then she dashes past Atticus—in sky-high heels, impressive—and she rushes me with her arm raised.

Is she going to hit me? Before I can react—I wouldn't mind putting her on her arse—the ward moves at least a foot, covering me. It sparks, ripples, and flashes a warning in her face.

Miss Peak halts her charge with an inelegant stumble. "What the hell is that?" Her voice wobbles. Her eyes flick down the property's boundary, and her raised hand shakes. She pops out a finger and points. "It moved," she whispers. "How did it move!" Oh, and the screech is back.

"You didn't just attempt to attack me, did you?" I ask.

"The ward moved. They can't do that."

*Well, clearly mine can.* I flutter my eyelashes. "Wow, the witches sure have nasty tempers. I think mandatory anger management might be required. Less spellwork and more social skills perhaps." I smirk, and her entire face goes as red as her lipstick.

Atticus firmly grips her upper arm and leads her away.

"I-I will get you," she sputters.

"And your little dog too." I grin. "Okay, bye-bye, wicked witch. I'll be sure to file a complaint." I give her a finger wave, and ignoring her and her screams, I drop my eyes back to the datapad and read through the not-so-standard-looking execution order.

When I first took the position of executioner, I was concerned I'd have to kill unarmed people. In my mind, I couldn't think of anything worse. I saw a hangman's noose or a block of wood with a neck-shaped wedge and me being handed an axe with an *off with their head* order. Not very sporting.

But the people I'm sent to finish don't stand still. No, they fight with every part of their rotten souls. The job isn't about murdering the innocent. It's about dealing with evil, a real public service. Rubbish removal. In the past three months, they've not once sent me to kill someone that hasn't deserved it.

Until now.

I read the document twice, and the words waver in front of my eyes. *How odd.* It's then I realise I'm crying. Tears stream down my cheeks, and for once, no one is watching me. I'm so grateful Miss Peak has everyone's attention. I turn my back and hurriedly wipe my trembling palm across my face.

I can't do this.

I can't. I won't.

The target's name is Caitlyn Croft. But what they have highlighted in bold is what's really upsetting me. The creature's race: an **unknown hybrid.**

The Grand Creature Council wants Caitlyn dead, and they want me to kill her.

A girl who has been masquerading as a human. The same girl who saved my life with a frying pan. And to top it all off, she's a hybrid, just like me.

It's a lot to take in.

I've never met another true hybrid, and everything inside me wants to fight for her. To keep her safe. I see myself in her. She's awkward, rude, and rough around the edges. I frown and wipe my face again.

No wonder she's so frightened. As it's not just about the witches; it's about her hiding her true nature. I've been there. I could never forget the daily fear of discovery, of being so frightened over the crime of being born.

The fear is constant and could drive you mad. I survived past infancy only through luck, circumstances, and fate. When I was discovered at seventeen, I had strong people in my corner to fight for me. If I hadn't had help from those influential people, I would have been killed.

Hunted down just like Caitlyn is now.

The datapad shakes in my grip. I owe my life to others, so I will not idly stand by while an innocent girl suffers. Is murdered. And just like others believed in me, Caitlyn needs somebody to help her. There is no way I can allow anyone to hurt her. This is my chance, now it's my turn to give back, to pay it forward and help Caitlyn.

I blink to clear my eyes and reread the order. I shake my head. This is a setup. It must be. The documents are off. Typically, they give me a complete breakdown, but there's nothing with this case, and what they have given me is heavily redacted. Blacked out as classified information. What is the point of that? There is a bullet list of horrible, unspeakable crimes that make little sense. If Caitlyn is such a monster, why haven't they given me the evidence?

They don't even say what type of hybrid she is.

This is all fabricated. It must be. It's the only thing that makes sense. Hybrids are supposed to be the big bad of our world, but I've done the research and never seen any evidence of it. I think it's made-up bullshit to control the masses. To keep people in their place and the bloodlines pure.

If I'm going to keep her safe, I'm going to have to be smart, and I'm going to have to be willing to put myself between her and the creatures that want her dead.

Oh, and those creatures—yay—let's not forget that I have a *team of hellhounds* hunting her down.

Eff my life.

Unless I'm meticulous and smart, I'll be putting everything on the line to do this, friends, family, life. I huff out a bitter laugh. Three months and four days; that's how long this executioner gig has lasted. *I don't care, not really. The job is a nightmare anyway.*

Gosh, my mouth feels so dry.

One thing for sure, the pixies and Dexter need to go to the Sanctuary. With the random attacks and the risks I face playing with the hellhounds, I need to know they are safe... before I set my entire life on fire.

Oh, I'll be super sneaky and careful, but in the end, they will know I helped her.

All my life, I've had my grandad's voice in my head, saying, *Can you live with yourself?* I've done some effed-up stuff. I know my moral code is wonky, but this... I have to help her, even though I can see this decision will ruin me.

I pull out my mobile and ring Caitlyn, and great, the mobile number is offline. It can't be that easy. Can it?

"She's dangerous, Tru," Atticus says behind me. "You can't save the hybrid. She's too far gone."

I can. I will.

I have to play this just right. If I agree too quickly, it will look sus as hell. I spin. "If she's so dangerous, sir, why is this report missing information?" I point at the datapad. "Where is the evidence, Atticus? Apart from Caitlyn being a hybrid—" I cut off my words as my voice rises. I sound distressed. I even called him by his first name. I blow out a breath with frustration. "I can't work with half-truths like this, and sending me to kill another hybrid is sick. What are the councils thinking?"

"The hellhounds will do all the heavy lifting, they will find her, corner her, and all you need to do is put her down."

Put her down like a rabid dog, eh? "Her name is Caitlyn," I whisper. "She saved my life, sir. I had coffee with her this morning, not even a few hours ago."

The pureblood vampire leans forward, narrowing those dark brown eyes. "You drank tea."

I flinch and stumble back. "You were watching me?"

"We had the café under surveillance, yes. This has been a long investigation on Miss Croft, and how you conducted yourself this morning convinced us that you are the right person to execute this target. From your distress, you clearly think the Grand Creature Council is being cruel by giving you this assignment. That is not our intention. We believe it'll be easier for you to get close because you know her. After all, you did kill your friend—wasn't he classed as a dependent on your work paperwork? A bitten vampire, no less." Atticus tuts.

Did he... that day, did Atticus know that Justin was there? *Oh, yeah, of course he did.* It was a test, just like this is a stupid test too. I will not be anyone's bloody murder puppet. My fingers dig into my hair. Even if I don't get myself killed, I'm done with this gameplay. This shitty job.

"Justin broke the law, and you didn't hesitate to take his head," the vampire continues. "If you're willing to kill someone you love, we don't think you'll have any problem with some girl you just met. Miss Croft is nothing to you. At least this answers your questions about the witches and why they are so adamant about killing her."

A memory comes to me of Caitlyn's house and when I was

speaking to the witches. The conversation didn't make any sense at the time.

"Go home," comes a reed-thin voice from upstairs. The other witches up there shush her, but she ploughs on. "This is coven business, Executioner. It has nothing to do with you."

"That's where you're wrong. Caitlyn is a witness to a crime, and she's under my protection. I won't let you hurt her. She's an innocent human—"

Another witch lets out a snorting peal of laughter. "Is that what she told you? Human? Look, we all know your kind likes to stick together."

It repeats in my head: *We all know your kind likes to stick together.* I'd thought it odd at the time, *your kind.* Now I realise they knew.

They knew what Caitlyn was. "They were going after Caitlyn that night because she's a hybrid."

"Yes. It had nothing to do with the male witch she killed, so your guilty conscience can rest easy. The witch didn't belong to a coven and was new in town."

Ah, that's why he didn't have anything personal in his flat but his clothing.

"Miss Croft is a very dangerous creature."

"*I'm* a dangerous creature. Is that why they keep attacking me? Is it open season on everyone different?" I point to the dead witches—well, the spot where they had been as they are already sealed up in their bags and in the back of a van. It didn't take long for the scene to be processed.

"The witches attacking you aren't from the same coven. They aren't even local; they're outside contractors. Perhaps friends of the male witch? The local witches don't have an issue with you, granted that one coven isn't happy about their dramatic arrests that night. You must consider getting different restraints; they really didn't like the cocoons." His lips twitch. "No, they aren't happy with your interference, but they've been made to understand that they are not above the law. They can't go around trying to kill creatures themselves even if it is well deserved."

"If they are not local, why is she so mad?" I point to the fuming Miss Peak, who has been locked in her car with a hunter standing guard.

Atticus shrugs.

Well, it looks like I have an excellent place to start: questioning the wicked witch.

# CHAPTER TWENTY NINE

WITH HER DATAPAD IN HAND, Story stands on my knee and reads. After a few minutes, she flops down, her bare toes wiggle, and she unconsciously picks at the hard seam of my jeans as she switches to watch the café footage I sent her.

"This girl? The kill order is for this girl?" She lifts her chin, and her sapphire eyes narrow as she glares at me. She then rereads the document.

Finally, Story puts her datapad down. "Were you coerced?" There's a guttural snarl to her familiar singsong voice. "As that's your signature, isn't it? That's the confirmation that you'll do the hit. Why? Tru, are you really going to kill that girl?" Her wings droop as she stares at me.

"I'm going hunting."

She licks her lips, and her nostrils flare. "For her?"

"No." I shake my head. "I'm going hunting for those idiots who think that they can come into our home and try to kill us. They're playing silly buggers with the wrong creature. I'm going to wipe them off the face of the earth, and while I'm doing that, I'm going to save the girl."

"How can I help?"

I close my eyes, and my bottom lip wobbles. I love her so much. "I need you safe." My voice cracks a little. "They targeted you and the kids. Even though they were at school, those pixies could have killed you and waited around to ambush Ralph and the kids when they got home. I'm too big. I wouldn't have noticed or been able to save you."

"If we stay, your attention will be divided. If I try to help you, it will get you killed." She gets it.

The tension in me releases.

For the first time in our history, she doesn't want to argue. I can see it written all over her face. Seeing those pixies frightened her. The witches might have been from out of town, but the vampire and the eight pixies were local.

Her wings droop lower. "Where do you want us to go? The Sanctuary?"

I nod.

Story straightens, squares her shoulders, and her wings rise behind her. "I always wanted to visit a pocket world. It sounds delightful. Someone told me they have a school that accepts temporary transfers. It's supposed to be out of this world." Story's lips twitch with her joke. "I'll go pack."

She's trying, but I don't miss the fear still in her eyes.

I change into my spell-repellent hunting gear, load myself up with easy-to-reach weapons, and tuck the Gary Chappell Reflect Me charm into my sports bra.

Dexter and I wait next to the Defender. The monster cat refuses to get in. He has his back to me, and his tail flicks from side to side with annoyance.

I cringe. He's really cross. "You're going to love it." I lean over him to make eye contact.

He moves away, and the fur along his spine and tail fluffs up.

"Dex, it's not that I don't trust or need you. I do. I need you to watch my back and keep me safe. But our pixies come first. It would be selfish to keep you with me. Please understand."

"Mert," he grumbles.

"Yes, selfish of me to keep a great and mighty warrior like you to myself. You are their only hope," I finish with a whisper. His ears twitch. *Keep that serious face, Tru. You need to sell this.* I grind my back teeth together, so I don't smile. *Please don't smile.*

"Breow." He turns and jumps through the open door and settles his furry bottom into the passenger seat with his nose in the air.

Phew.

Story comes out of the burrow, and I hurry to help with her bags. Even after all these years, I still get amused with the dinky pixie things. All the bags that Story was struggling with fit perfectly in the palm of my hand. It makes me feel like a giant. *Fee-fi-fo-fum.*

As I drive, we go over the plan, and when we get to the school, the kids and Ralph are waiting. When they get into the Defender, the troupe of pixies are solemn and quiet. Story hugs her children close, and Page cries.

We don't want to go home just to call the portal to the Sanctuary. With everything happening and all of us together, I can't help thinking we'd be sitting ducks driving home in the Land Rover. But we can't open a portal to a pocket realm on the school grounds, so we decide on the closest suitable space—the beach.

The tide is out, and the golden sand stretches for miles. On the promenade, I find a handy parking spot opposite the Tower.

The 158-metre cast iron Tower was finished in 1894, inspired and modelled on the Eiffel Tower in Paris. Although there were whispers of the coastal town being invaded by the fae, it was believed the Tower and the saltwater aquarium within its depths dissuaded them from attacking. The iron doesn't hurt the pixies or Dexter, which is all I care about.

We all pile out of the Defender, the pixies climb me and hang on, and Dexter trots by my side as we rush across the tram tracks and hurry down the thick concrete steps cut into the seawall.

When my boots hit the sand, I move sideways and stick close to the massive sea defence wall so we remain unseen from above.

*Okay, good so far.*

I don't know if this will work as I've never called a portal out of nowhere before. It's weird, and it shouldn't be a thing. But the Sanctuary is weird, and it's their magic. I've been told the pocket world can be accessed via invitation—they send you a portal—or as easy as wishing for sanctuary. Somehow the magic of the realm acknowledges your request, and if you fit their criteria, a portal opens. It's freaky magic.

I guess most people must be pretty desperate to step through a random portal and into an unknown pocket realm.

"Okay, let's do this." I make eye contact with Story.

She walks down my arm, stands in the middle of my palm,

and closes her eyes in concentration as she mentally calls the portal.

The minutes tick by, and nothing seems to be happening until... to my utter surprise, it works. A ball of black appears out of nowhere and cracks the reality in front of us, and the scary-looking mass blooms, opening like a rotten flower.

The power the growing portal creates whips the sand around, and little pieces of my hair not secured in my plait blow away from my face. Story clings to my index finger. I curl my fingers around her to brace her tiny frame so she doesn't blow away, and I cover Ralph and the kids with my other hand and arm and turn sideways to shelter them. The bloody portal is not pixie friendly, that's for sure.

The portal is an irregular shape, dark and smoky black at the edges. The outside seems to rotate turbulently, while the inside is calm and stable.

I wasn't going to go with them, but now I'm seeing that thing... I could be sending them anywhere. Story taps my finger, signalling she's ready to go. *Eff that.* I can't let them go on their own. Not until I check this Sanctuary out. I need to make sure they'll be all right. Safe. Otherwise, what would be the point?

"I'm going to come with you to ensure it's safe!" I yell over the whipping wind. "Ready?"

"Ready," the pixies chorus.

"Mert," Dexter agrees as he butts his big head against my leg.

*Okay then. Here goes nothing.*

My boots feel rooted in the sand, and I must force myself to move. One more stride and the portal swallows us whole.

# CHAPTER THIRTY

I BLINK. The portal spits us out into a fancy hotel lobby. If I ignore the modern windows, it's like stepping into a luxury Scottish keep. Wow, I wasn't expecting that. This place is pure magic made, and the power of the realm nips and bites at my skin. I fidget when I notice all my weapons have gone. *That's not good.*

A woman sits reading in a high-backed chair in the lounge area just off the lobby. She puts her book down on the arm of her seat. "Welcome." Her violet eyes shine with warmth.

Is this the creature who runs this world? Her beautiful face has swirls of silver magic, magic I've never seen on another before. It twists around, highlighting her eyes, cheekbones, and jaw. I have no idea what type of creature she is. As she rises elegantly from the chair to greet us, her thick, glossy purple hair slides from over her shoulder and falls like a curtain to her waist. She liquid prowls towards us.

I thought... I narrow my eyes when recognition hits. I know her. We know her. About five years ago, at the café, she helped me with a tiny vampire problem, and she healed Story. I owe her a debt. I instinctively know the pixies and Dexter are going to be safe in her care.

"Hello." I signal to the gang that everything is okay. Story zips from my shoulder into the air, and Ralph and the two girls climb down.

Jeff huffs and stomps his foot and gives me those big puppy dog eyes I can never resist. "Please, Tru," he whispers.

I roll my eyes and hold out my hand. Jeff leaps from my shoulder onto my palm with a grin, and I lower him to the floor.

The woman's smile gets bigger.

"I'm not staying," I tell her. Just in case she wants to kick me out. I'm not exactly the type of person who requires sanctuary. "The portal was kind of—"

"Freaky?" she interrupts. "Yeah, we get that a lot. Don't worry. I'll look after your family." She smiles at the pixies and Dexter. "Oh, and don't worry about your weapons. They will be returned to you as soon as you leave. My name is Tuesday. Tuesday Larson." She awkwardly thrusts a hand at me, which I reluctantly shake.

"Tru Dennison," I mumble.

"Larson? Any relation to Carol Larson?" Story asks.

"Yes, she's my mother."

"Oh, I'm so sorry about that," I say under my breath.

Tuesday snorts, and when her violet eyes meet mine, they dance with amusement. If Witch Council Carol is her mother, then… Tuesday is a witch? Whoa. She must be cursed or something, as I've never met a witch with such uniquely strange magic.

"I'm Story, this is my mate Ralph and my children Novel, Jeff, and Page"—Page squeaks and hides behind Ralph's leg—"and our beithíoch Dexter."

"Breow."

"It is a pleasure to meet everyone." Tuesday lowers her head and bows to Dexter.

I always find that move so strange. It's weird when the powerful do that. No one would bow to him if they knew how stinky his bottom got after eating an entire salmon.

In response to Tuesday, Dexter puffs up his furry chest.

"You're all welcome. I have a wonderful burrow picked out for you in the woods," Tuesday tells the pixies. "I adore fae guests. I wasn't sure what you'd prefer, Dexter. I presume you'd like to be close to your family?"

Dexter nods.

"Perfect. Well, let us see what we can find."

They all move away from the portal, which hasn't closed and is still swirling away behind me. I shuffle from foot to foot. I hate goodbyes. "So, um, I'm going to go." I point my thumb over my shoulder and smile awkwardly. "Thank you, Tuesday. I'll see you all in a couple of days. I love you. Have fun."

A couple of days is pushing it a little bit; I need to get this case wrapped up before Kleric returns in the morning. I don't want him involved with this either. I wince. It's two p.m. now, so no pressure. I wave and step back into the portal.

# Chapter Thirty One

THE PORTAL DROPS me off precisely in the same spot, and my weapons appear in the next eye blink. I go straight from the beach and directly to the rented house where the wicked witch herself, Miss Peak, is staying.

I might not have help from Ava on this, but I still have contacts. And from what I've learned on the drive over, Miss Peak is a visiting council member from the London borough. That's why her face is unfamiliar.

She's come to Lancashire to do a welfare check on some missing witches that were on holiday. Holiday my arse. Surprise, surprise: these *missing* witches are the ones popping up dead—the same ones who keep trying to kill me and end up killing themselves—and Miss Peak is up to her neck in this mess.

Why she thinks her shouting and raving make her and the other witches look innocent, I'll never know. It's so strange. Some wacky reverse psychology. It just makes her an easy target for someone like me to find. I guess in her head, guilty people slink about and hide in the shadows.

According to the paperwork Miss Peak filed, three missing witches are left on the list. Hopefully, she will know where they are and who hired them.

The rented property is on a fancy estate near Stanley Park. I leave the Land Rover on a quiet road and hoof it across the park to the quiet, vulnerable side of the development where I can jump the fence without being spotted.

It's ridiculously easy to find the right house and get inside. It's hard and expensive to ward a rented house properly, and they haven't bothered. This is why I'd stay in a hotel if I was going anywhere; security trumps privacy every time.

I use a simple unlock spell to get through the back door, search the house, and then settle in the living room to wait. She shouldn't be long. According to my source, she has a dinner meeting in a few hours, and there's a high chance she'll return to change her clothes—an outfit is laid out on the bed.

As I wait, the nagging, worried voice in my mind won't stop screaming that *the hellhounds are hunting Caitlyn*. The thought makes my guts twist and I feel sick. It's hard not to pace a trench in the living room carpet.

Forty minutes later and there's the scraping of a key as the front door is unlocked. The sun has set, and as the door opens, the streetlights cast shadows in the hallway. The door closes, there's a sigh, a thud of a bag, and then two smaller thuds when shoes are kicked off.

"Did I leave the television on?" she mutters and trots into

the living room on bare feet, her focus on the flickering silent television. Her breathing changes when she spots the bowl of half-eaten popcorn on the side table.

Hidden from view, I pause the film.

She lets out an angry growl and turns on the lights. "Who the hell are you? Get out. I've rented this house." Miss Peak—Gillian—even with no shoes, still manages to stomp her way aggressively around the sofa. Then she sees me curled up with a mug of steaming tea in one hand and a handful of popcorn in the other.

I wave my popcorn-clenched fist at her.

For a second, the witch freezes, and then with a cry she does an about-turn and attempts to run. With another sweep of my popcorn hand, I activate the temporary ward and lock the room down. She isn't going anywhere. Sobbing, she slaps the ward with her palm.

"Hi, Gillian. We're due a nice little chat. Why don't you take a seat? I hope you don't mind that I made myself at home. The popcorn is delicious. Did you buy that?"

She shakes her head.

"It's yummy. I'll have to buy some more. Okay, so if I can have a moment to ask you a few questions, then I'll get out of your hair."

"You can't do this. Do you know who I am?" Oh, and look at that. Her tears are miraculously gone—the little faker. "I'll have your job!" she screeches.

I cringe. My finger goes to my ear, and I waggle it. "Gosh, you've got some pipes on you, haven't you? Wow, they should hand out earplugs around you."

"Are you not listening? Get out!" She waves her hands in the air and stomps her foot.

"Does this look like a face"—I point to myself—"that gives a shit about a poxy job?"

She frowns.

"Gillian, I'm trying to be polite, so please sit the fuck down. We have much to discuss. For example, I'd like to know who hired you and your team to kill me and my family." I put the mug of tea down and pull a massive, serrated Rambo-style knife out from its sheath. "We can do this the easy way or the hard way." I rotate the blade with a creepy smile.

This thing is ridiculous. It's way too big, and the balance is completely off. But it's a perfect tool for threatening.

The witch sits. She almost flops to the floor but catches the edge of the chair. Her hands shake as she shuffles onto the cushion and stares at me with wide, frightened eyes.

"How many witches are left, and who hired you?" I get straight to the point.

"Three, plus me," she whispers. "There are four of us left."

I nod. That matches up. "And who hired you?" She stubbornly presses her red lips together and shakes her head. I throw the blade into the air, flipping it to encourage her to keep talking. Oops, I almost messed that one up and dropped the damn thing. My bad. I grin. The balance really is terrible. I better not do that again.

"Marcus!" she yelps out. "He set everything up for his necromancer girlfriend. She paid a lot of money to get our help. I don't know her name. I just know that she really doesn't like you."

Wow, she doesn't like me. *No shit.*

I hum under my breath. "I pissed her off, huh? What did I do?"

"Marcus said she was very unhappy about you being a hybrid and getting the executioner's position. You, the media darling, while everyone ignored what a disgusting abomination you are. She wanted you to mess up badly to prove to the world you're unbalanced and unworthy of the cushy life you have."

I guess the necromancer has a point. Not about me being an abomination; I mentally wave that rubbish away. But she's right that I'm not worthy of the job that wants me to kill innocent creatures—a position where the training was a crappy manual and half-hearted words of encouragement. *Go get them, psycho.*

It doesn't make sense, but when can you make sense of crazy? There must be something else going on with this necromancer chick. I'm sure it will come to light soon. I could understand if I'd executed a relative or killed a lover, but she's mad about the life I've got.

Heck, she will be so angry when I rescue Caitlyn, lose the job, have a price on my head, and ultimately end up dead. She will be livid when she finds out she's wasted her time, money, and the lives of the witches when all she needed to do was to wait me out. I'm about to mess everything up on my own. Thank you very much.

Or she'd be mad if I let her live. I'm planning on finding her first and finishing this sick game.

"We don't like her. She's bad news, but Marcus was spoiled. We indulged him. Loved him. Given enough time, he would have got bored with her. Marcus hired us at first to open the portals around town to run you ragged," the witch continues. "When that didn't have the desired impact, Marcus opened the portal underneath your car. When you killed him, it gave us the motivation to kill you. When we couldn't get to you, we planned to drive you mad by killing your family." She sneers.

Like it has a mind of its own, my hand snaps out, and the

blade flies a hair over her head and buries itself in the wall. She lets out a squeak.

"They're only pixies," she whimpers.

"Careful." I glare at her. "Do you really not know her name?"

"No, I don't have a name. Marcus knew, but he didn't say. It was for our protection."

"Describe the necromancer."

"She's short, long brown hair. I'm not good with faces." She holds out her hand as I shift my weight. "There are photos of her all over Marcus's place!"

Only one photo had been missed, and it didn't show a face.

"Where is this necromancer now?"

"She's with my coven, the other three witches."

"Where?"

She shakes her head until I pull out another blade, and she freezes.

"Hurry now, Gillian. I'll not deliberately miss if I throw this one." The edge of the silver throwing knife glints as it catches the light from the television.

"At the Tower. In the aquarium, the leisure group who owns the building closed the attraction this week for renovations. They're in there setting a trap."

"For whom?" As if I don't already know. I lean forward, and her wide, frightened eyes follow the knife.

"For you!" With a shaky hand, Gillian rubs her damp face. "For you. They're setting you up. Now let me go. Please let me go. I'm just the handler. My job was to stop the local witches and any creatures from interfering. I did nothing to you. I was just supposed to handle the local council."

I put the throwing knife away, she sighs in relief, and then she coughs, and her next breath leaves her throat with a squeaky wheeze.

"Have you anything to add?" I get up from the sofa with a little stretch.

"No, I-I've told you everything…" She gasps, struggles to breathe, and her mouth… The edges around her red lipstick are turning an interesting shade of blue. "Wh-what is happening?" she rasps. "Wh-wh-what did you do?"

"The chair. As soon as you sat down, you activated the spell for a slow-acting poison." My head tilts to the side. "Don't you recognise it, Gillian? It's your design."

It's horrible magic. I found it upstairs within her belongings. The contact I used to gather Gillian's information was very forthcoming and helpful. Miss Peak has a reputation for being a tad evil. Poison is her speciality.

"No—" She gasps, and her eyes roll into the back of her head.

I prowl towards her. "It looks as if your accelerated heart rate has moved things along." My voice is so soft. "I wonder if your victims felt the same?"

My mobile pings with a text as the wicked witch takes her last breath. I chuckle with disbelief as I read the message. The hellhounds have found Caitlyn. She's at the Tower, and they have her pinned down in the aquarium.

What are the chances?

I let out a frustrated scream and kick the leg of the dead witch's chair. It shunts across the carpet, hits the wall, and her lifeless body flops sideways across the seat's stuffed arm.

I wish I could kill her again.

Miss Peak must have heard me getting upset about the execution order, or the other witches saw us together at the café and presumed we were good friends, or more than likely, they knew Caitlyn killed Marcus.

"I'm so sorry, Caitlyn. You really are not having the best week." I tug at my hair and hang my head in shame. No good deed goes unpunished. I stare down at the mobile. *Look at that, a nice, neat little trap.* I shake my head.

# CHAPTER THIRTY TWO

I CAN'T GUARANTEE I'll be lucky enough to get another parking space for the second time in one day, so I text for a pickup at the park's main gate with an ETA of ten minutes.

I tip the remaining popcorn in the bin, pop the bowl and the mug in the dishwasher, and turn it on. I don't know why I bother. If they investigate, they will trace this unsanctioned kill back to me easily enough. My DNA is all over the place, and at this point, I'm beyond caring.

I get pickup confirmation, and as I go out the back door, I utter a silent apology to the house owner as I leave the crappy Rambo knife still lodged in the wall. At least I didn't make a complete mess of the witch, and if she's found soon, she won't even ooze.

I jump the fence and sprint through the dark park. As I settle into the rhythm of my stride, it begins to rain, and I think about Miss Peak. I'm glad I didn't leave her alive. I pass the Defender—it's best to leave it here where it's safe—and as I approach the park's black gates, a car is waiting.

"Miss Dennison?" asks the driver.

"Yes."

He opens the door for me, and I get into the passenger seat. I click the seat belt into place as the driver slides into the seat beside me. We take off, speeding down the road that loops the park. The driver doesn't say a word until he drops me off on Adelaide Street five minutes later.

"Go to the staff entrance of the Tower Buildings at the rear."

"Okay. Thanks for the lift." I close the door and dash down the street. The Tower Buildings is the name of the Tower's base. The three-storey entertainment complex at the foot of the Tower is made of tonnes of concrete with red brick and dozens and dozens of white windows and doors. The complex contains a kids' indoor play area, a world-famous ballroom, a restaurant, a circus, and the aquarium. The Tower has a lift within the building that takes visitors to the top and includes a glass viewing platform.

Hopefully, I won't be going up the Tower today, and things will stay contained on the ground floor of the aquarium.

The last time I was in this building I was around nine years old, when my grandad and I came to the circus. The Tower circus is located in the centre of the building and between the Tower's four legs. I remember the entire ring filling with water for the grand finale with dancing fountains. It was magical.

I jog my way around the early-evening shoppers, catch grumbles and moans about the weather and that the pedestrian-only road behind the Tower is closed. I turn left onto Bank Hey Street and slow down through the magical cordon blocking the road, where the three massive hellhounds await.

John, the hellhound I met the other day on the candle-witch scene, leans casually against the corner of the building, his shoulder propped against the red brick. As he watches me run towards him, his green eyes lack emotion, his face is blank, and he looks as if he's seen and dealt with this shit a thousand times. I'm sure he has.

"John." I nod a greeting at the other two hellhounds. It pays to be polite.

"Executioner, I'm sorry you got called out on this," John says, his voice on the edge of a growl.

This is all I need to deal with, angry hellhounds. "And I apologise for stepping on your toes. If it helps, this was not my idea." I'm exactly where I should be, but they don't need to know that.

"We appreciate you getting here so fast," says the shorter, blond hellhound with a friendly smile.

"Well, I've had zero time to prep. I'm running blind. So what have we got?"

John waves for me to come inside, and we prowl down the street and all pile into the narrow staff entrance. He uses his datapad to beam the building's layout on the wall before us.

*Handy.*

"Just after four p.m., a team of hostiles came through this entrance. They took out the building's cameras, threatened the staff, and killed a security guard when he tried to intervene." John clicks his datapad, and parts of the building's layout on the wall go green.

"Except for the circus, we evacuated the entire building, and currently we have three teams of hunters—here, here, and here—blocking these areas." He points to the upper floors, the ballroom, and the kids' area. That leaves just the circus and aquarium not secured.

"We confirmed the target to be here at the aquarium." John presses a button which marks an X on the layout. "Using camera footage from the street, we counted at least four hostiles. That doesn't account for any unfriendlies possibly already in the building before their initial breach."

With another click, an area incorporating the circus and aquarium goes red. "They control this entire section, and they've set up two wards. The one enclosing the circus is a simple, standard ward. The second is a killer ward. It's dangerous and will be a nightmare, if not impossible, to break. As it stands, we can't take this ward down without bringing the entire building down on top of us. It's around the entire aquarium." With another click, an area incorporating the circus goes orange, and the aquarium goes red.

*So I need to somehow get past the killer ward. No biggie.*

"They have witches?" I ask. Even though I know the answer to the question from Miss Peak's intel, it's always better to double-check.

"Yes, we believe at least three are strong witches."

"Any hostages?" I rub my temple. I need some water as I'm getting a massive headache.

"No confirmation. But we're missing staff, including the entire circus, who were doing a dress rehearsal when the ward went up and are still trapped inside. The hostiles aren't talking. Apart from the note pinned to the security guard, we've had zero communication," says the blond hellhound.

"A note?"

John waves me forward and points behind the desk. I peek over. The dead security guard is lying on his back, dressed in a red polo shirt with the word SECURITY written in bold black letters across his chest. My eyes trace the face of the young human security guard. A nasty spell must have killed him. On his shoulder, pinned with a butterfly knife, is a bloodstained note.

*We will talk to the executioner only.*
*She will be allowed through the ward if she comes*
*unarmed and alone.*
*And as an added incentive, we will let the circus staff go.*

"Poor guy. What a waste," I mumble.

"Yeah, and he isn't going anywhere for a while. We have to wait for the building to be secure before a team can come in and take him to the morgue," says the blond hellhound.

I pull two evidence bags and a pair of blue latex gloves out of one of my many pockets. "May I?"

John shrugs.

"Knock yourself out," says the talkative blond hellhound.

I put on the gloves, slip behind the counter, and tug the knife from the dead guy's shoulder. The butterfly blade goes into one bag, and the note goes into another. I hand over the evidence to John, and he lets out a grunt of thanks as he pockets it.

"So they will let me in if I go unarmed? For a chat? That's, erm, great."

The blond hellhound grins at me.

"I don't like it," John says.

"I don't like it either. Look, it's fine. I've been in much worse situations and have a few things up my sleeve. Sometimes you have to be on the inside to get things done."

"Okay. We can hold the building while you deal with the

hostiles in the aquarium. You have permission to terminate all targets in that area, and we'll deal with gaining control of the circus. The ward there is already fluctuating." John drops his voice into a super serious tone. "You know, when you go in there, you're on your own. There is no chance we can get you out with that ward active. To bring the ward down, you'll need to kill all the witches."

"I can do that. Just stop anyone from sneaking up behind me, and that'll be great."

The dark-haired hellhound that's been quiet up to now sneezes. "What is that rotten stench?" He rubs his nose. "Dead body rot."

I squint into the building. *Yay.* "Oh, yeah, about that. That will be the necromancer."

"Necromancer? When did a necromancer fall into the mix? Zombies, I hate zombies," the blond hellhound groans. As one we all look down the corridor towards the staff door to the circus and all the missing staff members. "They're all dead. Aren't they?" he continues. "The staff that they are going to let go. They're all going to be bloody zombies. Aren't they?"

It's my turn to shrug. "I don't know. Maybe, maybe not. That's why you earn the big money. Right? And everyone can hide behind you, as I bet you have tasty brains." I can't help but grin at the horror that crosses his face. "However, the necromancer would have to be freaky strong to rise and direct more than one zombie." I wave a hand. "It will be fine."

John groans. "They were in the middle of a dress rehearsal... Zombie clowns, that's just great. I hate clowns."

The other two hellhounds laugh, finding it easier than to get angry and upset. A joke to mentally distance themselves from the horror.

I catch a sound behind the desk and have one of my angel

swords out of its sheath and swinging before I realise what the heck I'm doing. I adjust the angle of the blade at the last second, and the zombie security guard loses the top of his head.

The blade scalps him and slices through his brain. *Ew.* It cuts all motor functions and magic. Predictably, the security guard's body folds, and he drops back behind the desk. Dead-dead. The putrid stink had a closer source. A zombie security guard.

*Bloody zombies. What did I say? I knew they'd try to bite me.* I shiver. I can't stand the idea of them chomping.

I think for a second and realise I had almost made a fatal mistake. Huh, I'm a soft-hearted fool. "When I removed the knife and note, it must have somehow activated him," I say to the hellhounds. "Not that I know if that's even possible." I bet Story would know.

I use a rag to clean the zombie brain goo off the blade. As I finish, I feel them staring at the side of my face. "Sorry about that." I turn to see all three hellhounds gawking.

"How the heck did you do that?" the blond says, then snaps his mouth closed.

I shrug.

John washes his hand across his face. "I think you're going to be fine." He shoves a closed-system mic into my hand.

"Thanks. I'll call you when it's done." The sooner I get in there, the sooner I sort this shit out and rescue Caitlyn. I undo and tug my body harness off. Now comes the uncomfortable process of removing all the weapons from my person. I take everything off, ending up with quite a collection on the counter.

"Is this area spelled for privacy?" I ask no one in particular, my fingers nervously thrumming a tune beside my weapons.

John lets out a grunt.

"Yes, you're good," the blond hellhound replies.

"Great." I dig into my combats and pull out the folded black silk bag, and the hellhounds watch as I feed everything on the desk into it including the mic. I then fold the handy pocket dimension armoury into a small square and slide it into an inside pocket. It sits flat against my left hip; hopefully, if I'm patted down, it will be mistaken for the lining. My attention goes back to the wall as I recheck the aquarium's layout and memorise the exits.

"Okay. I'm ready."

# Chapter Thirty Three

THE WARD menacingly crackles in front of my face as I stand outside the staff door leading to the aquarium. John wasn't kidding when he said this thing could take down the entire building. It's pumping out so much power my hair feels like it's standing on end. Behind me, the hellhounds are preparing to storm the staff entrance to the circus, and they trust me to do the same.

I need to keep convincing myself what I'm doing is right. I'm making sure Caitlyn and, with my very presence, the Tower staff will be safe. They all deserve to be rescued and go home tonight. And then part of me knows the grief I feel for Justin is making me not think straight, and my gut screams that I'm making a huge mistake, but I've committed myself to this now.

I feel jittery, and my nerves crawl. I'm also breathing too fast. I force my breaths to smooth, slow. I'm in control. I've got this.

*Got this? You are a devious idiot.*

I rock from foot to foot. The magic timer on my sleeve counts down sixty seconds to entry. The hellhounds trust me to go into the aquarium and kick ass. Instead, I'm deceiving them—lying by omission is still lying. I'm going in there to play nice with the baddies until I see Caitlyn. Once I have proof of life, then I'll deal with everything.

It will be fine. *It will be fine.*

I've made this mess, and I have to do the right thing and fix it. I look at the demon kiss with a sad smile and make sure my connection with Kleric is locked down tight. He doesn't need to know what I'm about to do. I swallow. Whatever happens now, I must keep going. I need to be the person who is good enough to be called his mate.

Thirty seconds. I feel odd, almost naked without weapons close to hand, and the pocket dimension tucked away in my trousers is burning an imaginary hole in my side. I ball my hands and out of nervous habit rotate my wrists.

Crikey, I miss the feel of my swords.

I can fight with more than just my weapons. *I'm* the weapon. I've got this.

At ten seconds, I square my shoulders, lift my chin, and glare at the ward. *I hope it doesn't bloody fry me.* I thrust out my hand. The magic sparks across my skin. It's like getting a shock from an electric fence, painful but not life-threatening. I grab the handle and open the door. *So far, so good.* One second. I take a deep breath and prowl inside.

Going from the harsh lights of the staff area to the soft, fish-friendly blue lighting of the aquarium makes it difficult to see for a few seconds. I let my eyes adjust as the door closes. With the ward at my back, no one will be able to sneak up behind me.

Once I can see, I blink and take a good look around. According to the big sign on the wall, they modelled the aquarium on the limestone caverns in Derbyshire. I can see that. The dark, cave-like blue walls are an alien world of lumpy fake stone encasing dozens of fish tanks on either side of the room.

Each tank has a square blue light above it and tiny information placards with details of the aquatic animals inside. There is a massive central saltwater tank with colossal sea turtles lazily swimming over chunks of ornate white Roman-style pillars. Perhaps a homage to the lost city of Atlantis?

There's a gift shop in the corner and aquarium equipment scattered about, pipes and things. It definitely looks like they are upgrading.

Dexter would love this place with its peaceful soundtrack of bubbles and the humming of the tanks. He'd spend the entire time running from the bright orange-and-white clownfish to the sea horses.

"Hello?" I yell. You'd think there would be a baddie welcoming committee. "You requested the executioner. Well, here I am." I hold my hands away from my body and wiggle them. "You can let the circus staff go."

At this point, I've no idea if the witches and the necromancer know I know this is a trap. My head throbs with trying to untwist this mess. I haven't had a proper night's sleep in days.

"Caitlyn? If you can hear me, I'm coming. Don't be frightened. Hold on, and I'll get you out of here soon."

"Yes, yes, lovely speech. Now put your hands up," snarls a

female voice. "Higher." I turn and see a dark-haired witch. She's on the other side of the room, tucked in a dark, poorly lit corner close to the ward. I hold my hands up higher. This feels so wrong, handing myself over like a prisoner of war.

I catch movement and angle my body to keep sight of the witch as two zombies wearing red staff polo shirts shuffle their way out from inside the gift shop.

*Oh hello.*

All I can smell is the salt from the tanks. I'm glad my nose isn't as sensitive as a wolf shifter as these newly made zombies don't smell dead to me. Their eyes haven't even gone milky yet, and thank fate, nothing is falling off.

Zombie one groans as he gets closer. I shudder as he gives me a sniff. He still has a name tag on. I squint at the badge. He's called Steve. The second zombie doesn't have a name tag, but he looks like a Chris, so I'll call him that in my head.

"What will stop them from chomping on me?" I ask through my teeth.

"The necromancer, not that you can do anything to stop them. I'd watch happily as they eat your face. As you're a shifter, I bet the necromancer would let you grow it back for the fun of it. But you step out of line, stop them or any iota of violence, and the girl you want to keep breathing is dead. You wouldn't want your little hybrid friend Caitlyn to die horribly now, right? Her very life relies on you behaving."

"Fair enough."

*I'll play this game.*

"Lesley, stay where you are," she yells to the other side of the room. "Madie, check her for weapons."

A red-haired witch appears behind the zombies. She crab walks sideways, her back brushing against the main tank so she doesn't touch them. She stops in front of me, and rising onto her toes, she plonks her hands on my head and digs her nails into my scalp. Checking my hair, she runs her hands down my neck, pats down my shoulders, and moves on to inspect my torso and hips.

Then her hands go down each leg. Madie's technique isn't bad, but she misses the tucked-away pocket dimension at my waist. With a firm tap and a scowl, she makes me remove each of my boots.

"Why are you helping the necromancer?" I ask her as I hop on one foot.

"Shut up," the first witch says.

I put my second boot back on. "Is it the money? Is the money worth all the dead witches?" My head is down as I tie my laces, so Madie surprises the heck out of me when she swings her arm and backhands me in the face. My cheekbone and nose stings. Ah, I hate getting slapped. If given the choice, I'd rather take a punch. Slapping is so undignified.

"Madie, go maintain the ward," the first witch snarls.

The happy slapper glares at me, and with a shove of encouragement from the first witch, she moves closer to the ward.

The first witch looks me up and down and shakes her head. "You sneer at us for making money, but you're a hired killer. You're no better than us. We are just more honest about what we do." She drops her voice to a whisper. "And you're so stupid. I can't believe you fell for all this. Where's your dignity, Executioner?" She shakes her head, and then she smiles.

I hate it when a baddie smiles like that. It's never a good sign.

Out of her pocket, she produces a familiar white collar. I hold in a gasp and take a step back. She lifts the collar to her face and admires it. "Recognise this? The necromancer has a bright and delicious sense of humour."

*Right, yeah, I can see that. So funny. It's great that she's using my past trauma to eff with me.* I grind my teeth. How the hell do they know about the white prison collars?

The violent unicorn part of me wants retribution and urges me to rip her throat out and feed her to the zombies rather than allow her to put that collar anywhere near my neck.

"You don't have to wear it. But the consequence if you don't will be that the poor, sweet, innocent hybrid dies. It's entirely your decision. Are you scared?" She smiles, and Madie in the naughty corner giggles.

Damn it. My nostrils flare. She's trying to bait me. The hellhounds would never have let me in here if they realised how vulnerable and easy to manipulate I am. They were sure I'd kill everyone. After all, they think Caitlyn is the target, not a victim. A victim that is now being used to control me. With a collar, no less.

It's kind of pathetic. I'm pathetic. How far I've fallen.

I give the witch a flat stare as I think of my limited options. I can deal with the collar. I nod, widen my stance, and brace myself as I let the witch click the white collar around my neck. My heart skips as the plastic—not metal—touches my skin. Then I can't even think as the collar rips my magic away.

I expect fear and bad memories to roar out of my subconscious, where I've done my best to bury them deep. But... I'm fine. I'm mad. I'm so mad at myself. And I can't breathe. I sway. "No please," I whimper. I don't say anything else as I'm not that good an actor. I find it hard to hold my head up, so it's easy enough to sag a little more than necessary, much to the delight of the witches.

They think they've got me.

"Strong, isn't it? We had a bet. It is four times stronger than a normal anti-magic band, so I said you'd drop and be out for the count. Madie and Lesley said you'd have a heart attack and be dead. The necromancer said you'd be weak as a kitten but still on your feet."

She slams her palm against my shoulder and pushes me; I uncontrollably sway.

"Looks like, again, the necromancer is correct." She shoves me harder, and I rock back into zombie Steve's arms. I don't struggle. My skin crawls.

Zombie Chris shuffles up to the left of us. He's a few inches shorter than my six feet, which aligns his mouth with my neck. I flinch when he snaps his teeth.

Both witches laugh.

*Yeah, yeah, laugh it up.*

"Our fun is over, and it's time for you to meet the necromancer. As you have been so good, we'll be kind and reward you and let you speak to the hybrid first."

# Chapter Thirty Four

THE ZOMBIES GRAB my upper arms and drag me towards the gift shop. I can't believe they are touching me. This is horrible, but it could be worse; at least these poor guys are fresh. On purpose, I hang my head and allow the toes of my boots to scrape the ground as we follow in the wake of the first witch as she marches ahead with a slight skip in her step.

*Someone is having fun.*

As I dangle, I focus on how I'm feeling inside. Weak. But as the magic of this fake collar settles on me, it seems to slide off me like water, and with each second that ticks by, I get stronger. Having no magic is horrible, but I've trained for this, and whatever the first witch thinks, the collar is not that bad.

It's not even half the fae power of the original collar I wore in prison.

We weave around the gift shop packed with turtle teddies, mugs and keyrings. Zombie Chris knocks against a shelf, and a few glass fish take a tumble, smashing to the floor. They crunch under zombie Steve's feet.

The witch flings open a hidden door to a room tucked away in the corner of the shop, and with a bit of zombie bumping against the wall and doorframe, we stumble inside.

I peek underneath my lashes. The thin room seems to run the entire span of the left side of the aquarium, with rear access to the whole wall of fish tanks and what must be one-way glass. Through the water it offers a superb view of the customer side of the aquarium.

Shelves along the other wall are packed with fish food and equipment. A big commercial freezer and a couple of big commercial fridges stand in one corner, a huge metal sink with a countertop in the other.

"Caitlyn, your hero is here to rescue you," the first witch says with sick glee to the poor girl huddled on the floor.

Caitlyn sits with her arms wrapped around her calves and her head on her knees. Her long brown hair covers her face.

The zombies let go of me. I groan, and with a dramatic flair I'm pretty proud of, I let myself fall. My knees crack against the painted concrete floor.

"I'll give you a few minutes to catch up." The witch flounces out of the room, and the zombies shuffle out behind her.

The door slams closed.

Still kneeling, my head dangles. I don't know if we're still being watched, so I keep my pathetic cover for now. "Are you okay?" I ask with the barest of whispers.

She coughs and gasps for breath.

*Uh-oh.*

"Caitlyn?" Underneath all that shiny brown hair, her shoulders shake. I crawl to her and put my hand on her back in comfort. She likes hugs. I do my best. "There, there," I murmur. This is all my fault, and my guilt can't handle tears.

No, not tears... I tilt my head as a rough dark chuckle rips out of her throat.

She's laughing.

I drop my arms and, still on my knees, shuffle back. It's never a good sign when the person you have come to rescue manically cackles like a cartoon villain. *She must be going crazy with the stress, right?*

Right?

Caitlyn lifts her head, her brown hair tumbles around her shoulders in a pretty wave, and her sweet, rosy-cheeked face twists into something unrecognisable. I blink. The mask she wears for the world slips and falls away as if it was never there in the first place.

*Oh, now that's not good.*

She tucks her legs under and rises to her knees so we are on the same level, and with a creepy giggle, she lunges. I see the glint of silver a little too late. *A knife.* It slides into my stomach. *Ouch.* It's one of mine—I recognise the handle. *The thieving cow.*

I stare in shock as my blood gushes over her hands, and when I look back at her face, she smiles angelically at me. I gasp, and she gasps along with me and does a freaky shudder. She's getting off on hurting me.

*Nice one. Caitlyn is a baddie.* What the fuck? Who knew? I sure as hell didn't.

To kill me though, she really should have aimed for my heart.

"You shouldn't have left silver knives lying around your house if you didn't want someone using them on you. This was in the cupboard under the stairs. I couldn't resist taking it." Her head tilts to the side with a beatific smile, and she flutters her lashes. "Does it burn? The silver is making my hands tingle, so it must be burning your insides so bad. You can scream if you want." She licks her lips. "I'd like that."

"I'm sure you would," I say.

And then I clamp my lips closed. There will be no screaming from me. The pain in my abdomen is indescribably bad. Who knew there were so many nerve endings in there? I wish I had access to even a smidgen of my magic. Bloody collar. This right here is a prime example of how being cocky can get you killed. I breathe through the excruciating waves of pain without a sound and try not to move.

"Just so you know, when you bleed out and die, I'll ride your corpse for hundreds of years. I'll use your dead body to trap your demon mate and kill him too." She beams another unhinged smile. "It's going to be glorious."

*She wouldn't dare hurt my demon—*

My mental anguish grinds to a halt as I take in everything she has said. *Oh wow.* The combination of pain and the collar is making me a tad slow. If I had a free hand, I'd slap my forehead. I missed a few clues there, and I see them clearly now as I kneel in a pool of my rapidly cooling blood.

*What a clustersuck.*

Caitlyn was the one who brought the zombie through the portal. She was the creature sneaking through my house, going through my things, and stealing the silver knife that is now sticking out of my abdomen while leaving the staircase of knives and the zombie finger.

*Caitlyn is the bloody necromancer.*

"On Friday night when you bopped Marcus, your boyfriend, on the head with the frying pan"—I'm not even going to go there about how wrong that is—"you had a gateway witch and the big-ass zombie hidden inside your house. While we were waiting for hunter backup right outside your front door, you activated the temporary ward I gave you, and then you left the house to portal into mine so you could sneak around and steal a knife—all before I got home."

Caitlyn has sure got some nerve. Her audacity is mind-blowing. Eff my life. If I'd done a simple house check on Friday night, her entire dastardly plot would've unravelled.

"Yes, that sounds right." She dreamily smiles.

I whimper and grab hold of her shoulders. My fingers twist into the fabric of her top. She shudders again and lets out an almost sexual sigh.

Her eyes glow, and I recognise the dazed expression. I've seen that look in her eyes before. I had thought she was in shock when she killed the male witch with the frying pan. But this isn't shock, far from it. She got off on killing her boyfriend, and now I think about it, she must have set him up just so she could get close to me.

I fell for her help-me innocent act like a proper numpty. It's now all so bloody obvious.

Caitlyn was the girl with the long brown hair in the photo kissing Marcus. She got me out of the house this morning to meet her at the Lakeview Café so I'd be out of the way and her assassins could sneak into the farmhouse and the burrow to kill my family.

I remember the smell of strawberries on her breath at the café. She was bloody eating the strawberry sweets in front of me —the same strawberry Starbursts as the wrappers in Marcus's bin. I groan. Like a jigsaw puzzle, click-click-click, the pieces fit perfectly. I wish I'd put them together sooner and avoided all this.

"Are you really a hybrid?" Was that a lie too?

"Yes, I'm a necromancer and a corvid shifter."

"You're a crow shifter?"

She nods.

"Huh. Can you shift?" Oops, I guess not by her livid expression. She really doesn't like that question.

"No," she snarls. "Half breeds can't shift." She gives the blade in my abdomen an extra punishing twist. I wince. *Ouch.* "Only you. You. The famous Tru Dennison, who is such a special snowflake, can shift. You make me sick. I hate you. I fucking hate you!" As she yells, little bits of spittle pepper my face.

Okay, I get it. "Why?"

"You're dying, and that's what you want to know?" she scoffs. "Okay, I'll bite. I'm the special one. Me! My magic comes from within. I have so much more power than you. While you steal yours through blood, dirty, disgusting vampire. Unicorns are supposed to be pure and shouldn't be mixed with your filth. I'm perfection. Me. I should be the one with the fancy job. No one has any idea what I can do."

I'm sure she's going to tell me.

She takes an angry breath. "I do what I'm meant to, create beautiful death, and they get angry. Can you believe that? I kill a few hundred people, and they want me dead."

A few hundred people? Yeah, I wonder why they don't like that.

One hand lets go of the knife, and she taps her lips and gets my blood on her face. I mentally urge her to take a lick.

"While you, you're everyone's little rainbow darling. So brave, the rebel leader, the everyday hero. So easy to manipulate once I found out how you ticked. Some blood, a whisper in Justin's ear, and he was happy to spill the beans on all your weaknesses and fears."

My heart dips. *Oh, Justin.*

"You really root for the underdog, don't you? That was my way in. Your weird, misplaced honour code wouldn't allow me to get hurt because of you. It worked out even better than I had planned, and you were so easy to manipulate." She beams a smile at me. "Look at your face. The sadness just leaks out of you, poor Tru. It hurts, doesn't it? What he did. Justin. It broke you up inside. Eating little kids." She tuts, and her head clicks to the side.

She then clacks her teeth at me and sits back on her heels with a big fat grin. "It hurt you to kill him. So much delicious pain. Boohoo... Shall I put you out of your misery? You know what, I think I will. Do you know what zombie blood does to vampires?"

I close my eyes and shake my head.

"No? Dead blood slowly kills them, rots them all up. Not only that"—she circles a bloody finger next to her head—"it messes with the brain. A powerful, once-in-a-generation necromancer like me can feed a bitten vampire undead blood from a zombie and then be able to control them. Like a doobie-doobie-doo puppet," she sings and wiggles her hand as if she were a puppeteer.

So the fearmongering rumours about strong necromancers have merit. They can control vampires. They just need their victim to ingest zombie blood first. That is horrific.

"Truth be told, Justin didn't have long to live. He was dying." She wrinkles her nose. "All the vampires die around the fourth-month mark. You see, the vampire virus is tricky, and I've yet to perfect the transition to vampire-zombie. That's interesting, don't you think? I need more test subjects to work out the kinks. The printing company is my brainchild. With so many regular blood-drinking customers, I can add the tainted zombie blood to a wider audience and infect whenever and whomever I want."

Caitlyn's blood-covered hand waves in the air. Her eyes take on a fanatical glow, and she doesn't wait for a reply as she continues. "Instead of becoming mindless zombies, the vampires have some autonomy and blend in better than their stumbling, brain-eating counterparts. I've always found that weird, as they're both dead creatures, yet zombies are seen as repulsive while vampires get all the street cred. You know?"

She nods and smiles so brightly. "My process just gets rid of all those pesky inhibitions. The humanity. I killed him. Your Justin. Me, not you. I killed all of them. That nest of vampires was *mine*! I murdered your friend and turned him into the worst of his fears. And then you trotted in and spoiled all my fun! You got in the way and put them out of their misery before I was ready. They were supposed to be here for the grand finale!" she screams and slaps her hand into the pool of blood on the floor—it splashes.

*Oh, Justin.*

I will not cry. The past four days, I've cried more than I have in the past twenty years. It's time to suck it up. I'm glad I know the truth—that Justin wasn't evil. He wasn't bad, and I was on the right track when I thought he was a demon or he was sick.

*He was sick.*

The rotten smell of the vampire's breath was another clue. A necromancer was controlling all of them with dead blood. Caitlyn did that to my friend. She killed Petra. She killed Justin and all the other vampires she got her claws into. Yes, it makes a horrible sense. I tuck this evil revelation away to unpack later. If there is a later.

"The grand finale would have been so much more beautiful. It would have been so much better to hit you with all that betrayal at once. To see your face." She takes a deep breath, and the anger melts from her face and madness sparkles in her eyes. "But this has been the most joyful time of my life to hurt and manipulate you."

"What is the point of coming here, Caitlyn? Doing all this? You trapped yourself in this building."

She stares at me as if I'm stupid. "Duh. 'Cause it's fun." Caitlyn clutches her chest and laughs. "I'm coming, Caitlyn. Hold on." She mocks me in a high-pitched voice. "I tried my best not to laugh, but I was just done with the games after that. You are hilarious and so very entertaining. What a pathetic creature you are."

I slump. I keep my head down, and it's my turn to smile. I came here to save her life. I thought all the horror she had gone through was my fault, and in one villain speech, she has cleared me of all the guilt. Caitlyn has set me free.

Now I'm free to do what I do best.

I'm collared with a fancy anti-magic band and bleeding from the gut wound made by a silver knife. She thinks she has won. Silver stops the shift. It scars. It scars horribly. It is true shifter kryptonite. But then there's me and the type of hybrid I am... Silver doesn't affect me at all.

To me, it's just a knife.

I let go of her top and take hold of her wet, slippery wrist. I twist, dragging her closer towards me. Our knees knock together, and the blade bites deeper into my abdomen.

Caitlyn laughs a deranged chuckle, almost like a hyena. "Yes, that's it," she coos. "Kill yourself quickly. Falling on the knife is such a beautiful way to go. I didn't expect this from you, for you to give up like this, but I'll take it."

My head drops onto her shoulder, and she dares to stroke my hair with another soft moan and shudder. *She is one sick cookie.* One detail she has forgotten about... my fangs. Caitlyn's moans cut off abruptly when said fangs bite into her neck.

Then she screams.

# Chapter Thirty Five

I MAKE sure I don't swallow any of her blood. Although I might have some of her flesh stuck between my teeth. Gross. Caitlyn gurgles, and I shove her. She falls back, clutching at her neck, her eyes wide. I spit blood and bits of her throat onto the floor beside her scrambling feet.

It goes against my instincts to keep the blade where it is, but it's plugging a rather big hole. For now, I need to leave it there. As a matter of urgency, I need to get rid of this bloody collar, and then I can shift. Heal.

I drag myself up from the floor and stumble. My legs don't want to work. *Look at that. I'm doing my own zombie shuffle.* I bet they, as mindless monsters, don't feel pain. They don't hurt.

There's movement in the aquarium. I lean heavily against the glass, laughing when I see zombie Steve jump the first witch. "Oops," I murmur. "You just lost control of your zombies. They are eating your witches."

"I don't care," she rasps.

*She doesn't care?* The anger inside me wants to wrap Caitlyn's long hair around my fist, drag her from the floor, and smash her face a few times into the glass. But she'd probably like that.

On the other side of the glass wall, scaring the fish, the witch's blood splatters across the fish tanks as she gets ripped apart by the two arguing zombies.

I pull out my now-beloved pocket dimension, stick my hand inside, and grab an anti-magic key. It should... I press it to the collar—then let out a sigh of relief when it clicks open and drops into my hand.

Magic floods me.

I stare at the collar in my fist and think about keeping the thing for about a microsecond. With a shake of my head, I drop the anti-magic key inside the bag and pull out an acid spell. Within moments, the collar is a pile of goo on the floor.

Caitlyn watches me with a delicate hand clamped over her bleeding throat and a furious expression.

I smirk. "Watch this." I pull out the knife, let go of it, and shift. Instantly my cells heal, and I snap right back into my human form, catching the blade neatly in my right hand before it can hit the floor. "Ta-da."

Caitlyn's eyes bulge. "How?" she croaks.

"How did I shift with a silver knife in my abdomen and silver particles in my system? As you said, Caitlyn, I'm an extra-special snowflake." I take my time to clean the blade, and with sick fascination and not an ounce of compassion, I watch as

Madie runs around the big central tank. One of the sea turtles also watches her as she tries to avoid the two zombies. She's fast. She slips underneath zombie Chris's flailing arms and sprints into the gift shop.

All casual-like, I move to the door, block it from opening with my boot, and hold on to the handle.

There's a thud, and the handle moves frantically in my palm. Madie, the now-not-so-happy slapper, slaps at the door. "Let me in, the zombies!" she cries. "Please let me in. The zombies are—" There's a more brutal thud of impact, and she screams.

Her cries quickly cut off, and blood seeps underneath the door like a water leak. I move so it doesn't get on my boots.

"Wow," I say to Caitlyn. "Exciting, huh?"

Through the glass, I see the third and last witch, Lesley, whom I've yet to meet. She tries to get through the ward but falls to the teeth of zombie Steve.

"Look at that. All three witches are dead. That was real karma at work. I didn't have to lift a finger."

"Y-you're—"

"Angry? Yeah, just a bit."

"No, I made a mistake. You're like me. We can have so much fun together," she says as if I don't see her cunning smile.

"I'm nothing like you, Caitlyn." If she's what hybrids are like, no wonder they hunt us down. I had better deal with her before she heals. Her breathing is already getting better. I feed the clean knife into the pocket dimension and exchange it for a plastic evidence bag and one of the angel swords.

"You wanted to ride my corpse for hundreds of years? Kill my mate?" I prowl towards her. The weapon is warm in my hand. I squeeze the hilt and send a pulse of magic along the blade, and like a Star Wars lightsabre, it lights up. The rainbow of my magic glints off the room's dreary walls like a disco ball.

"See this? Well, I'm going to use this sword to remove your head from your body, and I'm going to put your mutilated noggin' into this here plastic bag." The bag noisily crinkles as I give it a shake.

"Then I'll put down your zombies. When I get home, I'll half-heartedly write a report"—or maybe I'll get Story to write it as I hate those things—"and then... I'm never going to think about you again." I smile and point the blade at her face, and with the tip, I bop her on the nose. "That is your legacy, sweetie."

Caitlyn drags herself backwards and this time lets out a genuine whimper. "No!"

"Shush-shush, Caitlyn. Don't cry." I prowl forward and plant my boot on her chest, flattening her torso to the floor. "This is for Justin." I raise my arm.

I swing.

The sword makes a perfect arc, and I sever her head from her body. The heat from the magic cauterises the wound, and there's zero blood. *Huh, handy.* I feel kind of numb as I scoop it up by the long brown hair and shove it into the bag.

I check her pockets, and she has a datapad and a phone. I don't want this to go into evidence until I delete everything that might incriminate me. I transfer all the intel off the unit onto my own, then chuck both Caitlyn's devices into the pocket dimension for safekeeping.

I pull up the documents on my datapad and read. Within the files are pages and pages of notes and ramblings. Caitlyn has been busy. She's genius-level smart but so unbalanced. She details setting up the print shop; it was all her. Justin had nothing to do with it. She involved him because she wanted to destroy my life.

She almost did it.

Caitlyn kept meticulous details on everything, especially on the vampires she had already infected. I don't know if they'll drop dead or go on a rampage. I can see a future me having to hunt them down.

Halfway down the list, I find the name I'm desperately searching for: Justin. There's no date, but it looks as if it was around three months ago when she went after him. A perfect test subject. A perfect way to get back at me. I squeeze my eyes closed and bite my lip till it bleeds. She spiked his artificial blood without him ever knowing. He was shopping, and she dropped the doctored blood, a couple of bottles of it, into his trolley.

*That's it. No big conspiracy.*

Justin didn't make a mistake by drinking from a bad source. Once he drank it, within hours, the Justin I knew and loved was gone.

Bloody hell, my chest feels tight, and I want to crawl into a ball. My hands shake as I close the file and put it away to go over later. I can't right now.

Now I've got to deal with the zombies and perhaps the witches. I frown. They say necromancy-made zombies are not contagious. But they also say when a necromancer dies, so do the zombies. I stare through the blood-splattered glass. Those zombies do not look dead to me. They are still eating.

I use a Clean Me spell to deal with the copious amounts of my blood on the floor—no need to leave that lying around.

I've lost so much blood. Shifting doesn't replace that. I'm lucky my demon gave me an emergency vial of his blood in a spelled tube to keep it fresh. I chug it, and energy fills my limbs.

Instantly I feel stronger, and I spend another few minutes strapping on all my weapons and gear.

Fortified, I open the door, and with the evidence bag swinging in my left hand and a sword in the right, I prowl through the gift shop. There's no sign of Madie's body besides the blood and drag marks. *That's not good.* Let's hope the witch didn't get up.

Starting a zombie apocalypse by mistake would be just my luck.

I avoid stepping on the crushed glass fish, and as soon as I move out into the aquarium, I spot the zombies, both still happily munching on a witch apiece.

Zombie Steve growls at me, a flap of witch between his teeth, but he doesn't budge an inch from his kill. Zombie Chris doesn't look up. I stare at the sword with a sigh. After the evening I've had, I don't fancy getting up close and personal with the two chompers.

I silently back away into the gift shop.

Freeing up my left hand, I prop the evidence bag onto a shelf, slide the sword away in the crossbody scabbard, and dip my hand into the pocket dimension for my favourite compound bow and two arrows with suitable heavy-duty broadheads.

I haven't shot the bow for a few weeks, but it's a weapon I'm familiar with, and it feels good in my hands. I check the bow over, and once I'm happy, I nock the first arrow. Moving back into the open, with both zombies in sight, I shuffle sideways to change my position so I don't damage a tank if I miss. No need to hurt any of the lovely fish. Not that I'll miss.

Zombie Steve goes down first. The shot hits him perfectly in the centre of his forehead, and with an almost sad-sounding sigh, he slumps over.

*Sorry about that, Steve.*

I nock the second arrow for zombie Chris. I might show off a bit as his is head angled perfectly, as if he's presenting his ear to me, begging me to take the earshot. It would be almost rude not to. He topples over with the arrow sticking out of the side of his head.

*Sorry, Chris.*

Thinking there's even a tiny chance that Madie converted, got up, and zombie-tottered away makes me extra cautious. So for good measure, just to be thorough, I put the bow away and use the sword to slice the three witches' brains, which is as gross as it sounds.

The good news is since their untimely death by zombie, I can feel the change in the ward. It has weakened. I don't attempt to leave, as it's still powerful enough to fry me on the spot. But I do get the mic out. "All clear," I say. "I'm now just waiting on the ward to go down." I put the comms away without waiting for a reply and send an all-clear message to Story.

Then I grab the evidence bag from the gift shop, and sipping some water, I wander around.

Story responds. She's relieved I'm safe. They are all having a wonderful time, and they'll catch a portal directly home in the morning.

I debate telling her what I found out about Justin. I'd want to know. So I send her a simplified version of the information—I hate typing. Story immediately asks for everything from Caitlyn's phone. I encrypt the data, send it, and ask her to forward the list of the sick vampires to Atticus and let him know that the authorities should be on the lookout for any vampires with eye-watering rotten breath.

## CHAPTER THIRTY SIX

Over the next hour, I ignore the dead scattered about on the floor and instead read the information about all the fish and aquatic animals. As I move around the exhibits, Caitlyn's severed head occasionally knocks into my leg.

*Finally*, the ward fluctuates once, twice, and then goes down. The hellhounds and Xander—yay—burst in and find me standing there with my evidence bag, watching the sea turtles.

Boots march towards me. "Okay?" John asks gruffly as he steps up to my side.

"Yeah, piece of cake. You? How did the circus go?"

John grunts and eyes the evidence bag in my hand. "No

zombies, and the staff were fine." He casually looks around the room, tracking the blood dripping down the glass tanks. "We've all been waiting for you."

I pull a face. Not much I can do to speed up the magic, so I don't even bother to explain. "I'm glad the circus staff are okay. Sorry, I had all the fun." I tip my head to incorporate the bodies behind me. "The necromancer, unfortunately, zombied another two members of staff. They're over there. I'll send you the incident report if you want it."

The hellhound's green eyes narrow as he swiftly changes the subject. "I have a question for you. You don't know about a dead witch in a house by the park?" John asks this in a low rumble that makes me clammy.

If I answer wrong, will he rip my head clean off? Scary guy. I'm glad I don't need to pee. They found the witch's body quickly, perhaps 'cause she missed her dinner meeting?

Eff it. I don't care anymore.

I draw myself up to my full height and jut out my chin. I refuse to break eye contact. "Yes, Miss Peak. I killed her." And John knows that as my scent and DNA were all over the living room. "She was running interference for the witches that were helping the hybrid. The witches that put up the ward and, on at least three separate occasions, have attempted to kill me." I smirk and fold my arms. "You will find she's part of all this if you dig into her background. There were nine of them, and she had valuable information. She needed to be eliminated as part of this investigation."

We take each other's measure.

He grunts. "I'll make sure the cases are linked."

"Do you need anything else?" *That's it?* I don't say it, but it's implied in my tone.

His lips twitch. "No. Good job."

I grunt and shrug. *Good job.* I bet getting a good job from this guy is rare, and I don't care. He can stuff it up his bum. I want to go home and, fate willing, get a hug from my demon in the morning.

I want to see Kleric with everything in me.

I wave half-heartedly to John and get the heck out of there. With the evidence bag swinging, I prowl away.

Something inside me has changed, and I've decided to go for it. To love my demon. Life is too short to let something like fear stand in the way of happiness. If it doesn't work out, the pain will be worth not ever trying.

Xander is looking at the bodies, but I know he has been watching me this entire time. Judging me. I ignore him.

As I pass the other two hellhounds, the blond pats me on the back. "Nice zombie earshot, Dennison." I nod my thanks, continue walking, and slip past the hazmat team as they enter.

*Oh.* I freeze.

"Excuse me, here." I thrust the evidence bag at a competent-looking woman. "This is the hybrid necromancer, Caitlyn Croft. Well, her head. The rest of her is in a storeroom you will find in the corner of the gift shop. I've left the door open." I point in the general direction.

She takes the bag from me gingerly. "Thank you, Executioner. I'll get this logged."

"Thank you." I turn and leave.

*I can't believe I almost took Caitlyn's head home with me.* I have no idea why I was carrying it around. It seemed like a good idea. The right thing to do. If her head was in a bag, it wasn't attached to her body, and she wasn't about to rise and start more shit.

I guess I'm still in shock. I'm hurting, and it's going to take me a while to deal with everything. I escape out of the staff entrance.

Somehow, it's still night. I feel like I've lived a lifetime at the aquarium. "Miss Dennison? A moment of your time, if you please," says a familiar voice behind me.

I close my eyes. All I want to do is keep walking, maybe run. I don't want to talk to him. But the pesky ingrained manners force me to stop. I spin on my toes and tilt my head back to look at him.

Xander's honey eyes take me in. I'm sure he notices the hole in my top from the healed knife wound. I cross my arms, awkwardly hiding my abdomen.

"I'm glad you are safe," he says softly. The angel still looks tired.

"Xander, what are you doing here? How did you even get inside the aquarium?" Ah, now I remember. John and the angel are good friends. "The hellhound," I snarl with a shake of my head.

"I was worried about you. No matter what you think of me, my motives, and my mistakes, I'll always care about you. Worry about you."

"Sure." *Sure.* I stare at my boots and scuff my toe across a small crack in the pavement.

"I'm sorry about Justin. He was a good man."

"He was." My voice croaks with the feelings stuck in there. I cough. "He didn't do what they say. He wasn't himself at the end." I clamp my lips closed, unwilling to tell him anything else until I know more. Even if I wanted to, the words would get stuck in my throat.

He sees on my face the unwillingness to elaborate further. And for the first time in—our... ex-friendship? Ex-relationship? Whatever—in the time I've known him, he doesn't press. Wow, a modern miracle.

"I didn't make any assumptions. I was waiting to speak to you about it. I'm here if you ever want to talk." He adjusts his cuffs, and his expression becomes pensive. "Tru, we left things in the air. Atticus contacted me. I will not stand in the way of you and the demon. Kleric." He says the name like he's taken a mouthful of poo. "I still don't like it. He's too young, too cocky. He's not good enough for you."

I scowl.

"But I'm the first to admit he's a good man, and I want you to be happy. I'll step aside. I'm sorry I didn't see you as an adult until it was too late. I'm sorry for the hurt I caused you and for not listening. I was wrong."

Bloody hell, did I die? Is this some alternative universe?

We stare at each other, and the silence is a living thing between us. *I could just tell him to piss off.*

No one is infallible. My friend is dead. I killed him. It turns out I did the right thing, I think. I'm still not sure. But... I didn't spend hours talking to him to get his story. I didn't give him a chance to explain himself. Not really. I made a quick decision in the moment, and Justin is gone, dead. He's never coming back. I have no idea if he could have been healed, and I can never ask for his forgiveness.

I fell for Caitlyn's lies and her hare-brained schemes. I don't know her history or if she was always so unbalanced. What I do know is when I was seventeen, if I hadn't had this man's help, if circumstances had been different, perhaps my life would have turned out similarly to Caitlyn's.

I loved Xander once. I guess that's why I still have so much rawness inside me. It hurt more because it was him.

I swallow. I need to let the hurt and anger go. Forgiveness

doesn't make me weak. Sometimes it's the right thing to do. Holding on to all this hate and pain is toxic to me.

I lift my chin and thrust my hand out. "Friends?"

Xander takes in my hovering hand; it must be a trick of the streetlights as his eyes shine with tears. His warm, surprisingly callused hand gently takes mine in a handshake.

"Friends," he says with a soft smile. "Can I walk you to your car?"

Ooh, the angel is on his best behaviour. Ah, my Land Rover. I forgot I'd have to ring for a lift. I cringe. "It's at Stanley Park."

"I can drop you off if you'd like."

"Thanks, that would be nice." We move down the street—both of us pass through the crime-scene-cordon magic easily and head down Bank Hey Street.

"Have you named the swords?"

I almost stumble. "What?" I've never named a weapon in my life. Except perhaps when I'm mad at it, and then it's not so flattering. "Um... They are beautiful swords." I hedge.

"They are. So have you named them?"

I tap my fingers against my thigh and then brush a hand over the closest one. I think about what to say to distract him from his question. And then my mind goes blank when the angel gives me a look like he's waiting for me to say something profound.

"Stabby," I blurt. I blame the pressure of the moment, and I'm not wrong. They do stab.

"Pardon?" Xander's entire face frowns.

"Stabby One"—I wave at one blade and point at the other—"and Stabby Two." I nod.

Xander rubs his forehead vigorously. "Let me get this

straight. You called the two priceless angel swords I had commissioned for you Stabby One and Two?"

My lips twitch. "Yes."

"Ah."

"Yep." I grin.

I think the angel regrets our newfound friendship already. That must be a new record. It only took me two minutes to make him mad.

# Chapter Thirty Seven

Kleric is coming back through a proper gateway so there's an official record of his arrival back to Earth. Nobody needs to know that, because of our connection, he can do the smoky magic thing and arrive under his own steam.

I'm anxious.

I've seen him recently, but it was an emergency, and I was completely out of my mind with grief. Heck, I snotted all over him. I don't know why I snot all over that man. At this point, it seems to be our thing.

I tilt my head back, lean against the purple door, and gaze at the sky. Kleric keeps seeing me at my absolute worst. The clouds roll above my head, and the sky is an angry dark grey in places. It's not raining yet. Fingers crossed—the morning has been good so far. I'd be out here even if it were raining.

I groan and wiggle. My left leg is going numb. The doorstep I'm perching on is far from comfortable, and there's a deep crack in the stone under my bum. That will be fixed when the driveway is done. But for now, it's there, and it's making this an uncomfortable endeavour. But I'm not budging; from here, I can see right down the driveway to the private road and beyond.

The ward will tell me as soon as somebody comes up the drive, but I can't wait inside. My leg bounces with impatience, and my heart pounds. I could open our connection, remove the shield from my mind, and ask him where he is. I gulp. I don't want to.

The big bad executioner is scared shitless that Kleric is not coming. He promised to be home this morning, and if he doesn't come back, I'm going to be disappointed. So I don't want to know. Not yet.

I'll sit here for a few more hours, far into the afternoon, until I admit defeat. There are so many what-ifs rolling around in my head, and now I've decided I want to give being his mate a shot—to be happy—I'm so bloody frightened that he won't want me.

I'm effed up in the head.

I wrap my arms around my waist and lower my head to my knees. My leggings stink of paint.

I lift my head and rub my arms. I'm paint splattered all over. I didn't stop painting when I came home last night. I needed to keep moving as my mind was way too busy for simple rest, and knowing Kleric would be here in the morning made sleeping impossible.

There are now three coats of paint on the walls and two

coats on the woodwork. It's all ready for the floor and kitchen to be installed. I still have to paint the hallway. As the builders still need to come in and out, you can guarantee that if I paint it, it'll get scuffed. I wanted to leave it till last. It's a minor job compared to everything else.

I should have showered and changed my clothes or at least shifted. I'm a mess—I got a side-eye from Story when the pixies and Dexter came home an hour ago. Tuesday's creepy portal dropped them off right outside our ward. Some frantic part of me is worried I'll miss his arrival, and I so want to be here to greet him that I can't seem to move from the doorstep. It might be my imagination, but for the past hour, I have felt Kleric coming closer.

I might be losing my mind. Something inside me clicked when I thought he came through the gateway—an odd mental game of hotter, colder. Everything is getting hotter, and the kiss on my hand is glowing.

I can't believe I'm here alive and that I, unfortunately, still have the stupid executioner job. Not for the want of trying. I huff. I wonder when it will be best to quit. I scraped through the Caitlyn nightmare by the skin of my teeth. I got lucky it worked out the way it did, and it still doesn't seem real.

My stomach flips, and my conscience nudges me. *Lucky isn't a word you should use.* Lucky. Yeah, right, Tru. One of my friends is dead. So lucky.

I'm going to see Morris tomorrow. He was the second person I told after Story. I called him when I got home. It's still such a mess. I pick at a splodge of paint on my knee, pausing when I hear the distant rumble of an approaching car.

I spring to my feet and bounce on the spot. Like a little kid needing the toilet, I can't stand still.

*Is it him? Oh fate, is it him?*

The familiar car slides easily through the ward, and it slowly meanders up the drive and parks next to the Defender. The driver's door opens, and a massive pale blue demon emerges.

My tight shoulders sag in relief.

His overly large eyes are an endless black. They sparkle with warmth as he takes me in, and he smiles.

I let out a squeal of delight and run to him. I jump. His big hands catch me midflight, and then I'm wrapping my arms around his neck and my legs around his waist. Kleric seems bigger if that is possible. He smells so good. I kiss his face, small silly kisses. I pepper his face with them. He laughs, and my heart almost bursts with the beautiful sound.

"You're home," I say breathlessly.

"I'm home."

His warm voice makes me shiver. "I've missed you so much," I tell him. "Let's not do this again."

Kleric flinches.

*Uh-oh. What now?*

Kleric drops his voice to a deep rumble. "Tru, your ward just licked me." I giggle, and then he swings us around in a dizzying circle. "Why would it lick me?"

I laugh. "I don't know." I laugh so hard at his mortified expression.

Kleric stops spinning. He smiles down at me, closes the tiny gap between us, and claims my mouth. The taste of him floods me, and my senses go haywire—it's overwhelming.

I hold his face, and my thumbs trace his chiselled, high cheekbones. The kiss at first is gentle. Then with swift graduation, it becomes more intense, harder, deeper. Kleric wraps his hand around my plait and gently tugs to angle my head. I gasp.

As if waiting for that invitation, his tongue slips into my mouth and tangles with mine.

We kiss each other as if we are starved.

## Chapter Thirty Eight

The newscaster drones on about the landmark deal with the demon realm's royal family. "The trade deal is worth billions of pounds—"

Nope, no more of that. I roll my eyes and switch off the phone. I throw the mobile onto the bed and finish tightening the second ankle strap on the delicate silver shoe when a warm voice rumbles in my ear. "You look beautiful." I shiver, and goosebumps rise on my arms.

Awkwardly I straighten and fiddle with the hem of the silver dress. It clings to my body and makes my legs look a mile long. "I might not look as beautiful now that my face is going tomato red," I grumble.

It's nice. It's really nice to be complimented.

I turn, and my mouth pops open. "Wow. You look beautiful too—erm, I mean handsome." I blink owlishly at him.

He's wearing a gorgeous suit, and he looks all demon prince. Kleric smiles and tucks a strand of my multicoloured hair behind my ear and caresses my jaw. "So we have our first dinner date tonight, and I was thinking... If it's okay with you, I'd like to make it a family one."

*Family? On our first date. Okaaay.*

I do a bad job of letting the disappointment show on my face.

Kleric clears his throat, and his black eyes sparkle. "We have been invited to dine at the burrow this evening."

"What?" I gasp. "But how?" Am I missing something? Did I bump my head? That's not going to work. "That's not possible. That is Story's house, and we can't..." I hold my hands out to indicate my size, our size, just in case Kleric doesn't get it.

"That's where this comes in, your surprise." Kleric pulls out a pink box from behind his back. "The angel isn't the only person who can buy you gifts," he finishes with a growl.

"Jealous, baby?" I tease him as I eye the pretty pink box in his hand.

His growl abruptly cuts off with my words. "Don't baby me." He's adorably indignant as he puffs up his—substantial—chest. "I'm all man."

"Yes, honey. Of course, you are. I'm sorry." I pull off what I hope is a sympathetic face and pat his massive biceps.

He shakes the box at me.

I take it and carefully open the lid. Buried underneath a mountain of tissue paper is a shimmery white charm shaped like a pixie—I stare at it, frozen.

*Is that what I think it is?*

"It's a Gary Chappell Alice charm." He brushes my frozen

fingers away to help pull the charm out of the box. Kleric places it onto my palm. My heart pounds. "It's named after *Alice's Adventures in Wonderland*. It will change your size whenever you want."

"Wow." I stare at it and then peek up at him through my lashes. I'm honestly in shock. "You got this for me as a surprise? This is mine? A Gary Chappell Alice charm. Really? This is... these are..." I sputter. "Is it real?" I whisper. It feels real. The magic coming off the little charm is massive.

"Of course it's real." He takes the box from my shaking hand and pops it onto the bed. "I know how sad it makes you not to be able to see the pixies' new home. If it's in my power to make you happy, I will." He shrugs self-consciously. "I negotiate well, and I managed to jump the twenty-year waiting list and bought it for you."

I sniffle and dab under my eye with the edge of my index finger. My entire body is now shaking. "It will change my size whenever I want? Wow. Just wow. Thank you, thank you so much. This is the best gift I have ever received." Kleric smiles smugly. I throw myself into his arms and sniffle some more. I then pull back with a frown and glaze up at him. "What about you?"

"I'm a demon. I can easily change my size."

"Oh! Oh yeah, that makes sense." This is a dream. It can't possibly be real. "Are we really going to dinner at their house?"

"If you want to."

I vigorously nod. "Please." His eyes meet mine, and the softness in his gaze hits me right in the feels. My squishy heart misses a beat.

*Can he be any more bloody perfect?*

On his way past, he kisses my forehead.

*Oh yes. Yes, he can.*

Maybe because of all the messed-up shit fate has thrown my way, I've earned some karma and can keep him. He's mine. I'm not giving him up. Not ever. I bound down the stairs after him.

We make our way outside and walk down the path to Story's home hand in hand. When we get close to the tree in which the burrow is nestled, Kleric gives me a nod of encouragement.

This is a huge moment. I let go of his hand and chant the words to activate the Alice charm. The magic of the charm hits me, and the world falls away. It's the best kind of rollercoaster ride. My stomach flips, my ears pop, and the wind rushes around me as my multicoloured hair floats. When it settles down heavy against my back, I'm pixie small.

I feel dizzy. I rapidly blink as the world comes back into focus. A massive shoe the size of a car is next to me, and as I gaze up, Kleric is as big as a mountain.

After a few seconds, Kleric shrinks to join me.

"Hi," I say with a wave. I rub my throat and pull a weird face. "I thought my voice would be all squeaky, but I think I sound the same."

"Hi." His lips twitch, and he shakes his head at the shock he must see on my face. "And yes, you sound the same."

"So do you." I lean into his side. "This is scary."

"It's okay. We will keep each other safe." He squeezes my sweaty hand.

It's weird being so tiny. I cautiously look around; I sure regret not having a sword. I'm glad it's winter, as I wouldn't want to meet a fly being this small. Everything feels odd and dangerous.

The path to the burrow is massive, and the tiny pea-shaped gravel are like giant rocks that are difficult to navigate in heels.

The trees around us are never-ending tall, and the solar-powered lights along the path are far brighter and bigger than any streetlight.

The world is a completely different place when you're pixie small.

We walk up to the burrow's curved front door, and before we can knock, it opens. I jump and stare inside with shock and awe.

The entire space twists and turns, working with the surrounding tree roots and the curved ceiling. A rainbow of lights, fae lanterns float about, highlighting the hallway's best features.

"Tru! You came." I make an *oof* sound as Page throws herself at me and wraps her arms around my waist.

This. Is. Surreal.

I hug the adorable green pixie. "You are so pretty!" Page mumbles into my abdomen.

"So are you," I say in an awe-filled whisper as I stroke her hair.

"I can't believe how long we waited for you to even get to the door. Some of us are hungry," says Jeff. He tilts his head and stares at me. "Yeah, I guess you're pretty for an old person. I'm so used to looking up at your giant nose and those cavernous nostrils," he jokes. I think.

"Thank you?"

"Come, Tru, come and see the burrow and our rooms." Novel grabs my hand and tugs me inside, pushing a still-clinging Page out of the way. Unconcerned, Page spins and grabs my other hand.

I can't speak. I'm in shock. I've known these children since they were born, and to see them face-to-face is the strangest, weirdest feeling.

There is the sound of running bare feet, and I snap out of my stupor when Story dashes around the corner. She skids to a stop in front of me, panting.

A huge smile blooms on her beautiful face. "Tru!" she cries.

"Story?" Oh my. Her skin is just as sapphire blue, but the details of her cheekbones, the shape of her lips, and the rose-gold flecks in her eyes... It's like I have never seen her before. We stare at each other. *We are the same height,* I think dimly.

And then we move, we throw our arms around each other, and we hug properly for the very first time.

"Bloody hell, this is surreal," I manage to choke out. My voice is full of emotion.

"We've been best friends, sisters, for almost ten years, and this is our first proper hug," she says, giving me an extra squeeze. "Why haven't we done this before?"

We laugh, and after a few more minutes, we pull away.

Story takes hold of my hand. "Welcome to our home."

"It's beautiful," I tell her.

"Come on, both of you. Ralph is setting the table. I hope you're hungry."

I look over my shoulder in search of Kleric. He's leaning against the wall with the biggest grin.

*I love you*, I mouth.

*I love you more*, Kleric mouths back.

Dear Reader,

*Thank you* for taking a chance on my book! Wow, I did it again. I hope you enjoyed it. If you did, and if you have time, I would be *very* grateful if you could write a review.

Every review makes a *huge* difference to an author—especially me as a brand-new shiny one—and your review might help other readers discover my book. I would appreciate it so much, and it might help me keep writing.

Thanks a million!

Oh, and there is a chance that I might even choose your review to feature in my marketing campaign. Could you imagine? So exciting!

Love,
Brogan x

P.S. DON'T FORGET! Sign up on my VIP email list! You will get early access to all sorts of goodies, including: signed copies, private giveaways, advance notice of future projects and free stuff! The link is on my website at **www.broganthomas.com** your email will be kept 100% private, and you can unsubscribe at any time, with zero spam.

P.P.S. I would love to hear from you, I try to respond to all messages, so don't hesitate to drop me a line at: brogan@broganthomas.com

# About the Author

Brogan lives in Ireland with her husband and their eleven furry children: five furry minions of darkness (aka the cats), four hellhounds (the dogs), and two traditional unicorns (fat, hairy Irish cobs).

In 2019 she decided to embrace her craziness by writing about the imaginary people that live in her head. Her first love is her husband and number-one favourite furry child Bob the cob, then reading. When not reading or writing, she can be found knee-deep in horse poo and fur while blissfully ignoring all adult responsibilities.

- facebook.com/BroganThomasBooks
- instagram.com/broganthomasbooks
- goodreads.com/Brogan_Thomas
- bookbub.com/authors/brogan-thomas
- youtube.com/@broganthomasbooks

# Also By
# Brogan Thomas

Creatures of the Otherworld series

Cursed Wolf

Cursed Demon

Cursed Vampire

Cursed Witch

Cursed Fae

Rebel of the Otherworld series

Rebel Unicorn

Rebel Vampire

Printed in Poland
by Amazon Fulfillment
Poland Sp. z o.o., Wrocław
09 April 2024

11cdeef9-32c2-4b0f-a56a-649f8c2c52c2R01